A Fight For Peace

Karen Jeffcoat

ISBN: 9781657000490

*To my amazing family Neil, Hope and Jeremiah
who constantly encourage me to be a better person.*

*To my amazing family Neil, Hope and Jeremiah
who constantly encourage me to be a better person.*

PART ONE

Chapter 1

A single cloud of dust that had been picked up and carried along by the breeze was suddenly deposited again onto the ground. A black boot kicked aimlessly at it, and lifted it up into the air once more. It landed back on the boot, changing its natural colour of black to grey. The boot rose up into the air, waved about in annoyance at becoming dirty, and tried vainly to shake it off. A hand reached down towards it, and long, slender fingers hastily brushed away at the dirt with a handkerchief.

Parlon Dremun stood upright again. He appeared a formidable figure as he stood silhouetted against the setting sun of Zaren. Tall and proud, he was a lone man in dark clothing, watching the workers in the distance as they concluded their labour for the day.

His dark, wavy hair had just a tinge of grey about it, as did his beard. In his early fifties, he was an attractive man, an air of strength and authority about him. Despite attractive looks, he remained single, preferring not to compromise on his habits and tastes. He was single minded, but never selfish; a man with plans and dreams for his beloved home planet. He enjoyed his own company, introvert in fact despite his position high in the Zarenian council. He steered away from any social groups and gatherings which made him feel awkward, uncomfortable and vulnerable. People unnerved him; he felt he never really understood them.

1

Absentmindedly he scratched at his cheek; the skin was red and sore from a day spent walking around in the blistering heat, observing. His brown eyes shone with concern – they had seen many things in his lifetime that others would never see in theirs. His memory was running through the day's events like a computer. Parlon Dremun could sense a change coming. He did not like it at all. His boots scrunched the small stones into the path as he made his way back down the hill, deep in thought.

Something needed to be done soon to stop the unrest that was beginning to take place in a few areas, before it escalated and spread out of control. The best way to deal with these things was to crush them while you had the chance, he tried to reassure himself. Somehow he had a feeling that it was not going to be that simple.

Zaren was a hot, dry planet; and dusty. Too dusty. There were long spells without rain that were almost unbearable. The relentless heat given out by the twin suns that rose each day from opposite sides of the planet, met at midday, and slowly passed by to the other side before they sank for the day, was something fascinating and terrible at the same time.

Personally, Parlon Dremun could tolerate the heat and the dryness, but not the dust. He couldn't stand it. You just couldn't get rid of it. It got everywhere and it was impossible to stay clean. During the periods of dryness and heat, the birds didn't sing, and the animals hid underground. It felt like everything died and the humidity tried it's best to suffocate everyone. At least, that's what Parlon Dremun felt. When the heat died down, and the rains came, refreshing everything and encouraging it back to life, he felt contented and at peace. The trees and flowers burst back into life, reminding him there was always hope in even the bleakest situation, and no matter how dead the countryside looked, it surprised him season after season by resurrecting itself. The animals came back out and revelled in the rejuvenated and replenished streams and rivers, and most of all, the birds began their glorious singing again, celebrating victory over another difficult season.

As he walked back along the dusty track, wishing those days would hasten along, he stopped as he heard an argument taking place between two men, only one of which he recognised. Apparently, they were arguing over their food rations.

"You haven't worked as hard as me. Therefore, I should have more of your food quota. Give it to me," the stranger was demanding.

"No, I worked just as hard, if not harder than you today. Take your own food, and leave me alone!"

"I said, give it to me. Now!"

"And I told you, no! You have only been here a couple of days, and already you have started trouble. We don't want anything to do with you."

"I'm warning you, give me your…"

"Hey! What is the meaning of this?" broke in Parlon Dremun as he drew nearer.

"Sir, this newcomer wants my share of food, and I see no reason why I should give it to him. We worked equally hard. You can check that by asking for the weights of rock we brought in." The agitated young man was flushed in his cheeks, and standing ready to defend his food rather than give in to this bully. Hastily, he brushed his sandy coloured hair out of his green eyes, leaving a streak of grey dust from his filthy hands in the fringe.

"Alright Saloe, calm down," he addressed the flustered Zarenian. Turning towards the second man, he enquired calmly, "Now, what's your name?"

"Why?" demanded the aggressor. His dark eyes showed anger and his fists were clenched by his sides tightly, the knuckles showing white through his skin. He didn't look as though he had been working that hard; his black boots were dirty, but his long dark coat, black trousers and relatively clean hands did not reflect a hard day of labour. His dark brown hair showed hardly any dust, unlike Saloe's.

"You just listen to me, whatever your name is. You were made aware of our rules and customs before you were accepted here on Zaren to live, when you arrived uninvited. You pledged to obey, may I remind you. You know that we live peacefully together, and no matter how much we work, we share equal food rations. If you wish to complain about anything, you do it in the correct manner as set out in the manual. You will not take matters into your own hands. Do you understand?" Parlon Dremun delivered the last sentence more as a warning statement than a question. He studied the man's face, and knew that this was not going to be settled easily. Here stood trouble.

"Now listen to me...," the stranger began to snarl.

"No, you listen to me. If you persist, disciplinary action will have to be taken. You will lose your food for the day altogether, and for as long as this attitude persists. Nobody here likes a trouble maker, so I suggest you watch your step and make an effort to fit in. Otherwise, we can always send you back to Spilon."

At this remark, the stranger shot a look of pure hatred at Parlon Dremun. Spilon's leaders had recently sent a few hundred of its men to Zaren, the ships returning to their home planet once they were dropped off. Their food supply was becoming less abundant, and they feared that over population would result in starvation of some of their people. They needed new ideas and knowledge from neighbouring worlds they said, to keep Spilon producing enough food.

Spilon was known for its emotional and turbulent people, who were prone to arguments and outbreaks of violence, so the chosen number who came to stay on Zaren were only accepted after they had sworn an oath to coexist in peace and harmony. The Zarenians way of life was simple, humble and peaceful, and had been for several hundred years. They did not want to refuse to help, but they were not enjoying their visitors company.

They had upset many workers, and were reluctant to labour in return for their food and shelter. They wanted to observe and let their hosts do all the work, but the council had insisted that it was only by helping with the crops, and indeed mining rock from the quarries, side by side with their own men, that they would only then truly learn how to successfully work in teams, sharing knowledge and building up trust and friendship. Unfortunately, it was placing a great deal of strain on many men.

Zaren, a relatively small planet, had once been nearly torn to pieces by a war, in which tens of thousands of people had been killed. Eventually, the rival leaders had seen sense, and called a truce. In the aftermath they discovered that the war had started, and escalated, over something very trivial which could have been settled amicably with a little more effort from both sides.

After much thought and debate, a new set of rules for the planet were put into place, which aimed to keep the population happy and undivided. Practically everybody had lost one or more members of their families, and neighbourhoods had been ripped apart. No one wanted to see a repeat, so the rules were accepted and adhered to. There were a few problems at first, but gradually the people began to see the sense in what they were doing, and over the years, Zaren became a united, peace loving planet where everyone was treated equally. They became renowned and admired among the nearby planets, as well as for the quality of rock they mined for its mineral content, its strength for construction, and the energy giving properties it contained for fuel. Things were gradually looking up for Zaren.

From the outburst that had just taken place, Parlon Dremun knew at once that this man was a Spilon, and Saloe had only reacted to his unusual and unjust demands. He sensed that no matter how the situation ended here, it would not be concluded. He saw it in the stranger's eyes.

The threat to send him back, Parlon Dremun knew, was a bluff actually, as for one thing, despite being a highly respected man who was consulted for most major decisions, did not have the authority to exile anyone, and even if he had, the space shuttles they had were few, and to be used for emergencies only. They had not refined enough rock yet for adequate fuel supplies. Contact with Spilon leaders was also out of the question, as they had very poor communication equipment; something they were hoping to trade rock for with neighbouring planets. The stranger knew of the communication link problem, but he didn't know about the shuttle craft situation – yet.

Parlon Dremun and the man stood looking at each other for a few moments, almost trying to read each other's soul, thought Saloe. He felt most uncomfortable and embarrassed for being caught reacting to this man's demands. Still, he would somehow find a way to make up for it, one day.

A group of co-workers had gathered around the trio, curious as to what had caused the loud argument they had heard echoing around the walls of the quarry. They stood unsure of what to do, waiting for a cue from their respected leader.

The Spilon looked undecided for a moment as to how to carry on the argument, then gazing around at the small crowd, he grunted, and snatched up his bag of food which was part payment, provided to all workers every day for their labour. Muttering under his breath, he stormed off. Parlon Dremun watched him in silence until he was out of sight, and earshot.

Saloe had just finished telling the other men of the events that had led to this interchange, and was about to leave, when Parlon Dremun took him by the arm. "Saloe, I have a bad feeling about that man. I would like you to watch him carefully, and listen for anything that sounds odd, or might indicate trouble brewing."

"I understand, and I will, of course. But do you think that he and the others from his world really could pose some sort of threat to us, and if so, how?"

"Those are questions that I cannot answer yet, my friend. But if we are not careful, I think that they soon will be."

His grip on Saloe's arm lingered meaningfully for a moment to reiterate what he had just confessed. Then, seeing the comprehension on Saloe's troubled face, he relaxed his hold, and walked away homewards, leaving the others watching him in silence.

Chapter 2

A few days passed and Parlon Dremun's prediction slowly began to come true. The stranger that he had previously encountered, seemed to be some sort of ringleader, and began to incite arguments and, so far, minor outbreaks of violence. The other Spilons had until now seemed peaceable enough, but they too seemed to be more aggressive and argumentative. Bad feelings were growing and spreading. The atmosphere was changing perceivably day by day.

It seemed Parlon Dremun's fear that something was afoot was justified, and he was summoned to the Zarenian council who were becoming deeply concerned. They wanted to know more about the incident he had witnessed, and what his assessment of the situation was. They had never known such unrest in their lifetimes.

As he walked along under the shade of the oldest tree on Zaren, he stopped to gaze up through the unmoving leaves. This was his thinking tree, as he called it. The place he came to when he had deep thoughts to mull over. He enjoyed the whispers the foliage made, as though they were murmuring deep, wise truths into his mind. He sighed. Today there was no breeze, and they had no wisdom to impart. He was alone in his turbulent state of mind. Still, he gained some peace as he gazed through the varying shades of green, yellow, brown and russet tones of the leaves. How much brighter they would soon be when the rains came. Even still, they were beautiful and comforting. Nature helped settle his nerves, and he felt a small smile creep across his lips as the sun poured through the gaps in the foliage as though trying to shed light on his jumbled thoughts.

He reflected again on how beautiful and green some parts of his world could be, while others would always be barren and bleak. Another sigh escaped as he realised the similarity of his observation to his personality. It wasn't only other people he didn't understand; he never really knew what made him work either. Sometimes, and only sometimes, he wished he had someone close he could confide in, share with, hold close to him at night. Someone who could make him feel loved. He had never really liked himself, so how could anyone else love him, he mused.

His fingers brushed over the roughness of the bark, and his gaze fell upon a small beetle trying to burrow into a minute hole. The beetle obviously was not going to fit in, no matter how determined he was. "I know how that feels," he muttered.

He looked across at The Great Wall of History, a high monument that told through intricate pictorial carvings the depravity Zaren had once fallen into. Bold images of people slain in pools of blood, women and children included, orphans crying beside dead parents. Men were running, screaming, pleading, suffering, dying, and rotting. Its honesty of the brutality it showed was deliberate. It was meant to shock, and after all these years, it still did. As a boy he had wandered along its length, chilled by the expressions he saw on the faces of children not much older than he, thankful he had only ever seen such expressions in the frozen faces on the wall, never in real life. He felt that chill again now creep over him, despite the heat of the sun. He wanted to make sure he never saw these expressions for real. He knew he could delay entering the council chambers no longer, and as he touched one of the stone tears shown falling down a young girl's face, so he was aware one was slowly trickling down his own cheek. He turned his tall, lean frame towards the council gates and strode resolutely towards them. As he disappeared into the shade of the interior, so a cloud passed over the sun.

"I fear that things are beginning to get out of control," exclaimed Yurel as he entered the inner chambers, as though Parlon Dremun had been present during the prior discussions. He shared the feelings of the old councillor, and nodding, he said so as he took his place among the nine seated men already in attendance. Yurel paced backwards and forwards in front of them, and for a few moments, only the slight rustle of his long, cream robes could be heard as he swished them around in his agitation.

Ten drawn and tired faces looked on, waiting for his next words. Nine of them had nothing to say, but the tenth did, and when Yurel had remained quiet long enough that he knew he was not going to interrupt his elder, Parlon Dremun broke the silence.

"I would say by the events that I have witnessed and been made aware of, that there is definitely some sort of plot against Zaren. The immediate plan seems to be to break the peaceful union of our people. What the ultimate aim is, I could not say for sure. However, I would hazard a guess."

"Which is?" Yurel's voice was tense as he demanded the response, though he feared he knew what it would be, even if the others did not.

"Possibly to cause a war."

At this, the councillors broke their silence, like an iceberg cracking, and muttered loudly amongst themselves, disbelief and shock rippling round the room. Yurel sat silently for a moment, his eyes downcast; his hands clasping the arms of his chair tightly, as though trying to extract some sort of inspiration from it. It struck Parlon Dremun that if the situation had not been so serious, he would have laughed.

Eventually, Yurel broke free of his bond with the chair, and stood up. He held his shaking hands out, gesturing for silence.

"Councillors," his voice though trembling, was still authoritative, "Let Parlon Dremun continue." He turned towards the younger man, his eyes riveted on him. "What would be their reason for causing such a war? We are not a rich people, with no great power, and nothing much to offer anyone. What would they hope to gain?"

Parlon Dremun stood still, aware every eye in the room was focused on him alone, and he tried not to let his expression waver. Stiffly his voice rang round the echoing chambers, as he told them, "Maybe they hope to incite violence among our own people to start the dispute. The Old War began with an ambiguous argument, as you well know. Others took sides, became involved, and the unrest grew, like a disease. More and more men joined in, and before long, nearly the whole population was fighting."

At his dark words, the council again fell into a stony silence. They were ashamed at the memories of what had come to pass on their planet, and were now terrified that such a thing could happen again. Their dark past was rarely spoken of, and Parlon Dremun was not sure if he felt hot or cold under the anxious stares.

"I feel that the Spilons hope to cause this altercation," he continued oblivious to his own discomfort. "They would wait for the war to begin and escalate so that our own people kill each other, saving them the trouble. Then, when the surviving numbers become more manageable, they move in and take control. Zaren would fall to them. They could then move people from their own planet over to ours, thereby avoiding overpopulation, and the

14

bloodshed of their own people – we will have done the job for them."

"Why our world? Why not one that has not yet been colonized?" one of the councillors interjected in a very nervous voice. He clearly felt his question was one the rest of the men were contemplating, as he gazed from one to the other, hoping for nods of assent. One or two obliged, the others looked as frozen as the images outside on The Great Wall of History.

"Because we are the nearest and the smallest, and would prove little opposition. With the work that we have already achieved here, they also would not have to start from scratch. Everything would be set out for them, ready to come in and take over." Again silence hung in the air. This time, no one could offer up a question.

Yurel had turned very pale. "We must stop this before it gets out of hand."

It seemed that the suggestion Parlon Dremun had proffered, had become the reality in all of their minds, without any alternatives being needed.

"I may be wrong in my assumptions."

"Councillor Dremun, we have learned over the years through experience, that you are very rarely wrong. For you to make these suggestions, you must have spent a great deal of time considering all the evidence you have been presented with."

Finally, the youngest and newest member of the council, Bedel, who looked swamped in his official gowns and head dress, found his voice, as high and uncertain as it was. "We should return the Spilons back to their own planet," he ventured.

"How? If we send our shuttlecraft, they won't be returned to us. If more Spilons arrive, we may need them, for ...something else. We cannot contact them with the communication devices we have, and even if we could modify them, what would we say? "Please remove your men, they are causing trouble?" If we give away that we know that trouble is brewing, they would only sense victory closing in and send more men to speed up the process. They also know that we would not harm their people if we bluffed we were holding hostages. If we make an attempt to imprison the men that are here already, how do we know they can't alert their people? Things could turn very nasty rather fast."

Bedel looked sheepish and embarrassed, his face flushing the colour of his outer garment. Clearly, he could see why Parlon Dremun held such a senior position, and the affections of the elders of the council. He had much to learn; and he hoped he could do it quickly.

"What do you suggest?" Yurel asked.

"I think we should continue as we are at present. Monitor

the situation quietly and discreetly, watch and listen for everything that goes on. Learn as much as we can. We must not let on that we suspect anything is wrong. Let them think we are assuming they are just keeping up their reputation for being argumentative and hot blooded, and leave it at that. We must warn our people separately not to become involved, or react to any situation they find thrust upon them. In the meantime, I think we should begin to "educate" small groups of men as to what is going on. They in turn can pass the information on to others."

A buzz ran through the council members at this positive response. They had not expected a plan to be delivered as well as the grim news. However, the atmosphere soon changed as councillor Dremun added, "If we are not too late to stop this, I think we have to prepare for the fact that we may have to fight to defend ourselves."

He knew they would be shocked at this, but found he still had to turn away from the eyes riveted on him in utter mortification.

"Fight?" the half whisper escaped from Bedel's lips and echoed around the room. His lips remained apart after forming the word and his face was no longer flushed with any colour at all.

"We have no choice. Negotiations are impossible because of our inability to contact Spilon, and would probably be futile anyway. Apart from surrendering, which we just cannot do, the only alternative is to fight to defend ourselves, and our world. We must prepare for this, as I suspect they are making plans as we speak. Time may be short."

"Why can't we surrender, and save the bloodshed?" Bedel was obviously not keen on the idea of fighting to protect their world.

"Because they will eventually do the same thing again on another planet when this one becomes over populated. We cannot allow that if we have a chance to stop it now. I also don't think our blood would be spared if we did surrender. I have heard that killing can be a source of pleasure to a Spilon."

For a long time, the council sat in deep, dark contemplation, considering all they had just heard. Parlon Dremun's mind wandered back to the beetle outside on the tree, and wondered if he had managed to burrow into the hole yet. He felt like doing the same thing. He left the men deliberating, and went outside for some fresh air. He headed for the tree and found the insect had abandoned his attempt and disappeared. That's where the similarity between him and the beetle ended, he decided. He never gave up on anything.

He walked around aimlessly, stretching his arms and stiff neck, wishing he had the elusive solution to end all of their problems, and just hoping that he was completely wrong.

Once again, he ran his fingers along The Great Wall of History and wondered at the skill of the craftsmen who had constructed it, imagining their hands and fingers as they deftly carved and chipped at the rock surface. He felt the emotion that had created each line and curve as he walked along slowly, tracing years gone by with sensitive fingertips. He became lost in time, reliving the achievements of their heritage, the hard work, and the devastating failures and their consequences. The craftsmen had in their minds eye how the wall would look when it was completed; after all, they knew how the story ended. He thought about the current predicament and wished he could have a glimpse of how it would finish; how the story on the wall would be added to as events unfolded. What new images would come to be depicted in years from now of the troubles they were living through right now? The length of wall that as yet remained a blank canvas for the future, if there was one, aside from the lichen and moss which looked a little like a map, offered no clues. He shuddered involuntarily, and then realised he did not want to know too much about the future after all.

Pulling himself away, and feeling more clear minded , he was about to re-enter the chambers to see how the debating was progressing, when Saloe appeared from around the far end of the arced wall, and ran up to him.

"What is it, my friend?" Parlon Dremun could see something was clearly wrong.

"An accident," he panted, "On the rock face."

"Get your breath, and tell me what happened."

Saloe leaned up against the wall, shoulders heaving, his breath coming painfully in great gulps as he fought to speak. "No, rest for a moment, then tell me." A couple of minutes passed by, and slowly Saloe's breath became less laboured and his shoulders came to rest. He turned his troubled face towards his companion.

"One of the youngsters, Vefa, was doing some surface digging above me. There wasn't much left to do up there and the rest of us in the group had moved down a tier, leaving him alone. We had been working for maybe half an hour or so and could hear Vefa still busy above. We had stopped for a break and called Vefa to join us. He didn't reply, but we could hear him talking to somebody. The voices became raised and we shouted up to him. I looked up to see what was happening but the suns were in my eyes and we were too far below to see who was up there with him. Then some dust and gravel started falling down over the ledge and we heard shouting and a scuffle. I heard the other voice clearly and recognised it straight away; it was the stranger who demanded my provisions the other day, I'm sure of it." Saloe hesitated.

"Go on," Parlon Dremun prompted. After a few moments pause, he continued quietly, "Shortly after, the voices stopped and Vefa began his work again, muttering something. We just carried on with our break thinking he was alone again. We thought the stranger had gone away and the row was over. But, then all of a sudden..." Tears welled up in his already red eyes, and he visibly shook.

The older man gently took his arm and said, "Tell me what happened next."

"I heard a yell, and looked up to see Vefa come hurtling past me and smash onto the ground below. I can still hear his screams and see his terrified face. It was awful. There was nothing we could do." He tried vainly to control his emotions.

"Did you look up again? Was there anyone else there? Think, man," the councillor demanded.

"Yes. No, Well, I think I saw..."

"What?" Parlon Dremun had again gripped his arm, this time much more tightly.

"Well, the suns were in the way; I can't swear, but I think I saw someone move back away from the edge. But it could have just been the light in my eyes." He hastily added, "I know what you're thinking, that Vefa could have slipped. But though he was young and hadn't been with us for very long, he was really keen on doing a good job and worked hard. He was always careful. I know he didn't fall; he was on a high surface, but it was flat, and he was well in from the edge. He must have been pushed." He had been almost afraid to say that, but now that he had, he seemed relieved and calmed down. His torrent of words ceased.

The councillor released his grip, sensing it was too tight and stepped away, his back turned towards Saloe. His head hung down on his chest, his eyes stinging to fight tears away. So, the pace was picking up already. Still facing away from Saloe, he said in a hollow voice, "We must remove Vefa's body, and inform his parents."

"It is being attended to now."

"Good. Do you know the stranger's name yet?"

"No, no one seems to know who he is, or where he stays, or anything about him. He's like a ghost. He just appears each day, generally late, and then disappears again in the evening, usually before anyone else."

"Saloe, it is vitally important that you keep your fears to yourself." Seeing the shock on the younger man's face, he added, "Just for the time being. There is so much at stake. More than you realise. I will talk to you later about this in greater detail, but for the moment, you must carry on as though today was an accident. Tell that to the rest of the men in your group. Now, go home and get some rest."

"Yes sir, I will."

"And Saloe?"

"Yes?"

"Thank you."

Saloe nodded and walked slowly away.

Returning to the council chamber in somewhat more of a hurry than he had left them, he saw the determined look that he had expected on Yurel's face. He seemed to have aged though he thought, since he had left the room. He knew then the decision they had reached before they announced it to him. He waited patiently for confirmation.

"We will not surrender to Spilon," Yurel announced resolutely. "Therefore, if necessary, we fight. However, only in order to defend ourselves and our planet. We cannot take another's life without extreme provocation."

"Of course. It is likely to come to that though."

"Accepted and agreed. You will be responsible for briefing small teams of carefully selected men, who will in turn pass on their training to others. We must prepare as many men as we can as soon as possible."

"I will begin immediately. Saloe has just informed me of another incident at the rock face. The most serious one yet. It could have been an accident, but he is sure it wasn't. His word is good enough for me. Whatever happened, it resulted in the loss of a young man's life."

Any councillor that had until now doubted that there was any kind of threat to their world, was now shocked to the harsh reality that there was. Unfortunately, they did not know they had already left their plans too late.

Chapter 3

Time passed and gradually incidents became more frequent and violent in their nature, and appeared to be organised rather than random.

Council meetings were now a daily occurrence.

"Someone is behind this, putting everything together. It has to be premeditated for this to happen so quickly." Yurel's agitation was apparent, and tangible. He was deeply concerned that they were not controlling what was happening as they had hoped to, and even more concerned that their ill-advised people were beginning to lose faith in them. As the majority of people were still in the dark about the councils plans, they felt there was no leadership and that the situation was being ignored. Grumbling and gossip were rife in the communities. Some men were staying away from work altogether, choosing to remain at home and protect their families. The neighbourhoods became empty and quiet at night before dark, almost as though they had placed an unspoken curfew over themselves. Women only went out in the daytime in twos or threes and kept their children inside to play. An atmosphere of distrust had evolved everywhere, and people were becoming more insular and disinclined to interact and talk to one another.

"There are reports of more "accidents" arriving daily."

Parlon Dremun shifted his position. He was sitting on the uncomfortable, cold, stone window sill, looking out across the Square at his thinking tree, deep in deliberation. The tree was beginning to shed its leaves, and he watched one drift slowly down to the ground. Then two fell together, floating in a beautiful dance around one another, softly and gently, gracefully landing side by side. He reflected that his ideas felt much the same; they were falling uselessly one by one. His failures didn't fall so gracefully, however.

His untrimmed beard, unkempt hair and red rimmed, sleep deprived eyes, betrayed his exhaustion.

"What else can we do? We must act quickly." Yurel's pacing was speeding up at an alarming rate, and Parlon Dremun jerked his attention away from the tree, and towards his elder. His gaze fell upon the old man's shoes, clicking on the stone floor, each step making him feel more and more agitated, like a pointed finger prodding at his conscience, highlighting his failure, inability, indecision, and weakness. His heart seemed to be joining the rhythm of Yurel's steps, beating harder and faster, trying to keep up. The feet seemed to be beating the words, "failure, failure, failure." He passed a clammy hand through his hair, his fingers catching in knots in the greying mass. It seemed to be getting hotter and hotter in the chamber. He was aware he had not responded to Yurel's demand for more answers; answers he felt he could not give; did not have.

"I fear there is not enough time. We began to notice things too late. I noticed things too late."

"Don't say that!" Yurel looked as though he were about to explode as he snapped at the younger man. "We will not give up. There must be something we can do...There must!"

The clicking of his shoes had temporarily ceased, but now they took up their relentless critique once more.

"Calm down, please. You are no help to us like this."

Yurel stopped his irritating pacing, and took a few deep breaths, thinking on his uncharacteristic outburst. He was not displaying calm leadership to his fidgeting council members.

"I'm sorry. Of course, you are right. But I feel so responsible; I should have seen this coming long ago."

"You alone are not responsible. You could say that we all are, however."

"What do you mean?"

"It's our own stupidity. We are so naïve and gullible; just because we are a peaceful people who trust everyone, does not mean that that is the way of all others. We took the Spilons word that they would obey our rules. Yes, we vaguely know of their historically disruptive background, yet did not for one moment think that they should be distrusted." Sarcastically he added, "They had given us their word after all. It is our own fault. For too long we have been preaching to ourselves about our world, our rules, our past and future, oblivious to the realities of what is going on in the worlds around us. For so long we have been so busy teaching ourselves to be tolerant of everyone and everything, that we have blinded ourselves to the dangers of who and what else is around us. We are not familiar with the way of life elsewhere, because there is no way for us to know. Our communication links are useless." Now he was pacing up and down, but didn't even realise it. The only difference between his steps and Yurel's was that they were lower in tone and sounded like a warning drum. The sweat was pouring down his face, and a distant buzz seemed to be filling his ears. Why couldn't he think straight?

Shaking his head hoping all the distractions would come clattering out, he persevered, "We were a prime target, without even knowing it. All we can do is hope for some divine inspiration, and pray that the Spilons decide they have made the wrong decision after all, and leave. The way things are going though, I don't think that's likely to happen. I doubt very much that ships will randomly arrive to pick them up in the manner they arrived in."

He realised he had stopped in his tracks and he met Yurel's steady gaze. They both read despair in each other's eyes. "Yes," thought Parlon Dremun, "How old you look."

Looking at the councillors seated around the large, circular, wooden table, he saw mostly youth and inexperience. They had not encountered any great problems before. Most of the time, all they had to worry about was simple, straight forward business matters, concerning the quarry and the mines.

Now they had a very real problem to deal with. Looking at the worried, pale faces, he could only hope they were readier than they seemed.

*   *   *

One after another, Parlon Dremun taught selected groups of men in his desperate race against the clock. Yurel watched him one evening going through his lecture yet again, still enthusiastic, animated and determined. His voice was weaker now though, drained of inflection he noticed. He was neglecting himself obviously, his hair growing longer and unruly, his beard untidy, his sunken eyes dark and heavy with the tiredness that hung on their lids, and his hoarse voice becoming hardly a whisper as the lecture progressed. Yet, he knew, his head councillor could not rest.

The Spilons were gaining momentum now, and a number of Zarenians had begun to cluster together in small bands, plotting their revenge, ignorant of what their seemingly uncaring leaders were trying to achieve. All they could see, was that the Spilons were literally getting away with murder, and although violence was at first abhorrent to them, began to think that it was their only way to counteract the attacks. It was no longer a secret about what was happening. That illusion was shattered long ago.

Unfortunately, some were completely immersed in what they were doing, to the point they were blind to the fact that they were losing their own self-control, and indeed, becoming as barbaric as their aggressors.

Scuffles and riots broke out regularly, arson was being frequently reported, and some families had taken to the hills to hide and live in isolation. These were flushed out though when they surfaced to get food or provisions from their old homes. They disappeared altogether.

The council could not keep up with the numbers of incidents being reported to them. The Spilons had become known as "The Greedmen," because of the way they set about taking everything, from their victims, with no remorse or hesitation.

The Zarenians who were now waging their own war, regardless of pleading from others, took up their own gang name, "The Opposers."

Parlon Dremun worked continuously to try to combat this and restore the peace, if only temporarily, to at least give them more thinking time. However, he knew he was personally fighting a losing battle.

Yurel continued to look on in admiration at the man who had given in his usual selfless way; his time and energy, and even his health now it seemed, completely devoted to their cause. It was such a shame he had never had a family, he thought. He was a man who gave much, but also needed much. His train of thought was interrupted as he realised the voice had stopped altogether, and wondered what was wrong.

He saw Parlon Dremun standing still, eyes focused on the ground as though transfixed by something there. His mouth was forming words, but no sound was audible. He began to sway slightly, backwards and forwards, his knees beginning to buckle, and his right hand reached out for something to steady him, but there was nothing close by. He grappled to find something, anything, to hold him up, but found only thin air.

Yurel realised what was happening, and dashing over, caught him just as he fell backwards in a faint. Two men from the group being taught, leapt forward to take his weight from the old man, and together they carried him to his private rooms where they laid his unconscious form down on his bed.

Taking in the mess, Yurel could see Parlon Dremun had taken about as much care of his room as he had of himself.

Dust lay on the tables, books were discarded on the floor, clothes were hanging off the backs of chairs, and the flowers in the jar by the window were long dead. The bed he was laying on was the only tidy thing in the room. His brow furrowed as he realised that was a bad sign – it meant he hadn't been sleeping in it.

A physician arrived and examined him, tutting as he did so. Eventually he diagnosed his patient as being "generally fit, but completely exhausted." He could not stir him at all but was satisfied he was just in a deep sleep. Collecting all his equipment together he left the two men alone once more. His parting words were advice not to leave him alone, and to call him immediately if there were any concerns.

"Concerns," thought Yurel, "there are plenty of those, but nothing you can help with, I'm afraid."

He went into the kitchen area and set about making him and his charge something to eat, ready for when he awoke, tidying up as he went along. He was disturbed by a knock at the door. It was Bedel, come to see if he could relieve Yurel from his watch, but the old man politely declined. He wanted to be here when the younger man awoke.

A few hours passed by and Yurel decided to eat his meal, as there seemed no sign of Parlon Dremun rousing. It was rather good he smiled to himself. He had not done much cooking as the council president, but when his wife, Tacia, was alive, they sometimes used to spend an evening messing around in the kitchen, throwing together ingredients and putting in herbs their son had picked for them from the meadows and fields. The smile grew as he reminisced.

The happier thoughts were occupying his mind as he himself allowed sleep to take hold of him. As his head lolled down onto his gently rising and falling chest, he joined his wife in his dreams.

That evening passed, as did the whole of the next day without Parlon Dremun stirring at all. Once or twice he muttered something inaudible in his sleep, and his head and limbs jerked, but he became quiet again, and his rest continued undisturbed. Yurel refused to leave him. The old man needed the break from the chaos outside, a chance to reflect, and look after his patient. He was doing something useful.

Eventually, late that afternoon, Parlon Dremun opened his eyes, responding to the touch of Yurel bathing his troubled brow. "Welcome back," he whispered.

Alarmed, the younger man found that he could not reply; his throat was so dry and sore. Yurel held a cup of water up to his lips, and supporting his head, watched as he drank the entire contents in a few moments.

"Steady, steady! When did you last eat or drink anything?"

Parlon Dremun was still squinting at the light, and trying

to focus on where he was, and how he came to be there. He looked past Yurel as he vaguely rasped, "Don't know, can't remember."

"Well it certainly hasn't been the last day or so, while you have been asleep!"

Incredulity filled Parlon Dremun's eyes.

Yurel refilled the cup, and this time made him drink in slow, shallow sips. He helped him to sit up a little, placing cushions behind his neck and shoulders. "I will heat up some food I made for you; then you can start to get some strength back."

"Can't. Need to get back...to my work," Parlon Dremun began to struggle forwards, but the room tilted and spun and he let out a groan. He clasped his head.

Restraining hands pushed him gently but forcefully back down again, as Yurel said quietly, "A very wise man once told me, "Calm down, you are of no use to us like this." It was good advice," he grinned.

Parlon Dremun actually felt his cheeks flushing as he surrendered himself back down onto the pillows.

"And you would like to impart this advice to me?"

"Quite!"

The younger man let out only a deep sigh as his reply.

"Acting like a scolded child will not help either," Yurel chuckled.

Weakly, Parlon Dremun smiled back and reached out for the silver haired man's gnarled hand. Clasping it, he murmered, " I'm sorry, Father."

* * *

During the couple of days of bed rest, Parlon Dremun became deeply dismayed at the increasingly bad news reported to him. Yurel had not succeeded in keeping things quiet from him, only in making him stay put. He had had to inform his son that two key members of The Opposers had been assassinated during one of their meetings. They had become careless and clumsy with whom they spoke to. The Greedmen had apparently attacked dressed all in black, from head to toe, including helmets with darkened visors.

"So, they came to Zaren prepared," was his only comment.

Yurel enjoyed the precious time he had with his son, fussing over him as he had when he was a small boy. Making him eat was difficult in the beginning, but once his sense of taste awoke to his father's culinary talents, he soon found he was making up for all the neglected meal times.

"You know, this is almost as good as mother used to

35

make," was all the reference Parlon Dremun would make to Tacia. He still hurt deep inside; still grieved for her.

Yurel understood, but wished his son would open up to him. He was tired and weak though, and now was not a good time to push him. He just wanted to enjoy time with him.

They had time to appreciate one another, even share a few laughs. As much as Yurel was glad to see his son's health returning rapidly, he was also sad, because he knew he could not keep him away from his work for much longer. He knew there was no point half killing himself for what was, as he knew in his heart, a lost cause, but he also knew there had never been any point trying to get his son to stop something once his mind was made up. Once his mother had passed away, despite all the love, time and affection Yurel could lavish on him, his son had retreated deep inside himself. For some reason, he blamed himself, and felt guilty, completely needlessly. Despite many reassurances that he had no influence on his mother's illness and death, he could not let go the feeling of it being his fault. He stopped going out with his friends, spent long hours in his room and shied away from the many visitors to the house. He felt everything so deeply and Yurel wanted to make sure he did not feel that the atrocities going on outside were his fault too. Sadly, the time he spent talking to him, made him realise that was a fruitless task.

Though they were well guarded inside the house and the

council chambers, nothing but chaos was reigning outside in the city. It was now too unsafe to walk outside alone at any time of the day, or even to remain alone inside the dwellings; children had been the only witnesses to their homes being broken into, and their mothers being brutally butchered in front of them. Sometimes the children themselves were not spared.

Fathers returning home from their hunt for the increasingly scarce food, found a trail of blood leading to the corpses that were their families.

The fields of cereal crops were burned down, and the market places raided and destroyed. Sharing supplies became a thing of the past; everyone was hanging on to what they had, scared they would not be able to replenish their stocks and feed themselves, let alone their families. The only thing people had in common anymore was their terror.

Parlon Dremun felt there was no point in returning to his teaching once he felt well enough to leave his sanctuary – it was far too late for that now. In what seemed an incredibly short space of time, complete destruction of a high proportion of property had been executed, and lack of food, shelter and hygiene were the newest enemies. Disease set in; terrible disease that swept through the remaining population, the children in particular. Their feeble, starving bodies could not cope without nutrition and medicine, warmth and sanitation. It was a pitiful sight, seeing the once happy children who filled the communities with laughter and ran up and down causing mischief, huddled together in rags to keep warm; sheltering under any fallen pieces of branch or debris they could find. Their once pink cheeks that were flushed with joy, were now pinched and pale, their eyes dim and hollow. Their chatter had ceased. Crying was all the noise they now made.

As more citizens became infected with the disease, the severity of the symptoms grew. There was no medicine available, as it had all been either looted by The Greedmen for their own private supply, or just destroyed in the raids. No medicine, no cure.

After enduring weeks of painful suffering, the children first affected began to die. Orphans were no longer taken in for fear of the disease coming into a dwelling, and if they were lucky, some died of starvation and exposure before the symptoms tortured their small frames. Nothing could be done to ease the terrible open sores, or the bouts of cramp and nausea, the pain that seared through their bones, their eyesight and hearing failing them.

Numbers affected increased from tens, into hundreds. The need for shelter became the healthy people's priority, and they began to dig underground. It was their only chance to offer their families at least some sort of protection from the violence, the pollution from the fires, and the smell of dead decaying bodies, of which there were now too many to bury.

At great personal risk, Parlon Dremun set about organising a truce to discuss the situation. At first, he really did not expect his invitation to be accepted. He had issued it by sending a messenger to The Great Wall of History; leaving a message scrawled in dye on a large cloth tied to a pole, like some macabre flag waving about. He was right, it had attracted attention, and the next day a reply was left anonymously in the same manner, agreeing to his terms.

He remembered his own warning, that they were a gullible race, and knew full well that he could be setting himself up for disaster if the Spilons were tricking them. There was little else left to try, his remaining options were as exhausted as his body. It was all there was left.

So now an agreement had been made, and the desperate people held their breath, hoping that maybe soon, they would be able to rebuild their shattered lives, and return to peace. A truce over a period of one night fall was agreed for the meeting to be held.

As that evening approached, the air was full of trepidation. At first, few people arrived at The Square. They were too afraid they were being tricked; that it was an elaborate plan to flush them out of their hiding places.

Gradually, however, as they saw others making their way warily along to the meeting place, more began to trust, and joined the groups. Gathering their families along with their courage, they led them vulnerably into the seldom used open spaces.

Nervously, Parlon Dremun walked to and fro along the top of The Great Wall of History. Where were the Spilon's? Had they changed their mind? Were they purposefully making a late appearance to make the Zarenian's sweat? Well, if that was the case, it was working.

He was feeling much stronger now, and couldn't account if it was because of the rest and nourishment, or the time he had spent alongside his father, remembering, talking, laughing, and hugging. Probably a mixture of both, he decided. Physically he felt strong, mentally he still hurt terribly.

He waited until he believed the majority of citizens who would come, to be present, and decided to start discussions amongst his natives, until the Spilons decided to show up. Talking would help him, as well as them.

He invited Yurel to speak first, to welcome everyone, and to show there was no need to fear attending the meeting; whilst he however, was scrutinising every shadow, every movement, and every hooded head as his father spoke.

A polite round of applause ended Yurel's welcome, and he moved away along the top of the wall, which was their makeshift platform, gesturing with his arm for Parlon Dremun to address the crowd.

Taking a deep breath to steady his nerves, he began. He echoed the welcome his father had extended, and gave a passionate speech about the crimes committed against them and their land. He empathised with the suffering they had endured, recognised the loss and grief they felt, the confusion and fear. He also recognised a new feeling amongst the masses – hate. There was shame that went hand in hand with that too.

He saw that he was connecting with them; they had fallen silent and were really listening. Hope began to pulse through his veins. This was what he needed to see. He felt the tension in his shoulders subsiding; at last he was relaxing. He was beginning to unite his neighbours once more.

All appeared to be going well, and he had even forgotten that the Spilons still hadn't shown up. He glanced across at Yurel, who remained standing resolutely a few feet away on the platform, completely absorbed by the speech he had given.

If anyone could make a difference to the people's attitude, it was his son. If he should be too late to succeed, he had at least tried with every ounce of energy inside him. Whatever happened, he would always be proud of his son.

Without their enemies, they could not negotiate and bargain, as the point of the meeting had been. So instead, he was making the most of the opportunity to boost morale. It was going so well.

Parlon Dremun introduced three families onto the wall with their children, who were now affected by the disease. He had kept them away from everyone, so there was no risk of infection, and they slowly sidled along next to him, a short distance between them. He hoped to shock the crowds into seeing sense. Murmurs again broke out amongst the crowd. They were nervous, but saw their leader setting the example they must follow. They settled again.

The families removed their hoods and pulled their sleeves up to reveal their arms. Gasps of shock broke out. Someone was crying near the front.

"You see before you, what we have done to our children. Is this what we wanted? All of us are susceptible to this disease now. It only requires us to come into direct contact with an infected person; a scratch, or a touch to an open wound is all it takes. Now we are killing our own flesh and blood, it's not just those that attack us. Ironically, The Greedmen protect themselves by their heavy uniform and masks, while we proceed to kill ourselves. We are doing their work for them. Can you not see that?"

Complete silence hung in the air as he continued, "A world with constant fighting has little future. A world where is no children has no future." As he paused for effect, the only audible sounds were made by the younger children, crying in their hunger and confusion. He had them, he could feel it.

"Keep going," he told himself. He had not planned to say any of this, he was thinking on his feet. Maybe it was better after all that the Spilons had not shown up.

"Look around you. See what else this petty conflict has done to our peaceful world. The destruction of our homes, built by our ancestors, forcing us to live below ground, the continual hunt for food, the contamination of much of our water. How many of you have not already lost a relative killed in the fighting, or know a friend dying of the disease? If we stop now, we can rebuild our homes, tend to the wounded, start nursing the sick properly, look for a cure, and maybe compromise with the Spilons. We could help them to begin a new life on an un-colonized planet. We can do it, if we all pull together, like we did not so long ago. Can none of you remember already? Look at this wall. It shows horror, yes, but it also shows hope triumphing over it. We are holding in our hands the ability to create the next scenes on this monument. Our future will one day be our children's past. What do we want them to see? A repeat of what we look at in our history? Or something better? What have we learned, my friends?"

He paused briefly before delivering his last line. "I ask for all of you to join together once again. A united Zaren, as before, does have a future."

He sat down on his heels, balancing purposefully near the front edge of the wall so he could hear the responses, while he rested and prepared to run through his list of proposals and objectives he had set out while he had been recuperating. He listened to the hopeful, optimistic comments he could single out from those nearest to him in the front rows. He afforded himself a faint smile, as he began to think he had actually succeeded in returning some sanity to his world.

However, it was at this moment, when from out of the shadows, The Greedmen appeared. Not together in a group, but intermittently around the perimeters of The Square, spaced out in a line. They had not come to negotiate. They had seen this as an opportunity to enforce their dominance and power.

Parlon Dremun's head jerked up so quickly that he nearly lost his balance on the wall edge. Now what were they up to? The Greedmen stood still, silently for a few moments as though waiting for an order. For what? A single man pulled back the folds of his cloak to reveal a weapon. This was the cue for the others to do the same.

But they had agreed; no weapons.

"No," screamed Parlon Dremun, as without a word from any of them, they let out unrelenting fire into the assembled crowd. He looked on helplessly in horror as the scene in front of him turned into a bloodbath.

Screams echoed around the walls of The Square, as people ran, jostled, tripped, and fell. Children were crushed beneath falling figures. Bodies fell up against The Great Wall. It seemed as though the images carved upon it of The Old War were being brought to life and replayed in colour.

He whipped round to see Yurel standing frozen to the spot on The Wall. "Run!" he yelled, "Run, Father!"

His own limbs began reacting, and seeing a gun aimed towards Yurel, pumped his legs furiously in his direction. Taking a flying leap, he pulled him down with him to the ground, as he heard a shot that seemed louder than all the others.

As they landed in a jumble of arms, legs, and robes, he felt his father's body jolt on top of his. He twisted his neck round so he was looking into Yurel's face, but knew he was dead, killed by the single bullet. He stared into his lifeless, dull, eyes, as if he could will the life back into him. He was only just registering what had happened, when he felt a sharp pain in his leg. He waited for another bullet to strike him and finish him off, but it did not arrive. Instead he lay pinned underneath his father's weight, feeling his body temperature gradually fall. Twice more, the corpse was struck by a stray bullet, and Parlon Dremun wished his time would come soon.

He lay in a pool of blood that was a mixture of his, and his father's, and looked on helplessly from his awkward angle, witnessing yet more carnage. It seemed the images of their fate were to be drawn in their own blood on The Great Wall of History.

Knowing he must move and try to help others, he inched his father's body off of his chest, and then as gently as he could pushed him to one side. The pain in his leg sent an agonising bolt through him, and he fought to get breath. One hand brushed lightly over Yurel's face, closing his eyes for the last time. He felt the agony of his despair rising inside of him, and the adrenalin pumped through his veins. Painfully, he heaved himself up onto his feet.

His mouth moved, trying to scream orders for everything to stop, but of course, it was in vain. He could not be heard above the bedlam, and he realised he was only making himself more vulnerable as a target.

Everything seemed blurry to him; a mass of dark colours moving about, running, lunging, and falling. Still the screams of women and children frightened for their lives filled his ears, as they cowered against the walls, too afraid to move.

Who should he help? Which direction should he go? Everybody was moving so quickly, he didn't know what to do first. His leg was throbbing and he was losing blood. Spinning back round, he saw a young woman climbing desperately up on to the stage away from the crowd. She frantically clawed at the stone to grip it and climb up. This was where he could help. Hobbling across to her, he knelt down, stretching out his hands to help her on to the top. Her panic stricken eyes made contact with his, as he hauled her up and over beside him. He collapsed next to her on the ground, fighting for breath. Before she even let go of his hand, a Greedmen crouching further along the wall shot her, and her lifeless body slumped next to him. He gave into the waves of nausea that swept over him, and retched.

Saloe had been in the crowd, and was also stunned and horrified by what had happened. This had been the chance they had hoped for to heal the rift, and now it had been ripped apart beyond repair.

Helplessly, he had looked on as he saw Parlon Dremun rush to protect Yurel with his own body in vain, and saw the desperate look on his face, as a son realised that he had lost his father. He had seen what he had been trying to do, and was pushing his way through the chaos to help. He knew he was too far away, but he had to try. It was too much for him when he saw Parlon Dremun also injured, and not seeing any reaction, had assumed it was a fatal wound. He paused, and let the crowds push him about from side to side, as numbness spread over his entire body. Whereas Parlon Dremun had been overwhelmed by the noise in his ears, Saloe watched the scenes play in his head in slow motion and silence.

What was happening here? Throwing back his head, he let out the loudest shout he could, venting his suppressed frustration. As he let it drop back down onto his chest, he drew up his shoulders, and let out great sobs of anguish.

He dropped heavily to his knees and remained there, as what felt like hordes of people washed around him. Too absorbed was he in his grief, that he no longer cared what happened to him, and became unaware of everything going on.

Elsewhere, a woman lifted her screaming child into her arms, and ran blindly along the inner perimeter of the wall towards the gates and her freedom, oblivious to all else. She stopped in her tracks as she saw a Greedman step in front of her in the half light, and point his gun at her. Instinctively clutching her baby tighter, she backed away from him, and turned to flee. A second Greedman was blocking her way, and moving towards her. She spun round again towards the first. He was right in front of her, and she caught her breath. Her baby screamed louder as though sensing the impending danger, as her mother was pulled by her hair away from the shelter of the wall. Her screams drowned her daughters, as she was thrown down forcefully to the ground, and fell heavily on top of her. The baby stopped crying immediately.

The mother looked down at the tiny, lifeless body, and looked back up at her attacker, all expression wiped from her face in shock. Life ceased around her. Fear disappeared.

"You killed my baby," she whispered; then louder, "You

killed my baby." She hauled herself to her feet, and charged at the Greedman who had despatched the bullet.

Her move was barred as he brought up his weapon and butted her in the face. Her jaw cracked, and blood spilled from between her teeth as the second Greedman pulled her away, and pushed her forcefully into the wall.

She turned, ready to fight, and overcoming her fear, flew at him; lips stretched back across her teeth, eyes dark and shining with fury. The Greedman let out a loud bellow of laughter as he levelled his weapon at her, and without hesitation, fired it point blank into her chest.

Her crumpled form fell to the ground, and with her last breath, she tried to inch her way across to where her child lay, wrapped mutely in death. Her fingertips stretched to their very limit, desperate in their urgency to reach her, as darkness and dizziness seemed to close in. Finally, she grasped her daughter's tiny, cold hand in hers, and let out her final breath.

Her departure from that world into the next, was marked only by the mocking laughter of the men who took her life.

*   *   *

Eventually, The Greedmen had taken their fill of blood, and ceased their massacre. They left The Square, leaving less than one quarter of the people who attended, alive. They had got their message across.

Saloe had roused himself to leave long after nothing but silence filled the now dark night air. He could not believe he was still alive, but found himself wishing he wasn't.

The next day, he returned to look for Parlon Dremun's body. There were too many to bury, but he wanted to do that one last thing out of respect for the man who had tried so hard to rescue their land. It had been assumed by others helping that he had been placed in the mass grave they had started to fill before they gave up, though nobody could remember seeing his body. That wasn't surprising; no one was in a state to be registering the identities, and some bodies were too badly mutilated to be recognised anyway.

He was either in there, concluded Saloe looking at the pile of corpses in the hole, or maybe he was badly wounded and had dragged himself off to die alone somewhere. That would be typical of him. He could not have survived, he decided, or he would be here, trying to lift the low spirits and offering comfort to others, despite his own suffering and loss.

Any hopes the people had of resolving the rift had died with him.

Chapter 4

Days of violence, despair and misery dragged on mercilessly, unrelentingly; followed by another and another. Attacks were more sporadic now; there weren't so many large communities left to target. Whole families had now been completely wiped out. Those that had survived the massacre, or had not attended the meeting, and those that had watched loved ones die of the disease, sometimes took their own lives in the only way they could see to escape the insanity.

A small group of men whose children were still alive and healthy, and who had attended the meeting, had been deeply affected by the wise words of Parlon Dremun. They had seen for themselves how he had tried vainly to save his father by attempting to sacrifice himself. It had been what they needed to sting them back into hope and strive to find a conclusion to this terrible nightmare.

They began circulating coded messages left in secret places. They discovered information about The Greedmen from a few gang members who had become repulsed at what they had done, and, although they did not have the courage to admit this to their leaders and leave them altogether, they did what they could to help prevent as many killings and raids as possible, by working from the inside.

They spread the word, and when The Greedmen struck

their targets after days of detailed planning, they found the premises had already been abandoned.

Any men who were found to have been providing information were instantly labelled as traitors, and executed as examples to the others who may have had wavering loyalties.

Numbers swelled, along with the anger and desire for revenge, and still using the name The Opposers, groups became larger and more organised. They were able to counter-attack The Greedmen, and abandoned the idea of using the minimal amount of force necessary to gain results because of the extent of the barbarity and depravity their enemies exercised.

After what seemed like an eternity, hope began to pulse once again through the veins of the Zarenians.

Inevitably though, The Greedmen eventually employed the same tactics that had been used against them, and spies infiltrated The Opposer groups.

Although they had struggled against the odds, and to their surprise, achieved some incredible victories, their strength began to crumble.

One evening at a group meeting held in an underground dwelling, morale appeared to be decreasing rapidly among the numbers. Tempers were running high, and emotions were shown freely in the confusion and fear felt by all. How much more suffering would they have to endure? Could they endure?

Dissent began to filter through the crowd, and murmurs of discontent became very audible from a couple of men among one particular group. One of them rose to his feet, followed by a second, who shoved the first hard on his chest with the flat of his hand. The second retaliated, but with more force.

Within seconds, the two men's arms locked together as the fight broke out, and the rest of the men scattered, making room for the flailing limbs.

The anger rose between them, and the brawl became more intense, drawing blood from the nose of one, and the mouth of the other. It seemed neither wanted to back down.

The men in these groups had become very close knit, and fighting among themselves was a very rare occurrence. The rest of the crowd looked on in stunned disbelief. Within a few minutes, the fight appeared to be becoming too violent, as the men unleashed all their pent up frustration and rage against each other.

A figure at the back of the room slowly stood up, and with difficulty made its way to the front where the melee was taking place. He was dressed all in black, his face covered by a tattered hood. Though he was slightly stooped, his height was still obvious, and he walked with a limp. Despite his obvious discomfort, the tall man suddenly swept between the fighters, parting them decisively and forcefully.

They let themselves come to rest, as they stared in amazement at the figure before them, still standing in silence. The man who had begun the scuffle, looked up into the shadowed folds of the hood, and demanded, "What business have you got, poking your nose in where it's not wanted? Leave us be. There's only one way to settle this argument."

The stranger remained still and quiet, and although his face was hidden behind the dark creases of cloth, the fighter could feel his eyes boring into his own. He suddenly felt very uncomfortable, and ashamed of his actions. He knew full well that he was at fault. Bowing his head, he looked down at his feet, like a reprimanded child.

The second man, also ashamed at what he had done now he had calmed down a little, especially as his opponent was his best friend, asked, "Who are you? Why are you interested in what's going on here?"

There was no reply from the hooded stranger. Instead, he slowly raised his gloved hands, pulling back the heavy cloak from over his face. Something about the man's presence and gestures had commanded complete silence in the room, and the attention of every person present in the room was arrested.

Both men's jaws dropped as they recognised the face that was now exposed to them. Could it really be...? They found they could not speak a word or move a muscle, as the shock began to sink in.

Sweeping his cloak majestically behind him, the newcomer turned to face the rest of the people, who were now watching with even more avid interest at this sudden change in events. Gasps of surprise and shock echoed around the room. The hair was greyer, the beard too, and thicker. The eyes were more haunted, but the face was still distinctive.

"Parlon Dremun!" someone whispered. The silence in the room made it seem more like a shout.

"Indeed!" answered the now familiar figure, and unexpectedly sat down cross legged in the centre of the circle of men. One leg was obviously more awkward to bend than the other.

"Where have you been?" asked another voice, "We thought you were dead – from your wounds at The Square."

"So it would seem. I have been...everywhere, and nowhere. Listening and watching, remaining unheard and unseen."

His words seemed very deliberate and slow; the opposite of the way he used to speak, when his words had been full of passion. Yet, he still held a captive audience. "I have seen terrible things; much worse than we have seen before."

Murmurs of disbelief escaped from some lips at this remark. How could anything be worse?

"Shhh!" came several reprimanding voices.

"I have been collating information, assessing the situation, and watching developments. I see that it is now too late, my friends, to salvage this planet. So much damage has been inflicted, too many of the population massacred.

"I see from this evening's events, the disquiet now among these groups. Soon, even we will breed hate, and fight among ourselves."

More murmuring broke out among the crowd. He continued, "I see, brothers, that the only hope we have of survival, is to escape from this planet, and seek refuge elsewhere."

This time as his words ceased, not another sound could be heard. The pause seemed to hang in the air for an eternity, before questions began erupting from every direction.

"Where will we go? How will we get there? How will we manage to transport everyone? What about the disease?

Supposing the same thing happens again in the future?"

Parlon Dremun had anticipated all these questions, even though he could not be entirely sure of delivering all the correct corresponding answers. He sucked in the breath over his teeth as he rose to his feet, and removing his gloves, stretched out his scarred hands for silence.

"Brothers. These are the questions that we have to work together to find the answers to. It will take time to finalise all the details, of course, but we must be as organised and ready as we can, as soon as possible. We don't have much time. However..." Here he paused. "There are many difficulties and restrictions we must adhere to, for everybody's sake. We can only allow a certain number of people to leave, and then under very strict restrictions. It is hard, I know, but it has to be this way in order for it to work. No compromises.

"There is one functional and safe shuttlecraft remaining. There will only be enough room and provisions for two hundred and sixty people."

He appeared to be rather reluctant at relaying this last piece of information, as he knew the reaction that it would provoke. In the groups meeting here tonight, there were at least a few hundred people, and not everyone had attended. What about them, their families, and everybody else?

Continuing as though he could not hear the questions

that were now bombarding him, Parlon Dremun said, "Because you will be settling on a planet that is as yet uninhabited , as far as we know, we must ensure that the best possible start is made. It will be crucial to your survival. Therefore, I regret, only the healthiest men, women, and children may leave. The rest must remain here. The first born children must be given every opportunity to be perfectly healthy in every way, if you are to establish a population."

"Why do you keep referring to "you" all the time? You are going to oversee the project, surely?"

"I can't. I am no longer a healthy man. You recalled my injuries earlier. During my convalescence, I became unwell, and very weak. My judgement was impaired, and I scratched myself while obtaining some bread from a beggar girl. There is no medicine. The wound remained untreated, my immunity was low. Needless to say, I have contracted the disease that has laid claim to so many of our good people's lives. The beggar girl was obviously either infected, or carrying the disease."

Moving back a few steps, he pulled up the long, heavy sleeves of his cloak to reveal open sores. His face showed not even a flicker of fear, or self-pity. There was nothing that he could do now, except to help his people become organised for their escape to a new world, and to re-establish their numbers successfully.

This was his final opportunity to help before he became

too weak to be of any use at all.

All around, stunned, ashen faces stared back in pity at him. Tonight he had been resurrected from the dead in front of them, only to be facing the grave again.

Chapter 5

The next few weeks were taken up with the preparations and arrangements for the journey. The hum of excitement was almost audible. Everyone was again working together with a common goal and thinking of others instead of themselves.

Throughout all the activities, a lone hooded figure watched in silence, lost in thought and remorse that there was no other choice than to desert the planet that the people had loved so. Their home.

Parlon Dremun walked along the debris covered road, sidestepping holes and craters made by bullets and grenades. Occasionally, a dull red patch would be noticeable on the ground, where blood had been shed, and not cleaned away. He remembered back to the day he had been at the rock face and when he had witnessed the argument between Saloe and the Spilon, and how irritated he had been at the dust on his boots. Now, he realised, that was energy spent on something completely trivial, and wondered how anything like that could ever have been so important to him.

He considered how things had escalated so quickly since that day, and how nobody had ever expected the terrible twist in events since. He did not want to send anyone to another planet they knew so little about, especially without him there to safeguard and advise them.

"And yet, it is the only alternative," he kept reassuring himself aloud. He had been constantly haunted by the thought that there was something more he could do to save their world; but if there was, it kept eluding him. It drove him to the point of distraction, and caused him to spend many sleepless nights.

His hood now not only covered the scabs and scars of the disease that fed upon his skin, but also hid his pale, troubled face, and dark puffy eyes, away from people. He had to keep up the pretence that all was well, to give an air of confidence and encouragement to the others. If he failed in this, and they lost heart, then the plans and work would suffer, and delay the planned escape date. Any hold ups could mean complete abandonment of the project, so delicate were the plans. This must not happen at all costs. Each day that passed made it more dangerous to be caught by The Greedmen; the penalty would be instant execution, and possible discovery of their secret. Parlon Dremun shuddered in revulsion at the thought, and forcibly turned his mind back to what still needed to be done.

The majority of preparations had been completed; the limited food supplies stocked, including amount of grain, and seeds to sow crops immediately upon arrival. Maps and charts had been drawn up based upon the little they knew about their destination, basic training given in case any engineering problems were encountered during the journey. As much first aid and medical supplies as were available were also included, and a special glass compartment made to contain a scroll, listing a code of conduct, laws and rules under which the new colony should be established and maintained.

The engines had been modified and adapted, prepped and primed, checked for faults and then checked again. Nothing could be left to chance. Quantities of mined rock were placed in as many crevices as possible for additional fuel for arrival. The hardest job of all was the one deliberately left until last; choosing who would leave on the journey, and who would have to stay behind to meet their predestined fate. Parlon Dremun kept the name of the destination planet to himself. It would be dangerous for anyone else to know. It must not be talked about casually, for fear of being overheard in the wrong places. Now he dreaded telling the crowds which of them would have a chance at starting a new life, and who would be condemned to death here.

There were two other reasons he had waited before announcing his decision; the work and preparations needed to be carried out quickly and efficiently, and he knew that once his choice was known, those who were to stay might not work as hard, or stop helping altogether. He needed everyone who was involved to play their full part. He was also aware that as time ticked past, some of the people believed to be healthy might contract the disease. He would not be able to bear breaking the news to someone that their hope of leaving had been denied after all.

The torment of all this constant pressure was nearly tearing him apart. Great waves of doubt, anguish, failure and guilt washed over him; sometimes one at a time, sometimes all together, until he thought his sanity would be irretrievably swept away. Momentarily, at times of crisis like these, he would lose faith in himself and his final plans.

All his life, he had dedicated his time and energy to helping others, and for the improvement to the quality of life they enjoyed. He had worked tirelessly in his research and experiments, and had indeed been successful in many of his attempts, bringing him not only respect, but the satisfaction of seeing many of his ideas put to working use. For him, the reward was in seeing the benefit his work brought to others.

His failures were few, but he regarded these with disgust and dismay, and often spent whole nights in despair of his attempts, trying to correct and modify ideas so that they finally did work.

Never before though, had anything counted quite so much on being a success. This time, he had only one chance. If the plans failed first time, then that would be the end.

Suppose they were found out? They would all be executed on sight, or maybe captured, tortured, and eventually killed. The voices inside his head argued on loudly against each other.

Well, what was the alternative? Not to try at all, and the last survivors eventually be killed by the disease? That would be a longer and more excruciatingly painful death than to be executed by The Greedmen. Should they live life, such as it was, in the shadows, afraid of being captured?

He shook with worry, and the long suppressed tears welled up, and ran down his pale, pinched cheeks. Why should he have to take all the responsibility for these people's lives and futures? Why couldn't someone else take over and make all the impossible decisions? The voices grew louder and became more and more jumbled until he thought he would scream in agony. He was so very weary.

At that moment, he became suddenly aware of another person's presence in the room and he turned, startled. Saloe stood facing him, regarding him with what appeared to be complete awe. He didn't know how long he had been standing there watching him, but in that moment, he knew that although he had had to suffer the burdens and pressures alone, it had been his idea. It was him that had given the people at least a chance of survival. Without him, they would almost surely have been swamped and drowned in their own misery and hopelessness. Instantly, he knew that he had to keep the sole responsibility, and bring his plan through to the conclusion. If someone else took over and it failed...He had to see it through. If failure was to be his destiny, he would carry its weight alone.

"Yes?" he enquired of Saloe, already knowing what he had come to say.

Saloe found his voice quietly announcing, "The people are assembled, and ready for your decision, sir." His eyes burned brightly with anticipation; he had worked hard, and was still free of the disease. He believed that his name was on the list of the selected.

"I am ready." Patting his pocket to check he had the papers he needed, he marched resolutely from the room, knowing what they contained would lead to relief and exhilaration for some, and despair and destruction for many others. He clasped them tightly between his gloved fingers. He must keep a tight rein on his emotions. It was not for much longer, he kept reciting in his mind. It was nearly over.

He hardly sensed walking out to the waiting crowd, and was only aware that they were suddenly in front of him. He stopped and gazed around the sea of expectant faces, all exhibiting a range of differing expressions.

Taking a deep breath, he decided he may as well get it over with. They had waited long enough. Pulling the papers from his pocket, he removed his gloves so he could handle them more easily and slowly began to read the names of those selected from the list. He did not dare to lift his eyes from the pages even once for fear that he would not be able to continue.

His voice successfully managed to portray a false air of confidence, but as he read the last name, his voice slowed even further, for he was loathe to receive the reproachful looks of disappointment that he would surely meet.

When he finally looked up, he was taken aback; for though he could sense in the atmosphere that there were those who disagreed with his decision, the majority were actually regarding him with a quiet sense of approval.

Slowly, he shifted his gaze towards Saloe, whose name had not been read out. Saloe moved forwards, and whispered, "I understand."

Now that he knew he wasn't included in the journey plans, and nothing else that he did as an individual could jeopardise the mission, he reached out his own scarred and cut hands, and before Parlon Dremun realised what was happening, shook his hand before he could snatch it away. Saloe was now almost certain to contract the disease too.

Parlon Dremun saw the complete understanding of Saloe's actions reflected in his eyes, and could not find a steady voice to reply with. Instead, he gripped Saloe's hand back with equal force, and held it fast.

The crowds began to applaud, and he turned in amazement.

"We all knew you were burdened with the hardest decisions," Saloe began to explain, " And it was inevitable that there would be disappointment among us. But you have given us something very important – hope. We cannot criticise or condemn. We can only thank you for not giving up on us, and making survival at least a possibility for some of us. And for being strong enough to make the decisions that none of us had to."

Again, Parlon Dremun felt unable to speak steadily and waited for a few moments with bowed head.

"My friends," he began at last, sweeping his arms to show that he included every person in the room, "I am deeply relieved that you all understand, and I thank you for reassuring my doubts to the contrary were wrong. I can do nothing else now, except wish those who are leaving a safe journey to their new world; the name of which is...Vantil."

Applause again broke out, this time even louder, and the excitement was apparent at this choice of new home. Wishes of good luck were exchanged among those were leaving, and sympathetic hugs and handshakes to those who were not.

Parlon Dremun, unable to contain the stress of his feelings any longer, took his leave, and made his way back to his lonely dwellings.

Chapter 6

Two evenings later, the escape plan was ready to be put into action. The Zarenians who were leaving made their way under cover of darkness excitedly to the shuttle in groups of twenty without any problems.

Only Parlon Dremum and a few others would be present to ensure they left safely; large numbers of people wanting to bid farewell would only have attracted unwanted attention. As the selected men, women, and children waited patiently for their names to be checked off the register before boarding the craft, Parlon Dremun's hands again shook terribly.

When the last names were finally crossed off the list, and there were no more to follow, there were seven names that remained unmarked.

That meant that there were seven new contracted cases of the disease, or they had decided not to go, or perhaps The Greedmen had killed them. If it was because they suspected symptoms of the disease, the affected had bravely and wisely opted to stay completely away from the group. Parlon Dremun must now find seven replacements. He became anxious again, because he knew there was the possibility that someone on the shuttle who appeared fit and well, may have the disease, and would not be aware of it until after departure, but that was something he had no control over.

He checked the list that he had drawn up, and his eyes scanned down to the names which he had prepared as reserves. He felt the wrench inside his heart as he read the third name - Saloe. He knew what it said, he had written it after all, but it was yet another cruel blow to see that name, picture that face, and know there was nothing that could be done. If only his reactions had been quicker when Saloe seized his hand to shake it. If only he had not removed his gloves when reading the names out. If only, if only, if only.

Forcing himself to carry on reading the replacements names was probably the hardest thing of all he had had to do yet.

He would never tell Saloe if he saw him again that his name had been included in the reserves, for by now the disease would probably be well established in his system.

What made it worse, was that he alone knew there was a small amount of antidote aboard the craft. One of The Greedmen had been working on a cure and had had some success. Primarily it was for his own people, but he had been disgusted at what they had been doing, and was trying to develop the antidote for the Zarenians. Ammay, the young Spilon, had approached Parlon Dremun and given him a small amount, promising him more as he made it, but out on a raiding party one day, he had refused to kill a Zarenian child, and his superiors had shot him as a traitor.

The antidote would only be discovered after the shuttle had left, and be enough for each person to take one dosage during the journey if needed, with some left over for when they reached Vantil in case of any future problems of recurrence. It would only work for those who had begun to show symptoms of the disease up to twenty four hours prior to taking the medication, and would keep the others completely immune from it.

Saloe had held his hand two days before. Parlon Dremun could have administered the drug among the healthy staying on Zaren, but knew the disease was so widespread that it would only have had short term success for a minority of those suffering. He could have taken some himself, and hoped by some miracle that it would be effective, but he had had enough of life now and its cruel blows. It would be a waste. He knew it, and was not even tempted to try. But Saloe, he could have still had a chance.

"Damn it all," he cried out, " Saloe was so close to keeping hold of life."

The seven replacements were sent for, and shortly began arriving and boarding the craft in a bewildered state of euphoria, scarcely able to believe that they had literally been saved at the last minute.

Once everyone was safely on board and doors and exits locked, secured, and checked, everything happened very quickly to despatch the shuttle. There was no point in waiting. The sooner the precious cargo was transported away from Zaren and its death throes, the better.

As the craft finally lifted off, so Parlon Dremun felt all the strain and stress lifting from his shoulders too. He felt relieved he had succeeded, but also sad, as he realised that he would no longer need to torture himself trying to conjure up impossible alternative courses of action. He was no longer needed. It was all over. Zaren and its remaining inhabitants would just eventually die out completely.

Although they had not admitted it, The Greedmen must have contaminated men among their numbers too. Disease would also spread among them, and unable to return to Spilon, they would be wiped out. Their plan had failed dismally. Strangely though, Parlon Dremun felt sad for them, but did not know why. He surmised that it must be because the whole thing had been triggered off over something as basic as greed among such a few people, which ironically, had spread as quickly as the actual disease that it had caused.

Zaren would become uninhabited, the disease would spread and eventually have nobody left to infect, and it would therefore also die out. Maybe Zaren would be re-colonized in years to come by travellers from another planet. Perhaps they would be fleeing from the same threats, he wondered. He stopped his imagination from running away with him that in the future, the same thing would happen all over again.

He would never know.

He walked slowly along the uneven road from the meeting place, wondering if this time was the last one that his feet would dodge the ruts and grooves in the hardened mud. He had been absently picking away at a thread from a bandage he had put round his damaged left hand, which was no longer throbbing with the intense heat and pain that it had for so long. It was now completely numb. Was that good or bad, he wondered. Probably bad, he decided. He felt so alone, and in desperate need of a companion. Someone he could let the confined screaming, demanding voices in his head out to, so they didn't torture him anymore. These possessed and obsessed voices had been constantly arguing among themselves for weeks. They were incessantly telling him what he was doing was wrong, then right, then undecided, then not caring, then unfeeling, then in torment.

His limping frame dropped to its knees, and again the tears fell down his cheeks, preceding sobs of pent up anguish and grief. He thought about his dead mother, his murdered father, his phantom wife, and his unborn children. He hurt everywhere; physically, but more so mentally. He felt a choked and ignored cry coming from his stomach, and suddenly he was bellowing. Over and over, releasing everything he had not allowed himself to feel. It poured out of him, taking energy he did not know he had left. He fell down flat on his face, his unfeeling hands useless at wiping away his tears. The roaring carried on until there was no voice left, and he lay exhausted on the ground, partly trying to regain his breath, partly hoping no more inhalations and exhalations would come.

Eventually, he lay still, completely spent. He had no idea how much time had passed. Then, he slowly became aware, the voices had ceased. He listened, expecting them to start up again. They didn't. At last, they seemed to have died out altogether. Now he felt calm and peaceful.

As he hauled himself to his feet once more, he concluded that the most important task he had ever set out to do, was working; as far as he could tell. What happened to the occupants of Thalok 4, the shuttle, was now up to them, and out of his control. The forces of destiny would decide.

There was no way of communicating with Zaren at all. Parlon Dremun had anticipated that even if they could rig up some way of contact, the messages could be intercepted, and traced to Vantil. The consequences did not bear thinking about.

He began limping along once more, his last task once he returned home, to destroy the list of names and information he held in his pocket. He had not entrusted anyone else to do this for him. He could so nearly cease from dragging his exhausted body about. These thoughts gave him some comfort, and the strength to walk this last path.

Suddenly, he found he was lying down on the road again, but this time with a peculiar nauseous and dizzy feeling that left him unable to lift his head for several moments. He had not known that to be one of the effects of the disease. Buzzing filled his ears; then gradually subsided into silence.

"Stay where you are, Parlon Dremun," a low voice growled.

"What...?"

In the moment that he had half turned his head to see what was happening, realisation hit him that these were not effects of the disease at all.

So engrossed in thought was he, that he had not heard anyone coming up behind him, and striking his head. As his eyes focused, he guessed The Greedman standing over him had struck him with the weapon he was holding. It had caused a mighty jolt. Panting for breath and trying to remain calm, he rested his head on the ground, waiting. As he blinked rapidly, partly to steady himself but also partly to gain time to think, a pair of hands roughly pulled him to his feet. He stared transfixed at The Greedman who had struck him the blow. He had not seen one this closely before. His face was covered by a black mask and visor, and no part of his body was visible. He found it unnerving that he could not see the eyes or expression of the man who was veiled entirely from head to toe; veiled to protect him from those infected? Or maybe so as not to spread it to someone else? Even in a dire situation like this his brain could still not stop dissecting, analysing and asking questions

Terror seemed to freeze the blood in his veins, although his heart continued to beat wildly inside his chest. Was this a chance discovery, or had the escape plan been found out? Nothing could be done about it now, but what did they know? He refused to show his fear. He himself had worn a mask - of pretence - for several months, and a few moments longer would make no difference. Just until The Greedman decided to pull his trigger, and end his life. How many more seconds did he have left, he wondered?

To his surprise, the guard made no attempt to do any such thing. Instead, his hands were tied tightly behind him, and his shoulder wrenched painfully in the process. The stinging made him feel sick again, and he fought to mentally stay in control. He realised that he could only feel the cord around his right wrist and nothing at all on his numb left side. Perhaps that was an advantage, he mused. So, what was going to happen to him? He thought he could probably imagine; The Greedman had called him by his name. He either had been sent purposefully to capture him, or he had accidentally stumbled upon a prize catch to take back to his superior.

Either way, the day was not going to end in quite the way he had anticipated. His painful leg struggled to take his weight as he was half dragged, and half pushed to the makeshift headquarters of The Greedmen's camp. He thought they had been travelling for about forty minutes. Or maybe it was longer. Or it was quite possible it wasn't anywhere near that long. His head hurt, his thoughts were even more jumbled than usual, his shoulder felt like it was on fire, and his leg pulsated with pain. Trying to remain upright to avoid kicks and punches from his captor took all his energy. He didn't know how long it had been. However long it was, he was exhausted and wanted to sleep forever; which he realised, was probably what he soon would be doing. His captor had not uttered a single word to him, except to goad him when he stumbled and fell, and the pain brought gasps to his lips.

Finally, as they reached their destination hidden deep in the trees, he was propelled through a thick, wooden doorway, guarded by several more uniformed men, into a brick tunnel that wound slowly down to several tens of feet underground. This must have taken a long time to dig out, Parlon Dremun considered, and he partly felt admiration for what they had managed to achieve. As they proceeded downwards, he felt it getting colder, and his heart felt like it was joining in. Along with the falling temperature, he could feel the dampness in the air, and he could not help shuddering. They continued along and his heart began to steady again. However, as they reached a further door, which seemed to herald the start of something very sinister, he felt it give a few more erratic lurches. As he heard the door grate shut behind him, he felt perhaps his heart would cease to beat altogether.

For a moment they stood still in total darkness, and he wondered, what happened now? Were they alone? In answer to that, burning torches were suddenly uncovered, and his hood was snatched down from his head. His eyes gradually adjusted to the new light so that he could see his new surroundings. There was nothing to see, however; just a long corridor with stone walls, a sandy floor, and the torches which were now hanging periodically from dingy, shabby archways. A Greedman appeared and sat heavily down at a makeshift table and without looking up, demanded his name.

"Why don't you tell him?" rasped Parlon Dremun at The Greedman who had ambushed, captured, and forced him here from the surface. "You know it."

This comment was rewarded by a sharp blow between the shoulder blades that winded him and forced him to wince in agony. He gasped, trying not to show he had a weakness from earlier, knowing full well he had to hide anything they could take advantage of. When he had recovered his breath, he risked a further comment.

"You are good at that, aren't you?" He refused to be seen to be humiliated by them. This time, the force of the blow sent him crashing to the floor, his numb leg crumbling beneath him. Another wave of dizziness washed over him. A yell that could not be stifled escaped his lips, and again he fought for breath and composure. When he was sure he could stand, he got back up onto his feet, supporting his weight by his shoulder against the wall; his balance affected by his hands still tied behind him.

"Name?" the demand came coldly again.

"Why, haven't you got one of your own?" He even managed a half smile. They were clearly going to treat him like a toy before they decided to kill him, and he saw no reason why he should not play with them too. Death was inevitable. He might as well enjoy himself while he could.

This time, however, he had pushed his luck a little too far, and he did not even feel the blow that completely knocked his senses out of him.

*   *   *

Saloe had left the meeting place shortly after Parlon Dremun had. He had hung about, anxiously wishing to catch him quietly to seek his advice concerning the symptoms he could now expect to experience from the disease.

Seeing him exit, he had gathered up a few of his belongings and followed after him. He had nearly caught up when he had witnessed his friend breakdown and sink uncontrollably in grief to the ground. He could not bear to let him know he had seen him like that. As his friend's cries and moans had begun to subside and he was thinking about going to him, he saw The Greedman approaching. Quickly he sank down behind a pile of rubble, and peered over the top cautiously to see what was happening.

There was absolutely nothing he could do to help; he had no weapon with which to come to his friend's aid. Instead, he was forced to watch in horror as Parlon Dremun was knocked brutally to the ground. He too was surprised that they did not kill him immediately.

As he watched breathlessly to see what would unfold, he noticed a piece of paper fall from the councillor's pocket, unseen by The Greedman, and seemingly unnoticed by Parlon Dremun as he was frogmarched away.

As soon as it appeared safe to do so, Saloe crept out into the open and made his way cautiously over to where the paper lay, gently fluttering like a butterfly on the ground. Kneeling down, he scooped it up, and his eyes swept down the page, as he realised it was the list of passenger names, and final details for the departure. It was fortunate for everyone that the page had not been noticed, for its discovery of the escape plan and those involved would mean...he didn't even want to think about what that would have meant. Thank goodness Parlon Dremun had not been captured earlier – whatever was he thinking, keeping that paper on him? He was normally so careful and meticulous. He could only assume that he would have destroyed the list once he had returned home.

He knew he must destroy it now, so that there was no possibility of it falling into The Greedmen's hands. As he began to tear it up, he wondered whether Parlon Dremun would be relieved when he discovered it was missing, so that he could not pass it into those butchering hands, or whether he would be concerned about where he had mislaid it.

As he continued shredding it up, so something caught his eye. Pressing the remains flat out into the palm of his hand, he read his name near the top of the reserve list. So, he thought, as he swallowed slowly, that was why his friend had seemed so quiet.

He realised what a strain it must have been not being able to give away that his friend had been included after all, and then to know that it would have been to no avail anyway.

He decided what he must do. He must get back to the meeting place, and try to gather as many men as possible to help the one soul who had done so much for them. Tucking the shreds of paper firmly beneath a rock, he turned to run back in the direction from which he had come.

As he did so, he saw a party of Greedmen guards

advancing. He skidded to a halt, and then stood rooted to the spot as he gathered his thoughts and wits about him, before ducking back behind the pile of rubble once more.

It was too late. He had been seen, and The Greedmen broke into a run after him. As he looked over the top to see how close they were, so a bullet struck a rock about five inches away from him.

"That near!"

He looked back over his shoulder and saw an old deserted building. Keeping low, he sprinted towards it, dodging more bullets discharged at him, and scurried inside.

Pressed against the wall, panting for breath and straining to hear anything over the pounding of his heart, he edged his face up to the window and glanced out.

The Greedmen were only a few seconds away from entering the shack. He ran to the back exit and out that side, straight into one of the guards who had been sent to cover any rear escape.

He yelled in despair as he changed direction, and saw that way cut off too. He stopped, and began edging backwards, until he felt a gun pressed into his back. He closed his eyes expecting to be shot, and wondered if he would die before he felt the pain.

Instead, he too was bound by his hands and marched roughly away. Somehow he knew that it would have been much better for him if they had killed him there and then.

Chapter 7

When he came to, his body ached and his head was throbbing. Almost a relief, Parlon Dremun considered; at least the disease had not yet completely numbed his body. He opened his eyes and saw nothing, only blackness. At first he thought he had been blinded by the blow that he had received to his head, but after a few moments of blinking, realised that it was just the room he was being kept in.

He grunted as he tried to move. His hands had been untied, but the wrist he still had feeling in throbbed where they had been cruelly held. No matter which way he tilted his head, there was no trace of light anywhere, and he began to feel around him. He realised that he was lying on some kind of material on a cold, dusty floor. It wasn't a bed, just some scratchy cloth on the ground. It smelled of something rotten, but he couldn't tell what, and probably wouldn't want to, he mused. Carefully, he pushed himself into an upright sitting position, trying to ignore the protests his body made. He felt above his head to ensure if he stood up that he would not strike it on anything. It seemed to be clear.

Slowly, he edged his way up against the wall into a crouching position, and then onto his feet. As he did so, he noticed the terrible stench seemed worse; a smell of decay, but what? He shuddered and wondered what could be worse than the smell on the blanket. Was there a dead body in here with him? Maybe it was a previous occupant. With seemingly no ventilation, the smell could not dissipate. Perhaps they intended to leave him here to starve and suffocate. He couldn't imagine that – what pleasure would that give them?

He placed his good hand up against the wall, and was dismayed to find that not all of his fingers had feeling in them. With the palm of his hand, he felt along the rough, uneven surface, while his feet edged forward one after the other very slowly and carefully. He counted his steps to get an approximate size of his room, and shuffled to one corner twelve paces later.

Changing direction, he felt his way ten steps forward until he came to a second corner. A frown crept across his face; this was hardly a room, more of a large box.

Making his way along the third wall, he became more confident of his bearings and took larger, less careful steps. Suddenly, his foot struck something, and he heard a clang of metal striking the wall. He was relieved it couldn't have been a body. Gingerly, he eased himself down into a crouching position, and felt around like a blind man for the object. His half unfeeling fingers groped and stumbled about in the dirt until they found it.

Feeling all around its smooth shape, he concluded that it was just a metal bowl. His fingers explored inside, and discovered some kind of remaining liquid. It was thin, not sticky, at room temperature, and had no odour. He decided it was a fairly safe assumption that the liquid was water, and tentatively tasted it. After all, it could only kill him.

A few moments later, his suspicions were confirmed when he came across a lump of what felt like bread, embedded in the sand. Where a prisoner had bread, he generally had water!

Hoping that he had wiped off as much dirt and whatever else was on the floor onto his robes as possible, he bit off a chunk and chewed, pondering how much time had elapsed since he was rendered unconscious. He felt like a scavenging animal but he wanted to survive a little longer, if only to determine some more of the rules to the game that he was playing.

When he had eaten, gagging on the dry bread with hardly enough water left to help it down, he continued to feel his way along the third wall, and then the fourth, but came across nothing else.

Wondering if there might be anything in the middle of the room, he set about crossing from side to side, and then diagonally with his arms outstretched in front of him. Nothing.

He felt his way back to the third wall where he had found the bread and water. Logically, that must be where the door was. He felt around and found a groove. Tracing it with his fingers as much as he was able, he now knew where the entrance was; the opposite wall to his blanket. At least he now had some idea of his bearings and did not feel so disorientated. No point in trying the handle – it wasn't going to be left unlocked, and if he rattled it about, he might bring unwelcome company in sooner than he wanted, and perhaps another brutal beating.

He held up his arms above his head, as high as he could manage, to find out how tall the room was. He felt only air; cool air. Then there must be some sort of ventilation. He took a little jump, then a bigger one, and then the biggest one he could. Still nothing. At least he did not feel entirely like a caged animal. Rubbing his hips, he returned back to his blanket, and sat down with a sigh. His initial inquisitiveness had faded, and he realised just how tired he felt.

Sleep crept up on him while he still sat propped up against the wall.

* * *

Upon his capture, Saloe had not put up such a chivalrous show of bravado as his friend had done. For he knew that he had been the only hope of alerting The Opposers and launching some sort of attack to free Parlon Dremun.

More than anything, he felt angry with himself for being caught. It was highly unlikely that anybody else had witnessed their abductions. They were on their own.

When he had reached the base, Saloe had experienced the same sense of impending doom as the door sealed off the daylight behind him. He knew he would never leave again.

He had cooperated fully when asked for his identification, and thereby avoided the beatings Parlon Dremun had gone through. He had then been led to a room of which the door was guarded on either side.

The two guards escorting him pulled at his arms, gesturing to stop outside. Regarding the two men at the door, he wondered if they were reciprocating the enquiring look from behind their dark visors that he gave them. Why weren't they entering?

Just as he began to wonder whether they were going to leave him there and wait until he died of boredom, the door opened from within.

Two Greedmen emerged carrying a man between them by his arms and legs. His clothes were ripped, and huge sores and wounds were visible through the tears. His head lolled about from side to side like a broken doll, his face was battered, swollen, and covered in blood and bruises. His eyes were closed through unconsciousness. Or was he dead?

Saloe realised that his own jaw had dropped open in horror, and felt the blood draining from his face. His knees suddenly felt like they could not hold him, and his stomach, though empty, suddenly felt like it needed to dispel any contents urgently and forcefully. Trying hard to ignore these feelings and look unperturbed by this terrible sight, he tore his eyes away from the poor, unfortunate man, and fixed them firmly on the doorway.

Through his spinning thoughts and feelings, he realised he had been shown that deliberately, to unnerve and frighten him. It had worked.

Resolute to meet his fate with dignity and courage, he forced himself to remain composed, and continued to stare unblinkingly ahead, trying to stop his legs from buckling.

As the lifeless form was dragged past him and off to goodness knows where, he was only faintly aware that a form from within had appeared at the doorway, and beckoned silently for the guards to bring him inside.

Completely unable to move any of his limbs, his escorts gripped his arms more tightly and lifted him off his feet, carrying him into the room.

* * *

Parlon Dremun was awoken by a pair of hands shaking him roughly. Groggily he squinted against the light streaming into his cell through the open door. A Greedman stood before him. Temporarily blinded by the light, he didn't move quickly enough, and The Greedman gave him a kick to hurry him along. Clearly he was supposed to understand the silence meant he was to get up. He couldn't force his stiff body to coordinate itself, and still silent, The Greedman just pulled at his arm, dragging him to his feet.

"You only had to ask!" he muttered indignantly. He did so hate being rudely awoken.

Not a word was spoken as he was pushed out of the door, his feet unable to take him in a straight line, and his escort pushing him every time he fell against the wall. He recognised the corridor from when he had first arrived. They had probably placed his unconscious form in the nearest vacant room out of convenience, he thought.

Still shielding his eyes from the bright light, he stumbled along in whatever direction he was prodded. He was thirsty, hungry, tired, and hurt everywhere. Strangely, he wasn't scared or worried.

They must now be in the main part of the base, and guessed he was some way below the surface, as it grew colder and colder the further they progressed. He then noticed they had ceased to move downwards, and were now standing on level ground.

Approaching a doorway on the left hand side of the tunnel, they stopped. A guard outside rapped on the door, and waited until a voice from inside barked an order to enter.

Once inside, he gazed around at these new surroundings, and knew instinctively that this must be the Leaders office. He had expected to see lavish and rich trappings of the countless raids, and souvenirs and trophies on display. Instead, he found bare walls and floor, and just a cabinet, desk and two chairs; upon one of which sat the Leader.

He didn't speak, but indicated with a careless motion of his hand for Parlon Dremun to be seated.

"I will remain standing." As much as he longed for rest after the walk from his cell, he was determined not to appear weak, physically or mentally.

However, from the corner of his eye, he saw a guard raise his weapon, and wisely he hastily added, "Actually, perhaps I will be seated."

Facing the Leader, he did not try to hide the vehemence he felt towards the man who had ordered so much terror, pain and death to be inflicted upon his people. The Leader sat with his elbows upon the desk, his gloved hands together in a pyramid, regarding his prisoner through his black visor in silence. The sudden movement he made as he sat back in his chair made Parlon Dremun jump.

"I am Thalez, Leader of The Spilons, or Greedmen as you now call us." The words were delivered as though announcing he had done something he ought to be congratulated for.

"How nice!" came the retort.

"And you have caused us a great deal of trouble."

"Oh dear, what a pity!"

This sarcasm obviously agitated Thalez, but he was trying not to let it show. Unclenching his fist that had voluntarily closed into a tight ball, he stood and paced the length of his desk several times, trying to maintain an air of calmness and control. Obviously he had not encountered this sort of resistance before.

He continued, "You are a prisoner in our base…"

"Really?"

"…Where you will remain…"

"Thank you for the invitation."

"…And cooperate fully."

"One likes to be of service."

This interchange was clearly too much for Thalez to endure, and he stormed towards Parlon Dremun, who, because of the visor, could not see his face crumpled in rage, but could feel it none the less.

"Enough!" he cried, lurching at his prisoner, and

smashing the back of his gloved hand across his face, "I will not tolerate such insolence." Though Parlon Dremun expected punishment for his answers, he was taken aback by the strength this man possessed. Maybe he should be a little more thoughtful and wise before provoking him further.

For a moment there was complete silence while composure was gained on both sides.

"Tell me what you have done," Thalez finally said in a voice that sounded rather exasperated. "We know that a number of Opposers cannot be accounted for at this moment in time, and we also know a shuttlecraft has "disappeared"."

Now did not appear to be the relevant time for being flippant anyway.

Thalez had been walking around the room, his gloved fingers rubbing his masked chin thoughtfully as he spoke. Now he moved to behind his prisoner's chair and bent forward, until his head was a few inches away from Parlon Dremun's own. He fancied he could feel his breath despite the thickness of the mask. The hair on the nape of his neck stood erect. As he turned his face slightly, he saw his distorted reflection in the visor, but hardly recognised who stared back.

"You know exactly what happened, don't you? It was your plan, wasn't it?" he rasped in a low, menacing voice.

No reply.

"Wasn't it?" he demanded, straightening up.

Parlon Dremun closed his eyes, and tensed every muscle in his body in anticipation of the inevitable blow. Nothing happened. Warily, he opened his eyes.

Thalez was apparently regarding him quietly now, and Parlon Dremun could not help thinking that the mask probably concealed a wry smile, stretched across thin, cruel lips. Somewhere in the back of his mind, a voice was screaming that he knew the identity of his captor; but that was impossible. How could he? The familiar sound of Thalez's voice broke into his thoughts.

The tone in his voice changed, as he drawled, "I expected such resistance from you. You have proved to be strong and brave, and a good and loyal leader for your people. We have enjoyed watching you. You could almost have become one of us."

Parlon Dremun felt his skin crawling at the very suggestion and hoped his look conveyed the hate that he felt.

"However," Thalez continued, "although I believe the threat of physical violence to yourself will not break your silence, I believe that your reaction and willingness to talk might change dramatically if somebody else was involved."

Parlon Dremun could not hide his shock, and suddenly became very worried. Who else had they captured? It hadn't even crossed his mind that they might be holding another captive here.

"Particularly if it was someone you knew," he realised Thalez had just added.

Gripping the edge of his seat, he leaned forward and asked in a drawn voice, "Who?"

After a moment of silence, Thalez motioned to one of his guards, who immediately left the room. They sat in unbearable silence until his return. Parlon Dremun wondered if Thalez could feel his fear. His thoughts were again disturbed, this time by a sharp knock at the door, and he nearly jumped off his chair.

"Come."

It seemed to take an eternity for the door to open, until finally a guard entered backwards, stooped over, pulling at a man, who, unable to stand, was being dragged along on his knees. The huddled form was hauled moaning and groaning into the room, and deposited in a heap on the floor, face down. The guard straightened up and stood beside him.

Thalez strolled over to him, and addressing a grey faced Parlon Dremun said, "Perhaps this will loosen your tongue."

He placed his boot underneath the man's chest, and pushed him over onto his back. At first, he was unrecognisable through the blood and bruising that covered his face. Parlon Dremun felt sick.

"Saloe?" he cried, and flung himself down at his side, despite the pain that tore through his own body as he did so. Cradling his head gently in his lap, he carefully wiped away at some of the fresher blood with his cloak.

"Saloe." This time he whispered. In response, one bloodied eye opened as far as it could to look at him. The other was too swollen to open at all. A gurgle escaped his throat as he recognised his friend, and a hand reached up desperately to grab his own.

In a low voice, Parlon Dremun demanded, "What have you done to him?"

"He too was loathe to cooperate – at first. A little "gentle persuasion" was needed to encourage him to talk. Once he began...well, shall we say, he simply could not stop himself."

"You enjoy this, don't you? You actually enjoy it."

"Perks of the job."

"You must be completely insane."

"Why so worried?" We have hardly started yet. There is much more to come. He has merely provided us with a warm up – an appetiser."

Parlon Dremun was shaking with rage, desperate to help his friend, but fully aware that there was nothing he could do, except try to comfort him.

"Of course, they do have an annoying little habit of dying before the real fun begins. It does so spoil our enjoyment."

"I bet it does. Exactly how many have you tortured like this? Hundreds, it must be."

"A mere trifle."

"I fail to see how you can live with yourself. Have you no conscience? No feelings at all?"

"In my job, I cannot afford to have a conscience or feelings. I just have a good sense of job satisfaction at the end of the day."

A range of emotions swept through him, as he battled to comprehend how such a monster could exist. In fact, they were all monsters; he gave the orders, but they all obeyed him. Why didn't they stop? What was wrong with them all? He tried to stifle the feeling rising in him that until now had been alien. He felt anger so intense, that it was threatening to make him violent towards another living being. He was trying hard to quash it, but was not succeeding.

Perhaps now he was beginning to understand how some of the other men had been unable to quench their rising emotions and had become aggressive. He felt sorry now that he had not tried to understand and sympathise with them more.

"Anyway, your friend eventually saw our point of view, and told us everything," Thalez continued, as though he was pointing out what a lovely day it was.

For a moment, Parlon Dremun almost believed him. The state Saloe was in, he wouldn't have blamed him if he had talked.

He instantly dismissed the thought, for if Saloe had revealed everything, he wouldn't have been kept alive, and he himself would have been instantly executed instead of being interrogated. Besides, Saloe was one of the loyalist men he had ever known. No, they needed information.

"Then why are you asking me?" he countered.

At this, Thalez was visibly stuck for words, and he struggled to find a suitable answer standing stiffly.

"I need you to confirm his story." He seemed satisfied with his reply, and appeared to relax a little.

"You're bluffing. You don't seriously expect me to believe you, do you?" All right, if he talked, what did he tell you?"

Again, Thalez seemed distinctly ruffled while Saloe was still trying to gurgle something unintelligible to his fellow captive.

"If you had a degree of intelligence," he faltered, "you would realise that if I told you his story, which may turn out to be a pack of lies, you would hardly deny it and tell me the truth, would you?"

Parlon Dremun could tell by his voice that he believed that statement about as much as he did.

"However did you manage to become elected as Leader?" The instant that he let that remark slip out, he knew that he had made a costly error that Saloe would pay dearly for.

"Because I am not afraid to use methods like this to get good results." He lifted his boot sharply and Parlon Dremun tried to block it.

"No! Wait!" he cried, yelping in pain as the boot connected with his side. Two guards rushed forward and held him back as Thalez's boot this time thudded heavily into Saloe's side, who instinctively tried to curl up into a ball as he let out a scream of pain. For a second time, the boot lashed out and ferociously knocked him over onto his other side.

"Stop it! Stop it, please!" he begged. "I'm sorry. Just stop!"

Laughter echoed around the room from Thalez and the guards, mingled with the cries of Saloe's agony. Parlon Dremun's head fell forward down onto his chest, and as tears rolled down his face, he murmured, "I'm sorry Saloe, so sorry."

Saloe's cries died and he lay motionless; a heap of dirty rags in a pool of fresh blood.

When Thalez had grown tired of his assault on a body that no longer reacted to his violence, Parlon Dremun broke free of the guards grip, and knelt down beside his friend again. Grasping hold of Saloe's hand tighter than before, he hoped for his understanding as he told Thalez, "I cannot tell you want you want to know. My life is nearly over. I have the disease. You can only make my death come sooner, but perhaps more painful. It is of no consequence to me. Saloe too has the disease, and will probably only live a short while longer than me, after the way he has been treated."

He had to force every word out of his throat. It was true that he did not care for himself, but he could not speak for his friend. He could only hope that Thalez believed what he said, and would not force his hand further.

At least, he appeared to be digesting this information, as he walked slowly back over to the other side of the room, where he stood facing the wall.

Taking this opportunity, Parlon Dremun quickly leaned

over Saloe more closely, and whispered an apology in his ear. In response, his friend tried to pull himself up, and a cough escaped his lips along with dark, red blood.

"Don't...tell...him...please,"   he   managed   finally, "Whatever...happens...don't tell... him."

"I won't, I promise. Too much is at stake."

"I found...the ...list of...names...I...destroyed...it."

"What? You found it?" He realised he had completely forgotten about the list in his pocket. It must have fallen out when he was apprehended. If Saloe had found and read it..."Oh no, Saloe."

The sound of voices reached the ears of Thalez, and he spun around, catching sight of Parlon Dremun gently lowering Saloe's head back into his lap and wiping blood away.

"What did he just tell you?" he spat, thundering back over to the pair.

"Nothing."

"This is the last time I will ask. What did he say?"

"Merely that his lips are dry. He needs a drink of water. I suppose that's out of the question? Come to think of it, I too am very thirsty." He did not even raise his head as he uttered these words, for he was always loathe to lie, even if it was to this tyrant before him.

"You lie." Thalez again lashed out his fury at Saloe with his foot. He cried out again, and Parlon Dremun felt the agony inside of him as though he were the recipient. He wished he was.

He draped himself protectively across the now outstretched form, just as the second blow was delivered, catching him in the ribs. He was winded, but determined not to flinch away.

The guards moved in again, and tried to pull him off. He held on with all his remaining strength until the very last moment he could. Making a gargantuan effort, he pulled back towards Saloe one last time, and whispered his farewell.

"Goodbye my friend. I thank you for your courage and strength. Be brave in your last fight." He sensed their time together was nearly over.

Now, he allowed himself to be pulled away, and he closed his eyes to shield them from the horror he knew would take place before them.

The cries, screams and laughs all blended together into one interminable sound. Saloe eventually fell quiet after what seemed like an eternity, and the only audible sounds were then those of Thalez punching and kicking, and his maniacal laughter.

Parlon Dremun felt his strength and consciousness ebbing away, and he wished inwardly that he could just be allowed to die at that precise moment, so that he would never have to see what they had done to Saloe.

Chapter 8

The dizziness began to subside, the walls again became vertical, and the nausea left him slightly. Aware that he was still kneeling where he had been held by the guards, Parlon Dremun had reluctantly opened his eyes, and lifted his aching head.

He remembered.

Only seconds, or at the most, a couple of minutes, could have passed since his senses had left him. The blurry shapes in front of his eyes began to take a definite form, and he saw Thalez standing near Saloe's body. His boots and trousers were stained with blood, and a big puddle grew under Saloe's back, creeping further across the floor, as though it were defiantly trying to reach Thalez.

Parlon Dremun watched fascinated by its movement and the way the colour changed as it trickled across the floor. He determined to hold a strong countenance and not show his emotions; although inwardly he was being torn apart at the thought of the suffering his friend had endured. He knew that he was now dead.

Stinging him was the realisation that he himself would not be alive to tell The Opposers just how brave Saloe had been, and he resented that he would not be remembered as he should be.

Wrenching himself free of his captives grasp, he dragged

himself across the floor to Saloe. He felt his neck for a pulse, and then again with his other hand, to be sure it wasn't just his unfeeling fingers lying to him. As he expected, he found none.

The tears welled up again and spilled out as he embraced his friend one final time, and found that he could no longer pretend he was not affected by all this. He sobbed uncontrollably and freely as another wave of his long suppressed emotions tore free. At least they had let him hold Saloe, he was grateful for that.

Then through his grief, he could still hear Thalez laughing as he heard him say, "I told you they spoiled the fun by dying, just when you are beginning to enjoy yourself."

Suddenly, Parlon Dremun had a focus as his anguished cries unleashed his hidden feelings of shock at being badly injured at The Square, the despair of so many families dead, his anger at the violence on Zaren, the worries he carried as Leader of The Opposers, the weight he carried since finding out that he had the disease, his distress at his father being murdered in front of him, the relentless exhaustion of planning and carrying through the evacuation; and now, finally, the ordeal of coping with seeing his friend tortured and murdered in front of him, while he was made to look on helplessly. His loyal, courageous friend.

As the minutes passed by, the sobs began to diminish, and he slid a hand between his face and Saloe's chest where it rested, to wipe away his tears. He would not give Thalez the satisfaction of seeing his distressed face.

When he felt composed enough to do so, he lifted his head and turned towards his captor, who was now sitting quietly in his chair, observing the scene and his prisoner, with interest. He was sure if he could see his face, there would be a smug smile grinning at him.

"You do not even comprehend what I feel for this man, do you? You have never felt the grief of losing anyone, or seeing someone suffer, have you?"

"On the contrary, I find this scene of devotion rather touching, and quite stimulating."

"I swear I have never known there to be such an evil, twisted, mindless, monster as you."

"Thank you."

"Don't you feel anything else – guilt, resentment, shame, pity, remorse – anything remotely human at all?"

"You are very amusing. I only feel immense pleasure, and much satisfaction. Although, as I said earlier, I do feel a little resentment; that he didn't live long enough to amuse me further. However, I still have you."

Parlon Dremun began edging his way towards this vile being as he spoke, and pulled himself erect before him. At his last response, he felt his fury explode, and he lunged forward at Thalez.

"Well, I am going to feel immense satisfaction at this," he cried, leaping at him. He seized him by the collar and hauled him to his feet. His movement had been so quiet and unexpected that the guards who stood by the door had been momentarily left reeling in confusion.

By the time they realised what was happening, and grabbed hold of him, he had ripped the mask from the terrified Thalez.

The Greedman's face had at last been exposed, revealing cruel, hard features, with small, close set, dark eyes, and eyebrows that practically met in the middle. Beads of perspiration ran down the creases made by the frown he wore, and dripped off a long, narrow nose, down to the crooked chin which jutted upwards; the evidence of the effort involved in torturing Saloe.

"Somehow I knew it would be you," he whispered, recognising the man that he had seen arguing with Saloe all that time ago about his food rations. "And it was no accident that killed Vefa on the rock face either, was it? It was you. You killed an innocent young man, because he would not do as you said."

"Get him off, get him off. He has the disease," shrieked Thalez, as the guards tried to prise the two men apart.

"You're not enjoying your job so much now, are you?"

"Get away from me!"

"Not so smug now, eh?"

"Leave me alone, get away! Are you crazy?"

Parlon Dremun temporarily paused in his assault, for he found that last comment coming from such a man to be incredibly funny.

"Me crazy?" He relinquished his grip, and stood back laughing. "Me crazy!" he repeated, beginning to control his emotions again. He saw with great satisfaction that during the scuffle he had scratched Thalez's cheek, and a long thin line of bright red blood trickled down to his chin. As he was pulled away, he managed to free one arm and again deliberately struck out and caught Thalez's face with his nails, and made a second, deeper wound. He was amused by the squeak of fear Thalez let out, and wondered how such a brute who could inflict such pain on others, couldn't bear to be touched and hurt himself. He relaxed, and took deep gulps of air to steady his shaking hands.

"Well now, my treacherous friend. Issue your orders, and do what you will to me. I don't care. Beat me, torture me, hang me or shoot me. Whatever you please; for I will meet my death with gratitude. I have been given the chance to end your merciless brutality, your endless violence; your butchering and murdering ways."

As he delivered this speech, he staggered about, as though drunk.

"I have been given the chance to stop the war that you started on our planet. For, my spineless friend, in your stubborn ignorance, stupidity and arrogance, you have been most careless, and are now exposed to my disease."

Laughter again escaped his lips as he yelled at the top of his voice triumphantly, "You are going to die, and The Greedmen will die with you!"

This time the room rang with the sounds of his hysterical laughter, while Thalez looked on in mute horror. An ironical shift in role and power, in just moments.

During the following few seconds, a tumultuous mass of thoughts passed through his mind again. He could not believe that he had got through to Thalez so easily, and knew that once he was no longer capable of being Leader, The Greedmen who would also now be afraid of catching the disease from him, would probably become defunct. There was already an air of dissent among the men, but they had been too afraid to vent their feelings. This was the perfect opportunity for them too. Although it was too late to save the planet now, at least some kind of normality and rationality would be restored, even if only temporarily, for its final death throes. He found that reassuring.

Zaren, for a short while at least, would return to the quietness it once knew, before it completely died.

He had never condoned violence of any form, but felt that what he had just done was necessary and deserved, and surprisingly easily executed. Now he himself could die in peace, and was unafraid.

He was dimly aware that his own laughter had ceased, and he was now lying on the floor on his back, where the guards had thrown him.

He hadn't seemed to make any noise as he fell, and everything seemed to be moving in slow motion. He raised his head to see what was happening, and saw Thalez's mouth moving, but no sound seemed to be coming out.

As the guards moved towards him once again, he offered no resistance, and revelled in delight at Thalez's ashen face which was panic stricken now, instead of the perverted pleasure and joy it had shown earlier.

He resigned himself to the fact that his time was up now. At least he would not have to endure endless torture; not like poor Saloe. The guards reached him, and lifted him once more to his feet.

Everything now returned to normal speed, and he could hear the sounds of feet and voices again, and feel the anger and panic in the air. He felt himself being hurled against the wall, face first, and his nose cracked as he hit the hard surface with force. The sudden rush of blood nearly choked him, and fighting for breath, he turned with his back to the wall, and slid down until he sat propped up on the floor.

Instantly, he was hauled back up again and held against the wall, while Thalez vented his fury and frustration in his customary execrable display of physical violence.

Strangely though, Parlon Dremun did not really feel any pain after the first couple of blows; almost as though he had a protective barrier surrounding him. He hoped the experience had been the same for Saloe.

Did he just let out a groan of pain? He didn't know. His eyes drank in the scene, and he felt nothing but relief as he succumbed to his fate.

He saw Thalez stride away purposefully from him, and reach for his weapon. He looked at the threatening barrel of the gun as Thalez made the final adjustment to the setting, and watched in fascination as two pink, iridescent blobs exploded from it, and came hurtling towards him in quick succession. It occurred to him in an instant how pretty they were.

Then there was nothing but eternal darkness and silence.

Chapter 9

Perhaps it was a mercy that Parlon Dremun did not live. He was spared the terrible sights and sounds of yet more killing for a long time afterwards.

The Greedmen found out about the evacuation and shuttlecraft, but they did not find out how the plan had been plotted so secretly and quietly, nor the destination or numbers involved. In their arrogance however, they did not think for one moment that any plan the Zarenians had executed, could possibly succeed.

They didn't find out about the vaccine stashed on board the shuttle, and assumed that it was highly probable that the disease would be contracted amongst the travellers, and wipe them out before they landed at their destination to begin a new colony.

They continued their massacre, and The Opposers became outraged when an informant told them that Parlon Dremun and Saloe had been tortured and murdered.

Pointless battles raged on in the streets through the days and through the nights, for it seemed that both sides knew it was too late for anything to save either of them. The Opposers could not escape the disease; it was rife everywhere, and was only a matter of time before it claimed every last life on Zaren that had survived the bloody war.

The Spilons also had no chance of survival. For when their home planet finally sent a shuttle to find out how they were progressing, the officers were disgusted and outraged at what they found – they looked upon the whole mission as a complete, shameful, disaster. They left again; alone.

The Greedmen had been abandoned by their own people, and were looked upon as traitors for not completing the task they been set as efficiently and effectively as it should have been. It had never been an option for them to fail. After all, what possible actions could the Zarenians; a peaceful, quiet people, have taken to evoke such a shoddy, messy effort by a race regarded by all as dominant and superior? They were not given a chance to explain themselves, and were abandoned to die on Zaren.

The shame felt by Thalez was too much for him; much worse for him to bear than the disease ravaging his body. The fear of failure was seemingly the only thing he had in common with Parlon Dremun. He went into hiding, completely abandoning his post. He knew that his men would be so angry at the response from their superiors that they would probably kill him anyway.

A couple of weeks passed, and the disease established itself in his system, as Parlon Dremun had said it would. Curse that man! Even in death, he would not leave him alone.

When the pain became too great for him, both physically and mentally, he crawled away into an old ruined building on the surface, and sat dwelling yet again, on where it had all gone wrong.

He wrote an account of events in a journal, feeling a jolt of humiliation with every word he wrote, but hoping that he would understand how he had failed his mission, his people, and his quest for recognition and power. No matter how hard he tried though, he could not understand it.

He wrote to his wife and children, knowing they would never read what he had put, but feeling the necessity of bidding them farewell and asking for their forgiveness for his failure and inability to return home to them. Now he would never see their faces as they grew older. Would they be proud of him for trying? Would they be ashamed of him? Would they try to forget his very existence? Would his youngest son even remember him?

Finally, as he sat hunched up in his shelter, afraid of every noise and every shadow, and tears ran down his scarred and sore covered features, he placed the gun that he had used to kill Parlon Dremun to his head, and without any hesitation, fired.

His body was not discovered for many weeks, until one of the last few surviving Spilon's on Zaren stumbled across him by accident. He too was looking for a quiet place to die. Recognising the corpse only by the emblem on his uniform of the lightning flash through a crescent moon, and the red band on his sleeve denoting his rank, he stood over him and spat.

"Coward!" he cursed. "You killed us all. I show you no respect or honour in your death, for you never showed us any in your life.

He kicked at the stinking remains, and it fell down head first into the dirt.

"Huh," muttered the soldier, "How fitting." He scavenged through the coat and trouser pockets out of curiosity and found nothing.

"Like your head – empty."

Then, underneath one of Thalez's legs, he noticed a corner of the journal poking out and picked it up. Reading the last words about the shuttle leaving for an unknown destination, he sniggered, "I know where they went."

Finding the pencil Thalez had worn down almost to a blunt point, he scribbled the name "Vantil" on the bottom of the last page.

"Some of us knew more than others," he sneered, tossing the journal back at Thalez. "Except, now nobody else will ever know."

He stood up and looked down at the heap of bones once more before adding, "I don't want to die in the same place as you, you traitor."

He walked over to the doorway, ready to leave and look for somewhere to die where the company was better, but could not help looking back one final time.

Tears streaked his face as he murmured to Thalez almost as though he was going to reply, "What were we supposed to have been doing, eh? What was it all for?"

*　*　*

Dust settled, flames died out, bodies disintegrated, and time passed. Nobody came near Zaren for years and years, afraid that they might still be able to catch the disease. The Spilons had made it widely known about the disease, but not about their involvement and intentions. They wanted everyone to think that they really had been there on an "educational visit" and the disease was merely coincidental. It suited them nobody wanted to go there; it conveniently covered their guilt.

And so the people had died, the disease had died with them, and now the planet died too.

But somewhere, up past the stars aboard the shuttle, the hopes of one man, Parlon Dremun, lived on.

PART TWO

Chapter 10

During each century of its relatively short history, Vantil had been a beautiful, peaceful world to live in. Food was plentiful; hunger had never been heard of, and the people never found reason to fight, or have wars.

The exteriors of the dwellings were made of very simple raw materials, such as mud, stone, wood and straw, but not so the interiors.

They were richly decorated with extravagant and exotic silk like materials, carved and varnished wooden ornaments, and bright paintings on the walls.

Silks also made the clothes the Vantilians wore in bold and vivid colours draped about their shoulders, and flowing elegantly behind them.

Grace, beauty and peace reigned upon Vantil, and its people only had ideas for its continuity. They were happy and content in life. They loved and greatly respected Latnor, their Ruler, who guided them through the ideals of their land, set long ago by their ancestors when they lived on another world.

Then, war had necessitated their move to Vantil for survival and freedom from those who would dictate to others. War – a word rarely used by the people who were almost afraid that the very utterance of its pronunciation would provoke an outbreak of violence.

Latnor did everything in his power to ensure that Vantil remained the paradise that it really was. He held no ideas of higher status, or superiority over his people; just a whole hearted interest in the welfare of them and their land completely absorbed him.

There was no royal ancestry – Latnor was descended from the first people to arrive on Vantil centuries ago, and the leadership had been decided by vote, and the ruling line descended from there.

He was married to Cameen, who was expecting their second child any day. They already had a beautiful young daughter, Sahlin, and would have been contented with one child, but a son was needed to one day become Ruler when Latnor died. Everyone was hoping this baby would be a boy, and their future Leader.

According to the old custom, the Ruler must only ever marry once, and have one son. If a boy was not born, or anything happened to that child, the Council of Vantil would elect another to take his place when the Ruler died. So far, this had never happened.

Thoughts of a new baby brother or sister were greatly occupying the mind of Sahlin as she walked along by the river bank, her long brown hair neatly plaited and laying down her back. She often liked to walk here; it was perhaps even more peaceful and serene than the rest of Vantil. She paused to look out across the still water, which reflected the blue, green colour of Vindahl, their moon. Her slim fingers played gently upon the surface of the water, and Vindahl shimmered. A smile of contentment lay upon her lips, as her thoughts dominated her attention completely.

For a moment, she was vaguely distracted by a noise from behind her. Dismissing it as probably a Sonx, a small rat like creature that lived in the river banks, Sahlin's thoughts again wandered.

Picking up a long stick, she dipped it into the water, making Vindahl shimmer further, and became almost completely obscured by the ripples she made.

The water settled again, and Sahlin found not the face of the moon reflected there, but that of a man. As it had been so quiet, the suddenness of his appearance startled her, and she gasped with fright as she spun around.

Rusnan stepped forward. Sahlin's fright did not disappear when she recognised him. He was not a well-liked man, and she tried to avoid him whenever possible. The feelings he invoked in anyone who came across him were completely detrimental to their natural ones. He was not Vantilian. His space transport had crashed on the planet some time ago, and as all his radio equipment had been smashed on impact, he was unable to contact his home, Lospin. This was a planet alien to their knowledge.

The radio transmitter was beyond repair, he had said, and his shuttle certainly could not be mended; indeed, he claimed, he himself had been lucky to survive. He explained he would have to wait until his movements were traced on the tracking system before a recovery party came to take him home, which could be a very long time.

The Vantilians could not dispute what he told them; they had very limited knowledge of anything outside their own planet, they were very insular and preferred to keep it that way. He was making a lot of people very nervous and uncomfortable and they hoped he would be rescued very soon. They had taken him in, fed him, given him shelter and clothes, in return for him working on the land. It was no hardship; they had an abundance of everything. Fine silk-like strands grew from tall flowers which were woven together to make their exceptionally bright clothes. There were plenty of logs to build a hut, which after just a first meeting with him, they decided to place a small distance away from their own.

At first, people thought that his unwillingness to converse, and his rebuff to their friendliness, was due to being cut off from his own world. Attempt after attempt was made to make him feel comfortable and settled, but as time passed, they realised that their efforts were to be in vain.

Clearly, he did not wish to join in and make the adjustments to living in a new world as easy as it could have been. It was temporary after all, but they wished he would make some attempt to be civil and at least appear a little thankful. Instead he would sit and stare at the Vantilians as they went about their work, ignoring their requests to participate. Eventually, he did not even bother to go to the fields in the morning at all, and would sit on the hills in silence, alone, watching everyone.

He would disappear for long periods of time, without a word to anyone, and would never reveal where he had been upon his return. He chose to eat alone, which at least spared the awkwardness of the silence.

Gradually, their intolerance of the situation had grown so that people informed Rusnan that if he did not work with the others, he could not expect food and shelter in return.

Instead of this threat spurring him into action as they had hoped, Rusnan simply walked off into the forests, and began an even more solitary existence living in the shelter of the trees. Occasionally, he would appear in the trading places with wood, fruits and furs to trade for other materials and food, and then retreat quickly and quietly back to his hiding place. He visited no-one in the village, and they certainly did not try to find him. The day he left would be a day to rejoice.

"You frightened me, Rusnan," Sahlin gasped, turning back to look across the water once more. She couldn't help comparing his diminutive size, dirty, dark clothes, reddish brown hair, and small shrew like piercing eyes to the Sonx she first thought he was.

She hoped that that would be all there was to this meeting, and Rusnan would now continue on his way. Turning her back towards him was meant as a dismissive gesture, even though she felt uneasy not being able to see him. Unfortunately, Rusnan did not take the hint.

"I apologise, my dear Sahlin. I had not meant to," he replied in soft, mocking tones, adding mysteriously, "I knew that I would find you here."

The warm evening air had suddenly chilled at his words, and she turned questioningly towards him, wishing that she had not come out for a walk after all, and saw a maniacal look within his eyes. He was clearly in an unusually talkative mood.

She regarded him for a moment as she was subconsciously transfixed by the intentness with which he was staring at her. He was not handsome, or even a good looking man by far, and she was aware that ever since she had first met him, he had always conveyed a mysterious, devious expression, that had often made her inwardly cringe.

His long Sonx like hair was unkempt and greasy, and tied loosely at the back. As she looked at him, dark skinned, bony fingers emerged from beneath the wrap he wore, and brushed anxiously along his thin, wet lips. Sahlin swallowed nervously; she didn't know why she should dislike him so, afterall, he had never done anything to make her think like that – it was just his general appearance and mannerisms.

His behaviour and attitude towards those that had tried to assist him had also helped to convince her that he was not altogether the best man to socialise with.

In a slightly wavering voice she asked, "What is it that you wanted?" Her eyes rested on the lightning flash brooch on his wrap, noticing it was slightly chipped. Somehow it looked familiar to her, but she couldn't think why. She hadn't noticed it in her previous encounters with him.

For a moment, he made no reply, but let out a low chuckle, the coldness of which made her tremble.

"Please hurry and tell me what you want, for I am expected back home soon."

Still there was no reply, and keeping her gaze to the ground, she tried to pass by the squat, dark figure standing in her way.

"Wait one moment longer – please," he commanded her more than requested. Rusnan grabbed her arm roughly as she tried to move away, and she froze, her heart beginning to beat faster than it had ever done in her life. This was a new feeling to her and she didn't like it. She was glad that she hadn't experienced this before.

She looked about wildly hoping someone, anyone, would be walking along by the river, and hear her distress; but there was no-one, just her and Rusnan, alone.

Her head jerked back as he pulled her round to face him, and she looked up, defiantly meeting his steady gaze.

"Let me go!"

He pulled her closer, until she felt his breath against her cheek. His lips drew back, revealing dark, stained teeth, and Sahlin instinctively tried to twist away from his tight grip. The move was anticipated, and his fingers closed tighter around her arm. She felt her flesh burning beneath his grip. Still she gazed steadily back, defiantly blocking the rising panic within her from showing.

Then suddenly, he relinquished the grip on her completely, and moved backwards a couple of paces, still with that inane grin stretched across his features.

The surprise movement caught her off guard, and she stumbled and fell down to the ground. Her hand reached up and gently soothed the soreness from Rusnan's rough hold. Her instinct was to spring to her feet, and continue her bold stance against this man, but she was uncertain that her shaking legs would be able to hold her upright. Instead, she fumbled with her shoes, pretending that they had slipped off her feet as she tripped.

After a few moments she regained her composure sufficiently to stand, and drew away from the hands that offered mockingly to help her.

Anger was rising inside of her – he had no right to delay her like this, and certainly no right to frighten and touch her as he had. Her fury exploded out of her as she demanded, "What do you want Rusnan? I will not ask again."

"You surprise me, Sahlin. I don't think that such a temper is fitting for a Ruler's daughter; certainly it is not the behaviour one would expect from a young lady. Especially such a pretty one."

"As a rule, I am not used to dealing with such intolerable behaviour and bad manners."

"Such spirit, too. What a pity that it changes your whole face. Your features do not look so angelic and soft now."

"I am a patient person, but I too have my limits – even for a Ruler's daughter. Now say what you have to say, and leave."

"I merely came to warn you."

"Warn? What about?"

"Well, let me see. How shall I put it? Ah, yes. You see, I believe that being a Ruler's daughter living in all that luxury might cause some people to become slightly...jealous, I think would be the right word. Especially now, when there is a new baby on the way to your family. If it's a boy, there will be endless rejoicing

126

for the precious future leader of this wonderful world."

Sahlin trembled as he vehemently spat out the last sentence. He had become completely locked inside the thoughts his words conjured.

"What are you implying?"

"Merely that sometimes people can be affected by seeing what others have, and the way they live."

"You know that we all live equally. No-one holds themselves above anybody else."

"Your family does."

That stunned Sahlin. "That isn't true. To a degree," she faltered, "I will admit, we have to sometimes make hard decisions which are not always the most popular, but then my father is Ruler..."

"Is that so?" he sniffed sarcastically.

"...And that means we have to set an example by which the others must follow."

"Exactly. You say the word, and everyone obeys."

"That is what is expected of us. We have to adhere to the decisions made too."

"So, what if the others do not like your decision?"

"Nothing is our decision. Or not entirely, anyway. You know perfectly well that the council have to make their judgements collectively. Only if there is a stale-mate does my fa...the Ruler, have to cast the deciding vote. You know all of this anyway. It was explained to you when you first came. If you want to know anything else, you will have to come to the house." Realising what she had just said, she corrected, "Or preferably the council chambers."

She made a move to walk away, but again Rusnan seized her roughly by the arm, making her gasp.

"We will continue this discussion now. I want answers."

"You're hurting me. Please let me go, Rusnan."

"Then you will stay, and answer me?"

"Yes, all right. If I can," she conceded hesitantly.

"Very well." Rusnan seemed to relax, and again removed his grip.

"What else do you want to know?"

"Why I have been abandoned by your people, and forced to live in solitude. Why I am shunned. Why you all stare and treat me as though I am some kind of monster?"

"We do not. I resent your words. My people went to a lot of trouble when you first landed here, trying to make you feel welcome. We tried to ease the pain of your loss by helping you settle in. We made a home for you, and gave you work to help take your mind off your other problems. As I recall, Rusnan, it was you who did not respond. At first, we assumed that it was just your own way of readjusting. But you continued to shun our efforts, and showed no interest in anything.

"When you left - of your own accord – to live in the forests, we tried to find you, to ask you to try further, but you had hidden yourself too deep to be found. Nobody saw you for a long time, until one day you arrived at the market to trade food and supplies.

"After not seeing you for so long, we didn't know how to react towards you. We were embarrassed, and ashamed; we felt as though we had failed you, Rusnan. When, in fact, it was entirely the other way around. You have no-one to blame but yourself."

"You lie!" he snapped. "You have made no effort. The help that you speak of; making me work when I hadn't fully recovered from my accident. Expecting me to join in with all the others; you would call that help?"

"We thought we were. If you objected, you only had to say so."

"You and your smart words. You think you have the answers to everything. Well, let me tell you, young, sweet, innocent Sahlin, you are wrong. You don't know anything."

"Then why don't you tell me? What don't we know?
What have we done that is so wrong?"

"Everything. I tell you this, things will not always be as
simple and easy for you. You, in your life of luxury and
ease, who have experienced no hardships, no tragedies.
You, who do not know what it means to have no home,
or family. To practically fade away from starvation every
Period of Bleakness because of lack of food. To not know
if you will live to see the next Time of Blossoming. You
don't know what it means to suffer, Sahlin."

The frightened girl looked on transfixed by the intensity
his face had again taken on, and the bitterness of his
words. She felt completely numb and shocked; she had
never encountered such raw and passionate anger and
resentment from anyone before, and Rusnan's words,
expression and wild gesticulations terrified her.

"What is it you want me to do?" she quietly asked.

"Huh, help. Is that what you think I want?"

Sahlin's puzzlement was etched clearly across her face.
"Well, what do you want? I thought that was why you
were telling me all this."

"I told you, Sahlin; you think you know everything when
you really know nothing."

"What are you talking about? Are you saying that you're jealous? That something is going to happen? What? Tell me!"

"I think you will know soon enough."

Sahlin couldn't help hating him for the callous, cunning way in which he looked at her. He was playing games with her.

On purpose, he had worried and then frightened her, leading her up to expecting some great revelation, and at the point where she was practically bursting with impatience to know what he was talking about, he was just going to walk away. She started, as he suddenly found something immensely funny in his last words, and drew back.

Seeing the bewildered look on her face, he let out one final roar of laughter, and sprang into the deep, dark cloak of trees from whence he had come.

For a few moments, Sahlin stood looking after him, gently rubbing her arm, trying to comprehend everything that had just passed.

Trying to dismiss his threatening words, she walked quickly in the direction of home. She wanted to be sure that she didn't give him the chance of returning.

As she left the riverside behind, the bright reflection of

Vindahl suddenly vanished behind a bank of dark cloud.

Chapter 11

Four days had passed since her mysterious meeting with Rusnan, and Sahlin had not told anybody. She felt that there was enough to think about with the baby so near to being born, without her adding to the worries.

Besides, the more she went over the events in her mind, the more she decided that she had over reacted to the situation. Rusnan had probably not meant to scare her at all; it just so happened that he had appeared when she was deep in thought, and felt vulnerable. There. She had convinced herself that there was nothing to fret about. More or less.

Even now, after all the time she had spent mulling his words over and trying to erase them from her mind, she still felt threatened by him.

She leant down to draw the water from the well, as she sighed for what felt like the hundredth time she had tried to dispel her uneasiness, and dropped the bucket heavily into the depths.

As she wound the line up again, and pulled the heavy pail over the side, Tamek came rushing out in a state of great excitement.

Tamek had been a great and loyal family friend for many years, and always helped out during the times when the Ruler's family needed extra support to sustain the hectic schedules and work load. She had been visiting Cameen, Sahlin's mother, who had been feeling unwell for a day or two.

Sahlin looked up from her work to see what the commotion was. Tamek's almost white hair had fallen from its usually neat perch upon her head, and stray strands had fallen across her agitated face.

As she drew within earshot, she stopped dead in her tracks and fought to stay upright as she skidded in the dust. Pushing her hair hurriedly away from her eyes as though it would make her heard more clearly, she cried out to Sahlin, "Come quickly!"

"What's the matter?" called Sahlin, trying to hide the amusement in her voice; Tamek was normally such a quiet, placid, graceful woman, and the sight of her flushed cheeks and crumpled clothes were indeed something to behold.

"Quick! We need you." Taking a deep breath to calm herself down, she explained, "I think you are about to get the little brother or sister that you're always talking about. Hurry!"

It took a few moments for Tamek's words to sink in, and finally she spurred her legs into action, and ran towards the house with a broad grin across her face, and her pail of water completely forgotten.

A figure hidden in the trees nearby had been watching the scene, and as Sahlin gathered up her velvet-like skirts and ran after the fast disappearing form of Tamek, a nervous finger smoothed down a twitching moustache. Unseen, the figure moved away and merged into the shadows of the neighbouring buildings.

* * *

Throughout the still, warm night, Sahlin sat beside her mother's bed, joined by Latnor who had been summoned by a neighbour upon hearing the commotion outside. Together they held her hand, soothed her brow, and attended to her requests.

"This baby certainly seems determined to take its time making its entrance," thought Sahlin, as Cameen lapsed into a disturbed sleep. How much longer would it take?

Seeing her pale, exhausted face, Latnor squeezed her hand gently. She smiled back at him, thinking how radiant he looked.

"I have been here before in this situation...with you!" he beamed at her. "I will stay with your mother, but you should get some rest, my child."

"So should you, father."

"I'm alright," he chuckled, "I couldn't possibly rest. I'm too excited!"

"So am I!" ventured Sahlin, grinning.

"Please go, even if only for a while. It is nearly dawn already. I hadn't realised. But I am not going to have stayed here all this time, then go away and miss the birth!"

"No. Of course."

"No arguments then please. Go child, and rest."

Reluctantly, she forced herself up from her chair, kissed her father on his forehead, smoothed back a stray curl of brown hair, withdrew her hand and walked outside into the quiet stillness. The small crowd of well-wishers that had arrived earlier to await the birth had dispersed as the night had worn on, and all was as quiet as it should be just before the suns rose.

She stood for a few minutes gazing up at the dark sky which was becoming lighter every moment now, and delighting in great breaths of fresh, cool air.

Stretching her aching body, she wandered along to her favourite haunt by the riverside and sat down, her back resting against one of the oldest known trees on Vantil. It was surprisingly comfortable, despite its roughness.

Gazing out across the still water, she reflected that despite all the excitement, she was not in the least tired. As this thought trailed lazily through her mind, sleep pulled a sheet of drowsiness over her body and her mind drifted away.

*   *   *

When she awoke, she did so with a start, for momentarily she couldn't remember why she was laying by the river. Looking around her she realised that she had slept far longer than she had intended to.

The twin suns had already risen from their separate points, and at midday, they would overlap to create one great ball of scarlet flame, far, far away in the purple-red sky.

As she stretched the sleep and stiffness from her slender body, she was suddenly reminded of the circumstances that had brought her here.

Jumping lithely to her feet, she ran up the long, narrow path that led from the river back to her home. She paused as she reached the doorway suddenly feeling dubious about entering. Shrugging her fears away, she raced through the hallway and towards her mother's bedroom.

Carefully, she pushed aside the jewelled curtain that hung across the arched doorway, and tentatively stepped inside. She saw her mother instantly, lying peacefully asleep, and Latnor standing by the window, gently holding a tiny bundle of cloths in his arms. As

Sahlin moved closer he became aware of her presence, and turned towards her.

As he did so, she saw a little pink, wrinkled face staring back through half opened eyes at her.

"Sahlin, this is your new brother, and future Ruler of Vantil."

"Oh father, he is so beautiful. I can see by the look in your eyes that you're very proud and happy. May I hold him?" she whispered carefully as though the sound of her voice might break him.

"Yes, of course. He is a wriggly little fellow, and determined too. An early sign of his destiny, I would say!"

Very gently, the tiny snuffling infant was passed from his father's large, strong hands, to his sister's smaller, slender, pale hands.

"How is mother?" she asked, taking her eyes off her brother momentarily to look at Latnor. His face grew serious and the brightness that had been shining in his eyes faded, and was replaced by dullness. He heaved a deep sigh, and walked across to the window.

Although Sahlin followed his gaze to the distant rolling hills, she knew that he was not really taking any of the beautiful scenery in.

"What is it?"

In a strangely strained voice that was almost a whisper, he replied, "She is extremely tired and weak, and needs much rest."

He would say nothing else, and Sahlin did not know what to say either. Her gaze shifted from her baby brother, to her mother who was lying so quietly, and then back to her troubled father.

For a moment, Sahlin stood quietly absorbing what her father had just said. She knew that her mother must be very ill by the way he had spoken. The tiny body in her arms was forgotten temporarily as her mind whirled around the conception of life without her mother. What would she do? How would her father manage? Who would nurse the baby? The baby... what was she thinking of? Who said she would have to face the prospect of losing her mother? After all, her father had merely said that she was very tired. That was to be expected after having a baby.

Trying to put these terrible thoughts out of her head, she paced the length of the room and back, gently rocking her brother who had begun to gurgle and cry.

"Ssh, ssh, it's alright, little one, it's alright." So why didn't she believe her own words?

"Where is Tamek, father?"

As he answered, she saw the sadness in his eyes, and as

their gaze met he was aware of the way she looked at him, and immediately averted his eyes back to the window, trying to hide his worry from her.

"She has retired to your room. I hope you don't mind. She was here throughout the labour, and is completely exhausted. More from excitement than anything! However, she too had to be dragged away from tending to your mother."

"I'll go and check on her to make sure she's alright. Now then little baby, you must go back to your daddy," she cooed as she handed him back to Latnor.

It seemed such a pity that such a marvellous occasion was marred by worry and sadness. Things just didn't seem to be going well lately...

Treading softly along the passageway, Sahlin went to look in on Tamek. So absorbed was she by her thoughts, that she didn't realise that she was not even looking where she was going. Her feet seemed to know the route so well that they automatically led her there.

Pausing at her own doorway, she peered cautiously around towards her bed. There Tamek lay curled blissfully into a tight ball, her hands clasped together beneath her cheeks, her face completely expressionless in her sleep.

Sahlin thought about the many times that this role had

been reversed when she was younger, and Tamek had been looking after her. Often, Sahlin had feigned her sleep when she had heard her footsteps coming towards her room, and she adopted a suitable convincing position.

As soon as Tamek had retreated back along the hallway, Sahlin had immediately sprung out of bed, and continued to peruse through the old, ancient books that had been passed down from generation to generation. She loved the feel of the yellowed, well-thumbed pages, which were so old they made a crinkly noise when turned. She felt privileged to even hold them, and always treated them with the utmost care and respect, as though they were a living, breathing thing. They had been one of the few "luxuries" brought with the settlers those many centuries ago from Zaren.

The cherished memories held her entranced, reliving the feel of the pages, and she even fancied that she could smell the musty, dusty scent in her nostrils.

The movement Tamek made as she stirred momentarily, catapulted Sahlin back to the present, and she waited for her good friend to settle again before she tiptoed outside.

Not really knowing what to do with herself, she decided to go for a quiet walk alone. Instinctively, she was about to head for the river, when she remembered Rusnan and the unwanted encounter she had had with him there.

Shivering, she made towards the forest instead.

Wandering along the track that led up through the hills to the trees, she welcomed the shelter the canopy of the leaves provided against the sweltering heat already given off by the twin suns.

As she walked along, her thoughts dwelt upon the worried tone her father's voice had adopted when speaking about her mother's condition, and about the haunted look she had seen in his eyes. She had never seen that look before, even when council matters had been at their most pressing. He really was very worried indeed. But why? He had only said Cameen was tired. To cause him that much worry, there must have been something else wrong. Why wouldn't he confide in her? She was old enough to understand, and she wouldn't have told anyone. Perhaps it was because he just didn't want to cause her any unnecessary anxiety.

When she finally surfaced from the deepness of her thoughts to see where she was going, she found that she had completely lost herself. Her feet may very well have been able to lead her round familiar, well-trodden places, but she had never ventured this deep into the forests alone. She had no idea how long she had been walking for, but when she looked up past the canopy of leaves, she saw that the twin suns were beginning to separate again.

She spun around trying to get some sort of bearings. She

had even wandered off the track, and all around she could see only trees and grass. Whirling about she tried looking for anything unusual she may have passed that she remembered, for now that she had been walking round in circles trying to find out where she was, she had even forgotten from which direction she had come. Nothing seemed to stand out from the rest; every tree looked the same to her.

"Oh, how could I be so stupid?" she cried. "Father says I spend too much time with my head in the clouds." There was no point in calling out for anyone – who would there be this deep in the forest to hear her?

She had no alternative but to keep walking, and try to keep a calm head. "Don't panic," she chided herself, taking deep breaths. She walked on in a random direction, but seemed to have picked a route that led deeper into the heart of the trees however, for as she moved on, the light grew weaker, and the air became cooler.

Resting for a moment, she stopped and hugged herself as she gave an involuntary shiver. What was her father going to say when she got back? He would be so worried; but then again, she reflected, perhaps his mind was too occupied with matters at home to even have noticed she was missing.

For quite a while now, she had had the feeling that she was being followed, but dismissed it as just fear of being lost and alone. Her mind always had been overactive, and her imagination inclined to run away with her.

Who on Vantil would there be to follow her here anyway? Unless…

"Will you pull yourself together, you silly girl," she chastised herself. Still, as she walked she could not help feeling as though there was someone following, someone watching her, lurking unseen in the darkness of the shrubs…

"Will you stop it? There's no-one there!"

A little while later, she stumbled upon a stream and the relief swept over her in great waves. Now all she had to do was to follow the direction of the stream until it joined into the river, and she would be able to find her way home easily from there.

Stooping down, she scooped up some water in her hands to moisten her parched lips and dry throat. As she was about to swallow, she gave a start as she heard a familiar voice from behind her.

"Are you sure you weren't being followed?"

She jumped to her feet gazing wildly around her. Where was he? Where was he hiding?

"Come out Rusnan," she demanded, "Where I can see you."

Still he did not appear, and all she heard was that soft, mocking laughter.

"You may think this very funny, but I do not share your sense of humour. Will you show yourself?"

"You really should be more careful when you are out walking, Sahlin..." Rusnan stepped out from behind one of the thicker trees at last, "...Especially when you are alone."

Although his appearance still alarmed her, she was relieved that she could at last now see where he was and what he was doing.

He continued, "After all, something terrible could happen to you. Then what would everyone do?"

"What do you want this time, Rusnan? To tell me about something else we have done wrong, or have misunderstood about you?"

"Very funny, but I don't share your sense of humour, either."

As he spoke, he had been moving very slowly towards her, and she had been inching very slowly backwards away from him. She certainly didn't want to turn her back on him.

Stepping on a small tree root sticking up out of the ground, she almost lost her balance, and looked down to stop herself from falling.

By the time she looked back up, he was right in front of her with his hands outstretched towards her. Her eyes conveyed the fear she felt.

"I seem to have frightened you again," he muttered, his tongue slowly licking over his top lip.

"Yes, it does seem to be one of your habits," she ventured.

"You think you are so clever," he snapped, the smile vanishing from his face. "I think it is about time I taught you a lesson."

"Well, it won't be a lesson in manners."

His right hand dipped into the inside of his wrap, and reappeared clutching a knife, about five inches in length. Sahlin let out a scream, and moved back further away, even though she was now very close to the edge of the stream.

Keeping eye contact with the terrified girl, he moved the knife up in front of his face, and menacingly drew his finger over the gleaming blade. A small line of blood appeared as the point pierced his flesh. He seemed to delight in the horror showing on Sahlin's face.

"What do you want from me?" Sahlin whispered in a trembling voice.

Rusnan made no reply.

"Please leave me alone."

Her words only seemed to succeed in enticing him nearer. Glancing quickly behind her, she saw that there was nowhere to go; she would have to stand and fight. As she looked back at Rusnan, so he lunged and made a grab at her, and she nimbly dodged out of the way to the side.

This enraged him, and wiped the gloating smile from his face.

Bending down without taking her eyes off him, she felt around on the ground, her fingertips searching for anything that might serve her as a weapon. She touched a small rock, and her desperate hands seized it at once.

With her heart beating fast, and her legs quivering and unsteady, she realised that she had never hurt a living creature in her whole life. Even the Sonx, the small rodent that was the only threat to the planets crops, was trapped in a corner, and re-released as far away as possible from the vegetation. Life expectancy of a Sonx was quite short, and they did not breed very much, so were not really a problem, providing they were controlled properly. Furs were taken only from dead animals they found.

This situation was different, Sahlin told herself. This man

was threatening to hurt her; maybe even take her life away from her. She was not going to let that happen.

Gathering all her strength, she drew back the stone, and with a fierce yell, propelled it with great speed at the advancing figure, just as he was about to lurch towards her with his knife.

The stone caught a glancing blow to his forehead, enough for him to be temporarily thrown off balance. Inwardly Sahlin gave a little cheer at her small success. At least it had given her a few seconds to collect her thoughts and to re-arm herself.

Looking quickly around, she picked up a small fallen branch, and waved it about from side to side with an air of confidence that she wished she felt.

Rusnan advanced again, clearly unhappy that such a slip of a girl had got the better of him. When she dared to shoot a small triumphant smile at him, she realised that all she had done was to fire his anger towards her even more.

"Please Rusnan," she tried again, "Let us talk together, instead of fighting. Perhaps we can work things out, and start again. Please."

For a moment her words seemed to have had no effect at all. Then quite unexpectedly, Rusnan stopped dead in his tracks.

Looking at her with wide eyes, he said, "Do you mean that? Do you really mean that?"

"Of course I do. We have always helped each other. Or at least, tried to. Let us help you, Rusnan."

Very slowly, Rusnan placed the knife down on the ground, and stepped towards Sahlin, smiling weakly.

Reciprocating the gesture although not entirely sure she trusted him, she put down the branch and moved closer to him.

"There, that's much better. Now we can talk properly."

"Talking is not what I had in mind, Sahlin."

"What...?"

Rusnan seized his opportunity and quickly grabbed her arms as she let out a scream.

"You tricked me," she cried, "Let me go!"

His only reply was to roughly twist her round so that he held her by one arm behind her back. Pushing her forward he walked to where he had laid down the knife, and twisting her arm tighter until she screamed again, he stooped down and picked it up. Before she even knew what was happening, she was being held with a knife at her throat by a maniac, for reasons she did not even understand.

"How will you get out of this predicament?" he asked mockingly, as he teased the blade closer to her throat. She remembered the way he had done the same with his own hand and not hesitated to draw blood. She held her breath, daring not to answer, for fear that the smallest movement would cause the blade to pierce the delicate layer of skin.

Suddenly, she heard a shout from behind them. It momentarily startled Rusnan, and Sahlin seized her chance.

Taking a deep breath, she quickly drew up her free arm, and clenching her fist, jabbed her elbow back hard into his stomach; hard enough to wind him. He let her go as he fought for breath, and she stumbled away from him, taking great gulps of air herself in her relief to be free of his grip.

She looked up as she saw a man in the distance rapidly advancing. He was young, and seeing Sahlin was in obvious trouble, his legs were pumping at a furious rate to come to her assistance. In his hands he held an axe.

Hearing a groan, Sahlin caught a glimpse of Rusnan staggering to his feet out of the corner of her eye. He was completely bewildered by this chance turn of events, for it was highly unlikely that anybody would have been in such a close proximity to hear Sahlin's cries in this remote part of the forest.

He glared fiercely at the youth, and then at the girl who should have been under his control, but by some stroke of good fate seemed to have been saved – for now.

Weighing up the differences of height, age and build between him and the axe wielding youth, Rusnan realised he would not stand much of a chance against him with his knife, and cursed his bad luck. Casting a final hateful look at Sahlin, who was now positioned in a fighting stance again, he ran off at great speed and fled once more into the cover of the trees.

She watched until he was right out of her sight, for she did not believe that he would give up so easily.

The youth finally reached her side, hardly out of breath at all from his long, furious run, and at once enquired if she was hurt.

"No, I am alright, really. Well, actually I do feel a little shaken. Perhaps I should just sit down for a moment."

"I will fetch you some water," replied the young man as he helped her sit down on a rock near the stream..

As he knelt beside the water, Sahlin studied her rescuer. He was around nineteen she supposed, with a very athletic figure; the condition of which she had just seen a demonstration. He had blonde, straight hair, parted down the middle and swept back close against his ears, and was shoulder length at the back. Sahlin noticed his height straight away, for he was very tall; well over six feet. This was perhaps his most striking feature, for Vantilian males hardly ever reached or exceeded this height.

She was also somewhat struck by the clothes that he wore, which exposed a lot more of his body than most males showed. The men normally kept themselves well covered, especially when in public.

He had the most enchanting, kind, brown eyes she thought, as he returned with her water, and she actually felt her cheeks flush.

"Here, drink this. You will soon feel much better."

"Thank you. And not just for the water. Thank you for coming to my aid. I'm afraid I don't know your name."

"I am only too happy to assist you, Sahlin. My name is Menzin."

"You know me?"

"I think perhaps everybody knows the beautiful daughter of Latnor," replied Menzin smiling, and aware that it was now his turn to flush.

He too felt a strange feeling as he looked down into the pale, attractive face; an almost nervous sort of sensation, which was so silly as he felt completely relaxed with this girl. Looking into her eyes, he felt like he belonged there, and found he could not concentrate on anything else. He realised that he could hear nothing else either, almost as though there was nothing else.

Pulling himself back, he broke away from her gaze and found it was like trying to break free from some sort of huge, powerful magnet.

"I'm sorry," he spluttered. "You must think me very rude."

"Not at all," replied Sahlin, who without Menzin realising, had just undergone the same kind of sensation. Something she too had never felt before, but it was wonderful. Here she was with a stranger whom she felt completely at ease with after such a short time. So at ease, that there really did not seem a need for words. In fact, her terrible encounter with Rusnan seemed like a very long time ago...Rusnan! She had almost forgotten him.

Seeing her sudden change of expression, Menzin became worried. "What's the matter?"

"I'm sorry. It's just Rusnan – the man who was here with me before – he frightened me so much. I have never been as afraid as I was then."

"It's alright now. I'm here, and I won't let him hurt you. He's our unwanted visitor, right?" he said putting a protective arm around her shoulder as she nodded silently. "Hey, you're shaking. Would it help if you talked to me about it? Tell me why he was attacking you, I mean."

"Well, I wish I knew the answer to that myself."

"I've certainly never heard of such a thing before." He looked right into Sahlin's eyes as he added, "This hasn't happened before, has it?"

She shifted uneasily on the rock, looking down at her feet as though she saw something immensely interesting there.

"It has happened before, hasn't it?"

"Yes, but only once."

"What do you mean, "Only once"? Once is too often."

"I know, but it wasn't like today. He just threatened me verbally."

"What did your father do about it?"

Again, Sahlin looked about uncomfortably.

"Wait a minute; you haven't told him, have you?" Menzin sounded incredulous.

"No. He has so much else to worry about. The last thing he needs is to hear about this." Sahlin began to sound a little tearful.

"He would probably be more upset that you haven't told him, I would guess. Something really serious could have happened here today. It was only pure luck that I was working nearby."

"Yes, where did you come from?"

"Just over the rim of the hill there," he indicated. "My father has been unwell for a while. Well, since my mother died three months ago actually. I came up here to chop some fire wood before the rains come."

Sahlin noticed the fleeting look of pain that crossed his face as he spoke of his mother's death, and she offered her hand to comfort him, as he had done for her. "I am so sorry."

"Anyway, I'm glad that I was up here today to help you."

"So am I!"

Again their eyes met and locked in a trance for a few moments before Menzin continued, "Well, tell me about this Rusnan anyway."

"You know almost as much as me. He isn't Vantilian, as you know. He crashed here in that space shuttle a while ago."

"Yes, I remember. He wasn't very cop-operative if I recall,

but I don't know the full story, living further away from everyone else."

"You're right about him not being very co-operative. After he crashed he came to our village, saying he couldn't repair his vessel because it was so badly wrecked, and that he had no means of communication with his home planet."

"He found you?"

"Yes."

"Where is his shuttle wreckage?"

"I don't know. No one does. He wouldn't say." "So he crashed here in a shuttle so badly damaged that it's beyond repair, and all communications were knocked out, and yet he walked away from it and stumbled across us?"

"Well, yes." The unlikeliness of the story was just beginning to hit Sahlin for the first time. She had always been taught to unquestioningly believe others. After all, nobody lied on Vantil.

"He must have been injured?" pursued Menzin.

"No, not really. He said he could have been killed, but just needed to rest for a while and he would be ok."

"In your heart, do you really believe that he could escape

from such a severe crash as he described, without injuries? Do you?"

"No."

"And why wouldn't he show anyone where he crashed? If his story was true, and he had managed to escape from the shuttle unharmed, then he must have salvaged some belongings. I for one, know that if I was going to be stranded on an alien planet, I would want as many of my things with me as possible."

"Well, maybe that is why he hasn't adjusted very well; because he has nothing of his own world."

Menzin raised a questioning eyebrow at her statement.

"Do you really think that's the reason, after all we have just said?"

"No, I don't." She shuddered.

"I think we need to look into his story a little closer, and find out a bit more about him. If we can find the crash site, perhaps that would provide us with some clues."

"Do you think we should?"

"The alternative is to sit around and wait for Rusnan's next move. So, what do you want to do? I'll help you as much as I can if you'll let me."

"Thanks Menzin. I think you're right. I am afraid, I will admit. But our people must come first. If Rusnan poses any sort of threat to the harmony of our existence, then he must be stopped."

"Good. I admire your courage."

He squeezed her hand as a gesture of both affection and moral support.

"At the moment though, I would rather not tell my parents. Let's wait a little longer, and see what we can find out. When we know more, I promise I will tell them."

"Whatever you think is best. Now, I think perhaps I should get you home before you cause your parents any more worry. You can fill me in on everything that happened with Rusnan before while we walk. My father is used to me disappearing sometimes. He won't be worried, and he'll be fine on his own for a while.

Sahlin giggled shyly and began, "Menzin, I…"

"Yes?"

"Nothing." She fell silent, and again was distracted by his unusual height as he rose to his feet and offered his arm.

"May I?"

Nodding her assent, they started home.

Chapter 12

Her thoughts temporarily diverted from recent events by her new found friend, Sahlin was aware that she was in a happier frame of mind than she had been for some time.

All the way home, Menzin had talked and joked, and had made her heart feel so light that she felt like singing.

"You have a beautiful laugh," he had remarked. "It's very infectious."

"Well that's something else I should thank you for. I haven't felt so at ease for quite a while. I haven't forgotten the troubles we face, but I did need to rest my mind from it for a little while."

"It's not healthy to dwell on worries for a long time. It doesn't make the problem disappear. It's better to break from it, and then you can cope more easily."

"You're right, although I do feel a little guilty."

"Why?"

"I don't know, really. I suppose it just seems a little inappropriate."

Noticing the wrinkle across her forehead which was again occupied by a frown, Menzin cupped her face in his hands.

"You know I'm here to help. You can talk to me. I know we've only just met, but…"

"I know, I feel like we're old friends too, and I do trust you. I'm sorry. I didn't mean for you to feel shut out, honestly."

"It's alright, and please stop apologising!"

The eye contact remained after the words had ceased, and for a moment, each fancied that they could feel the other's heart beating in unison with their own. Menzin's face drew closer to hers, and at last she closed her eyes as she felt his lips gently kissing her. They remained closed for a few seconds after he had moved his lips away, and she felt she wanted the moment to last forever.

Opening her eyes again, she found Menzin had turned away and was looking ashamed.

"I'm sorry Sahlin, I didn't intend that to happen," he said in a low voice.

"Now who is needlessly apologising?" she laughed. "You may not have intended that to happen, but I did!"

His relief apparent, Menzin seized the laughing girl, and together they ran round the last corner of the track leading to her house.

As they did so, they saw a large group of people gathered

outside the house, and as they neared, could hear them talking in hushed tones.

Immediately, she knew something was wrong, and her broad smile vanished. Letting go of Menzin's hand she rushed forwards, pushing her way through the crowds.

The whispers subsided as she passed and was recognised, but as they once again filled up the space her path had made, the murmuring resumed as before. Menzin waited at the back of the crowd not wishing to intrude, trying to make sense of their jumbled words.

Inside, the atmosphere changed the instant Sahlin walked through the doorway. It was quiet, cold, and almost eerie. She shivered as she passed along the passageway leading to her mother's bedroom.

As she moved inside and her eyes drank in the scene, her mind seemed to jam, and refused to register what she was seeing. She stood motionless inside the doorway unable to comprehend, just watching. Suddenly, her limbs seemed to move all at once, and she lunged into the room.

Reaching her father's side at the window, she flung her arms around him, refusing to acknowledge that the lifleless body of her mother lay covered on the bed. There was no need for words between them as she held the tormented, grieving figure closer to her, and the heavy tears began to roll down her face. Her grasp on

Latnor grew tighter and tighter as though she were afraid that he would suddenly leave her, and there the pair stood wrapped in their grief.

Eventually, she felt movement from him, and sensed he wanted to be released from her grip. She looked up into his face and her eyes asked the question in her mind.

"I should tell you what happened while you were gone, child."

"I should never have left. If only I had been here. Perhaps I could have…"

"There is nothing you could have done. None of us could do anything." His voice broke.

"What happened?"

"Not long after you left, I was tired, and went outside for some fresh air, just for a minute or two. I only left her just for a few moments, and that was it."

Sahlin waited patiently as his voice trailed away and he tried to compose himself. Realising she was waiting, he continued slowly.

"Tamek, you recall, was asleep in your room at the time, and heard nothing. I was outside, for such a short while, just talking to some of the well-wishers, letting them know of the news, when suddenly, and I cannot explain why, I felt I should return inside."

"When I came in, Cameen was still asleep. I noticed an up-turned glass of water on the floor, and assumed she had knocked it over in her sleep."

He paused again, making an obvious effort to keep himself from breaking down again. Sahlin stroked his hair comfortingly and again waited for him to continue in his own time. She could see the pain as he relived every moment in his mind.

"A little later, I tried to wake her up to give her some food. As I touched her arm, I noticed how cold she felt. I thought that strange as she was so well covered in blankets. Something in the back of my mind started alarm bells ringing, and I turned her face towards me.

"She had turned the most dreadful colour, and I shook her harder; still no response. I quickly felt for her pulse, and there was none. She was dead. I had been sitting by her side thinking that she slept, when all the time, she was gone. I left her, and now she's dead."

"Oh father, I'm so sorry." She fell back into his arms, and he pulled her so close that she felt she couldn't breathe properly. Bitterly, she thought, "I don't care."

*   *   *

When Latnor's tears were finally under control, he set about officially announcing the news of the death. It was a very hard task for him to complete; how could he

163

announce the birth of his son, and the death of his wife in the same day?

Normally when the Ruler announced the birth of a son, the people celebrated for four consecutive days. This time however, the Vantilians found it hard to raise a cheer, for it would have been as though they celebrated the death of Cameen.

They felt that they should postpone all festivities until a later, more appropriate date, and the ensuing hush that fell over the land was very rare indeed.

Latnor seemed unable to concentrate much on important council matters. At first, it was only natural and to be expected, but as time progressed he did not appear to improve.

His people became very worried, and frequently expressed their fears to his daughter, and to the Council of Vantil, who reluctantly summoned him to warn him of his failing ability to rule.

This embarrassed him so much that matters deteriorated further, and did so for a period of around four Vantilian months.

Then, when everyone was least expecting it, Latnor suddenly decided that it was about time the birth of his beautiful son was celebrated in true Vantilian style.

Preparations began at once, and everybody joined in. Never before had they exerted themselves so much to make such a Feast Of Celebration; for they knew that this was the only way to show their Ruler how much they cared, and wanted it to succeed for him. Every ounce of their energy went into the preparations, for they dared not think what might happen if they failed to help him.

However, it seemed that they need not have worried, for their beloved Latnor appeared to enjoy all four days. Each day he moved to a different location, and spoke of the pride he felt for at last providing a son, and future Ruler of Vantil.

Ever eager to make him feel loved and appreciated, the people gave rapturous welcomes wherever he went. Much joy and relief was felt by all as he walked around seemingly back to normal and apparently enjoying himself.

"It's wonderful to see him out and about again where he belongs; amongst his people," Sahlin heard someone in the crowd say.

So why did she feel so uneasy? She couldn't help feeling that it was all a charade; a masquerade for the sake of his people. Yes, he smiled, but it seemed so false, and when he spoke to her she saw no depth of feeling in his eyes. Just an emptiness that frightened her. He had been with Cameen so long, she knew that he had been more devastated by her death than anyone knew.

She herself had battled with the tumult of emotions that constantly swept through her. The anger that she felt first of all towards her mother for leaving her, then the terrible, inconsolable sense of loss, the realisation she would never see her again, the awareness that she wouldn't be able to go to her for advice or guidance, or merely just to talk to and laugh with. The resentment that it had happened to her mother, the guilt she felt for not being there when she died, the ordeal of coping with the funeral arrangements, the inevitable numbness which followed that, and then the gnawing pain of loss that would not go away.

Whatever she did, wherever she went, it followed her like a shadow, even into her long, dark, demon filled nights; too afraid to sleep lest the visions of her dead mother's face came to haunt her there too.

What had finally helped her to begin to pull through the darkness was seeing her father's inability to cope. He needed her so much, and she was not there to help because of her own grief; like she had not been there to help her mother when she needed her most. She was not going to live with the sense of guilt that she had not helped her father either. He gave her the jolt she needed to begin to make the journey back into the real, everyday world she had to live in. His need for her pulled her back from her nightmare.

Now she had to live with seeing how her father had been affected, and try to find a way to pull him back too. It wasn't going to be an easy thing to do, she could see that.

At first, he appeared to almost resent his son, as though he were somehow to be held responsible for Cameen's death. It had since been discovered though, that she had been ill for some time before giving birth, and the exertions of labour had only brought her life to an end a little more prematurely than would have otherwise been expected for her condition.

She found it hard to cope with the fact that Cameen had been ill for some time without anyone knowing, not even herself. But, thought Sahlin, in reflection, maybe she had suspected, for she hadn't been her normal self for quite a while. It had been assumed by everyone that she was just pre-occupied with the forthcoming birth. She wished she had known. She would have spent longer talking with her, being with her, appreciating her, loving her.

Now she had to pick herself up, get on with her life, and help her father to get on with his.

Menzin had been a great help and influence in this, for he had shared the pain of emotions he had gone through after he lost his mother to help her realise that what she was experiencing was natural.

One unbelievably warm evening, the pair had sat alone in the light of Vindahl, talking and holding hands. They were waiting for Latnor to address his people, and chose to sit outside and watch everyone drift in, in front of the dais that had been erected for him to speak.

Menzin had seemed quiet and withdrawn all day, and nothing Sahlin did seemed to help.

Although she didn't want to pressure him, she desperately wanted to know what was wrong, for fear that it was she who had said or done something to upset him.

Finally, after she had enquired if it was something to do with his father, he had given in, and told her that he still felt the pain of losing his own mother. The trauma that he had helped Sahlin through had brought back his own grief. He had actually begun to cry in front of her, and had been embarrassed that he had appeared to be weak when he needed to be strong for her.

"For once, I want to be strong for you," she had comforted him.

"You shouldn't have to be."

"Why? Because I'm a woman, and you're a man? That is a stupid thing to say. It doesn't matter who you are. Everyone has to cry sometimes."

"This is the first time that I've...cried." He seemed loathe to even pronounce the word.

"You didn't cry at the time? That was months ago."

"My father was completely devastated, and I found myself pushing my own feelings aside to help him get through his. I suppose seeing you so upset has brought it all back subconsciously, even though I thought I was coping. But you're right about the emotions you feel. So many, all at once. It's the way the body and mind heal themselves."

"When will it get better though?" she asked.

"I wish I knew. Different times for different people, I guess, but I have faith that time will heal eventually, for both of us."

Looking at her father now, she inwardly wished that time would heal his suffering soon, for seeing his pain made her suffer more.

Perhaps the healing process had begun already though, she thought, for at least he had now ceased to pace up and down alone in the dark night hours, and was making an effort for his people here. Still though, she felt unsettled. Her train of thought was interrupted by cheering from the assembled crowd.

Where had they all come from? They hadn't even noticed how many people had gathered while they were talking. The place was filled. Surfacing back to reality, she realised that Latnor was making his way to the stage to make his speech.

The excitement had reached a climax, for this was the fourth evening of the celebrations, the time when traditionally the Ruler showed the heir to their world and its people.

It was also custom that this be held near the Ruler's home, and so the huge stage had been erected in the vast fields along the riverbank.

As Latnor made his way up the steps, Sahlin couldn't hear herself for the noise, but the moment he stepped onto the platform and turned to face the expectant crowd, a hush swept among them as though a breeze had blown through, and carried their words away on its back.

A fanfare of music broke the silence, and Brule, the speaker, stepped onto the stage beside Latnor. A ripple of applause greeted him, as he gestured for silence with one hand, while the other swept back the endless folds of beautiful red velvet material that made up his cloak. It fitted his slender frame perfectly; snug at the waist, spreading out into a wide tail at the bottom that swirled at his feet. The collar stood tall and stiff and was edged with golden thread, as were the cuffs. Gold coloured fastenings glistened down the front, although this was undone to reveal a white silk shirt, with spiralling silver patterns embroidered upon it. The silver perfectly complimented his grey, wavy, long hair, beard, and precisely shaped eyebrows.

His legs were wrapped in a light grey pair of silky leggings, which fitted tightly down to the knee, where they broadened out, and were then tucked back around the shins down to his feet, upon which he wore silver shoes made from a synthetic material resembling the hide of the Sonx.

He took a deep breath before addressing the crowd.

"People of Vantil. Tonight is a very special occasion, as you are of course all aware. We are extremely delighted and privileged to welcome the Ruler on this very happy evening, and he will be introducing another very important guest; we all know who that is! So, please welcome Latnor, Ruler of Vantil."

The quietness shattered in a deafening round of applause, and cheers erupted as Latnor stepped forward to the front of the stage.

His dress was similar to Brule's, except it was green, and more ornately embroidered. He still seemed rather pale, but looked much better than some of his more recent appearances, and when the clapping and cheering subsided enough for him to be heard, he eventually spoke. The gentle, quiet yet firm voice, resonated around the crowd, as his hands gesticulated for quiet.

"My people; I must first of all thank you for your support in recent times." He looked sad and pensive for a second or two, but then smiled again as he continued, "However, I am not here to dwell on the sadness that has touched us all, but to officially announce the much happier task of naming my son, and introducing him to you all.

"So, let me introduce him to you straight away, as you have already waited patiently for long enough to see him."

Turning to his daughter who was now waiting at the side of the stage behind the ornate curtain hangings, he called, "Sahlin, please bring out Fulmin, future ruler of Vantil."

She boldly stepped forward in her sky blue, flowing robes, edged with ruby red, into the eager gaze of the expectant crowd. In her arms she tenderly held her baby brother, and reaching her father's side, gently handed over the tiny bundle of silken clothes to him. She too was proud of him, and she felt very emotional.

The audience whispered amongst themselves, appreciative to the baby's need for quiet, but too excited to keep completely silent. As the level of chatter grew, individuals voices could be heard, calling out "Sssh!"

By their reception, Latnor saw that the delay had obviously been worthwhile.

His daughter stood looking out across the audience, amazed by the delighted, awed faces that looked back, including some of her friends. She was pleased to see

Tamek, even though she looked rather weary, and Menzin standing near the front. She smiled fondly down at him and he returned her gaze.

Once the audience seemed satisfied that they had seen Fulmin from just about every angle, Sahlin took him back, as her father still had a long speech to deliver about the new hopes for the future that the birth meant.

Looking down at her brother's wrinkled face, she thought how much like Cameen he looked already; closely set eyes, small nose, and long eyelashes. Something moving at the back of the stage in the shadows caught her eye, and the smile quickly faded from her lips as she saw Rusnan standing there. His face was the only one she had seen that evening that was unhappy.

Instinctively she hurried off, clutching Fulmin closer to her, anxious to forget the evil face who had forewarned of tragedy in her family.

The rest of Vantil would carry on celebrating well into the night once the speeches and toasts were over, but she was happy to return Fulmin home and look after him. She nearly dropped him in her fright as someone suddenly caught hold of her arm, but relief flooded over her as she saw it was Menzin.

"What is it?" he asked.

"Nothing really, I just thought...I saw Rusnan and he

173

frightened me. I thought you were him."

"Where?" His eyes instantly began scrutinising the shadows.

"At the back of the stage, as I left."

"Are you alright?" The smile that she had come to love so much had disappeared, and had been replaced by a look of total concern.

"Yes. Did you enjoy the ceremony?" she asked, trying to divert his attention.

"What? Oh, yes, and it was refreshing to see the people looking happy again. I know that she was your mother, but everybody felt the loss of Cameen deeply."

"Yes, I know." Trying to change the subject before her emotions overtook her she continued, "I have to look after Fulmin tonight. I hope you don't mind."

"No, of course not. That's why I came – to see you home."

"Thank you, I would love the company, even though its really not that far!"

As they walked along, he protectively placed his arm about her shoulders as he often did now, and Sahlin certainly didn't object. She felt safe and looked after in his presence.

Soon after they arrived home and had settled Fulmin down for the night after a feed, Tamek arrived.

"What a surprise! Why aren't you out celebrating with the others?" asked Sahlin.

"Well," explained her friend, "I knew that you would probably like to be out yourself, with Menzin. I'm on my own, so thought perhaps you would like me to look after Fulmin for you. It's such a pity to let that beautiful gown go to waste!"

"That's very kind of you, but…" Seeing the determined look on Tamek's face, she said, "Well, yes, if you're sure?"

"I am. So off you go, the pair of you, and enjoy yourselves."

Her gentle features showed a hint of mischievousness as she winked a twinkling blue eye at them, and her smile stretched into a knowing grin. She removed her outer pink garment, and laid it across a chair as she sat firmly down; brushing her white and silver curly hair out of her eyes, and folded her hands in her lap. Her look showed the matter was settled.

As the couple left the house, Menzin asked how Sahlin thought Tamek was coping.

"It's difficult to say. She has always been such a private

person, and you never really know how she feels inside. All I can tell you is that normally no matter what happens, she is cheerful, optimistic, and is always the one who gives others a boost."

"She knew your mother a long time, didn't she? It must be hard, even if she does cover it well."

"Yes, but I think that's why she wants to help out so much with the baby. He takes her mind off things, while at the same time, he reminds her of mother."

Seeing the very thoughtful look in her eyes, Menzin asked, "Where would you like to go this evening? Back to the party, I guess?"

"Anywhere. I don't mind. You decide."

"Well, strange as it may seem, I know today is really special and this kind of occasion doesn't happen very often, so we should be celebrating with the others, but I just feel like being alone with you, somewhere quiet; away from all the noise."

Looking up into his eyes, she replied, "That is exactly how I feel." The two exchanged smiles that each had come to cherish so much lately, and walked on hand in hand beside the river.

As they walked further and further away, they could hear the sounds in the distance of Vantil in the midst of celebration fading away, and could now only just make out the faraway lights.

They had covered some distance when they came upon a huge flat stone that Sahlin had often visited as a child, to talk to her imaginary friends.

Menzin motioned for her to sit down.

Chapter 13

Tamek had not had an easy evening with Fulmin. No sooner had his sister walked out the door, he opened his little eyes and cried and screamed for attention.

"There, there, little one, whatever is the matter?" she cooed as she picked up the little wriggling bundle and gently rocked him to and fro, "Ssh, ssh now."

Eventually he had cried himself back to sleep and Tamek went to settle down in the adjoining room. Several times, the baby awoke again, and she found herself once more rocking him.

"You are excitable tonight, aren't you? It must be that you can hear all the celebrations going on. It seems strange that it's all because of you, and you are too young to even know about it."

Fulmin's tear stained face watched her intently as she sang a lullaby to him almost as though he was really trying to understand what she was singing to him. His eyes remained open but he stayed quiet, just listening to her voice.

"You know, you are so tiny and yet you have already given so many people such happiness. You don't understand what I'm trying to tell you, but one day when you're older, I will tell you again what a special gift to us you are.

"Your destiny was clear the moment you were born. I just wish your mother...never mind. The important thing is that we have you. Now, I think we should put you back to bed, young man!"

As she lowered the baby back into his crib, she straightened up upon hearing a noise outside.

"Perhaps your sister is coming back early. Goodness! Is that the time? It's not so early after all!"

Tucking Fulmin's blankets gently in, she went to the door to see why no-one had appeared.

"Sahlin," she called softly, "Is that you dear?"

She listened for the reply, but none came. "Who's there?" she called again, "Who is it?"

She went to the door and peered out. Nothing to the left or to the right. She was about to go back inside, when she heard the noise again. It was coming from round the other side of the house.

Softly closing the door behind her, she crept around the side and edged her way along the wall. As she neared the corner, she took a deep breath and sprang round. She stopped dead in her tracks surprised there was no-one there. Puzzled, she murmured, "But there must be."

She was about to turn back, when she again heard a rustling noise. Creeping along, she made her way to a stack of old timber that stood by some bushes. She lifted up a corner piece cautiously, and still saw nothing. Bending down, she poked her face more closely to the hole. "Just darkness in this hole," she whispered to herself. "Honestly, these days, I'm just so paranoid. I don't know what's wrong with me."

Suddenly, she saw two eyes peering back at her, and before she had time to comprehend, something jumped out at her. She screamed. A mass of squealing fur ran away down to the river.

"A Sonx! Now I'm afraid of a Sonx! Honestly!" Her hands rested on her chest as though that would make her heart slow down a little. She began to laugh in relief at her silly mistake.

"As though someone is likely to be creeping around here anyway," she muttered as she walked back round to the door.

Rounding the corner, she stopped, puzzled, as she stared at the wide open entrance. She had closed the door when she came outside. There was no breeze to blow it open.

"Sahlin, are you home?" she called, although she knew she couldn't be; she would never have left the entrance open like that.

From Fulmin's room, she suddenly heard crying, but not

in the tone of voice he had cried all evening. This was a startled, frightened cry.

"Fulmin!" she screamed, running along the hallway, "Fulmin!"

Bursting through the door, she could not quite believe what she saw. A man dressed completely in black, was lifting the baby carelessly from his crib, and putting him in a sack.

Momentarily, Tamek stood still, trying to sort out some kind of logical reason to explain what was going on. Now, she saw quite clearly there was no logic in this at all. Rushing forward, she launched herself at the intruder without a second thought.

"Leave him alone. Get away, do you hear me? Get away! Help someone, help!" She pulled at the man's arm and tried to free his grip, but he was much too strong. Almost effortlessly, he swept her across the room, and she landed heavily on the floor. Her head struck the wall, dazing her.

Pulling herself giddily and clumsily to her feet, she lurched over to the small table and picked up the metal platter she had eaten her evening meal from. Creeping up behind him, she lifted back the plate and brought it down with as much force as she could muster. Unfortunately, the intruder turned at the last moment, and dodged out of the way. Instead of the force being enough to knock him out, it only temporarily slowed his attack.

Tamek felt her heart would stop as he walked menacingly towards her. "No, please," she whimpered, shrinking away from him. The last thing she remembered was a large gloved hand swinging towards her face.

* * *

Sahlin had obediently sat down at Menzin's request and wondered what could be on his mind, for he had hardly uttered a word for the last hour or so, and he was definitely preoccupied with something.

Perhaps all the celebrations had reminded him of how much he was missing his mother again, she reflected.

She watched as he paced up and down for quite a while, obviously grappling with something in his mind, and seeming to become more agitated with every step he took. She was beginning to feel anxious, so diverted her gaze across the river, admiring the pale, still reflection of Vindahl. She loved to see its beauty. No matter how long she looked at it for, she never grew tired of it. Momentarily she forgot Menzin then turned to see if he had ceased his pacing. He was still walking to and fro, decidedly uncomfortable. Perhaps his father was unhappy he was spending more time away from home, she wondered, and he was going to say he couldn't be with her so often.

She was contemplating how sad that would make her feel, when suddenly, a short distance away, with his back to her, he swung round and strode purposefully over to where she sat. She regarded him quietly, waiting for him to speak.

"I have something to say to you," he blurted, and her heart sank in preparation for the bad news.

"I have thought the whole thing through very carefully, and I need to ask you an important question. I have waited a long time for the right moment to speak, and I'm convinced that time is now."

Now she was curious, and could see he was not half as confident as he was trying to sound.

Finding new courage, he cleared his throat and continued, "Before you answer me, I want you to think very carefully. It's really important you don't answer straight away."

All this time, Sahlin had waited patiently and not uttered a word. At first she had been worried, then bemused and completely baffled as to what was making him so unsettled, but now she had quite a good idea. If it was what she thought it was, then she was about to become the happiest girl on Vantil; even happier than the rest of her people.

Menzin took hold of her hand, and looked her straight in

the eye – something else he hadn't been able to do since they had begun their walk. Now he was quiet and calm, as he slowly said, "Sahlin, by custom of Vantil, I kiss your hand and ask you to consider if you would marry me?"

He seemed completely drained after the prosposal, and had turned rather pale. Sahlin stood up and withdrew her hand, walking a few paces away from him. So, she had been right. That was what was on his mind all evening.

On Vantil, courtship was generally not very long; once a couple had met and knew they loved one another, a proposal of marriage was made quickly. Menzin must know in his heart she was the one for him; she certainly felt she would never want to be with anyone else.

Her mind was already made up; indeed she had dreamed of this day for quite a long time now, and of what her response would be. Determined to keep him waiting for as long as possible, and without turning her face to him, she spoke in a serious voice disguising the smile on her lips.

"It is a very serious question, Menzin, and I will indeed think it through very carefully before I answer."

Her voice had succeeded in remaining calm, exactly as she had wanted it to, even though she felt like jumping up and down and screaming in delight. Casting a sideways glance at Menzin, she saw how uncomfortable he looked, and thought she couldn't bear to tease him any longer. Her own heart pounded and she felt as though her face was on fire, so she could only imagine how he must be feeling.

She wandered up and down a little longer, and this time it was Menzin's turn to sit and watch her every movement in silence and agony.

Eventually, she swept over to him, still hiding her smile. Instead, she wore a very authoritative look which she very rarely used, but was most effective all the same.

"Menzin, by custom of Vantil," she began in a cold voice, "I have considered your proposal…"

"No wait, please don't answer now. Take time to think about it longer, please."

"Don't interrupt. My mind is made up and cannot be changed."

"I'm sorry, please continue." His eyes fell to the ground; where he felt his heart drop to as well. He knew he wasn't good enough to marry the Ruler's daughter. What had he been thinking?

"As I was saying, I have considered your proposal very thoroughly, and I'm afraid I could not possibly…" She paused, and Menzin closed his eyes, fearing the crushing rejection he knew was coming.

"...refuse."

For a split second, he didn't realise what his ears had just heard, and then it suddenly sank in. Opening his astounded eyes, he looked up at Sahlin who was now beaming at him, and he stared open mouthed at her.

She continued, " By custom of Vantil, I take your hand and accept your proposal of marriage." Informally, she then added, "I would dearly love to become your wife; I love you very much."

Menzin remained silent as he stood up and pulled Sahlin to him, kissing her soft lips.

"I love you too," he said. Then pulling away, he jumped up into the air as he yelled, "We're getting married!" at the top of his voice.

When he had calmed down a little, Sahlin told him that he had restored her happiness.

"Mine too. I didn't think I could ever feel this way."

"Let's not tell anyone just yet – it's nice to have a pleasant secret for a change!"

"You and your secrets! Come on, I'll take you home, it's really late."

The pair ran hand in hand all the way back, laughing and shouting, rejoicing in their happiness, not noticing as they arrived back that silence had replaced the jubilations they had left. As they reached home, their joy faded very quickly indeed.

*   *   *

Arriving back at the path leading towards her home, Sahlin's heart suddenly missed a beat as she saw the quiet crowds gathered, as they had before when her mother had died. Surely nothing else could be wrong? Please no.

Breaking free from Menzin's hold, she rushed forward, half of her desperate to know what had happened, the other half wanting to run the other way; away from the bad news that she sensed was waiting for her.

She feared in her heart that the grief of her mother's death, and the pressure from the Vantilian Council to pull himself together, had finally proved too much of a strain for Latnor to bear.

As she passed through the crowd to the front, she realised that there was a distinct difference in the atmosphere to the day Cameen died. Then, there had been an air of shock and disbelief, but this time there was a great feeling of anger. This was alien to her. Whatever had happened? She could palpably feel their anger emanating; throbbing almost.

As last, she was finally inside, and was almost surprised

to see Latnor pacing up and down, apparently not ill at all.

"Father?" she asked as he turned his face to her, "What's happening?"

She noticed that although the colour had vanished from his face, there was a mixture of anger, worry and intolerance etched across his features. As the moonlight pushed its way through the window, it struck her just how much greyer his hair had turned, since the day they had received such a shock in this very room just a few months ago.

"Sahlin, at last! Where have you been?"

The demanding tone in his voice made her aware that now was not the time to announce her engagement. Besides, her present confusion and uneasiness now made Menzin's earlier proposal seem like a distant dream. She was shocked to see her father so angry.

"I was...I was out walking with Menzin," she faltered hesitantly.

"Thank the merciful gods of Vantil you're safe. For the past few hours I have lived in the fear that I had lost both of my children."

Sahlin felt a lump rising in her throat, and stared wide-eyed at the agitated, upset figure in front of her. Fighting her rising fear, she demanded, "What do you mean, "Lost both of your children"?" Then as realisation combined with dread, she cried, "Where's Fulmin?"

The long silence and the look from Latnor told her far more than words could have, and she turned and fled to the nursery, almost knocking over Menzin who was just entering the doorway.

There she came to a halt, and looked about in complete incomprehension at the scene before her weary eyes.

Tamek knelt on the floor picking up spilled remains of food, and scrubbing at a red mark on the rug. As she did so, huge tears rolled down her cheeks, dripped off her chin, and mingled with the mess she tried vainly to clear. In the distance of the back of her mind, she heard Tamek's voice sobbing over and over, "My fault, it's all my fault."

As Tamek turned and saw her standing there, she saw the shock that she felt mirrored in her friend's face. Her gaze dropped from Tamek back to the stain on the rug, where she saw a trail of red spots that led to the window and the vast, dark emptiness beyond. Blood.

She didn't hear footsteps behind her as Menzin followed her to the nursery and stood mutely there.

"Is he dead?" she shrieked. "Well, answer me. Is he dead?"

"No, no, "Tamek sobbed. "I don't think so; I don't know," she howled, covering her face with her shaking hands. "It's all my fault," she continued, rocking to and fro, "All my fault."

The realisation that her brother had been kidnapped struck her like a physical blow to her body, and the sting swept her into action. Lurching forwards, she grabbed hold of her terrified friend and hauled her to her feet.

"What have you done? What's all your fault? Where's Fulmin? Answer me!"

"Sahlin, stop it!" she heard Menzin cry behind her, and felt his strong hands pulling her away.

"Leave me alone," she shouted stretching out towards Tamek who had fled to the other side of the room out of her reach. "I want to know what happened."

Latnor rushed in.

"You will," reasoned Menzin, "but you must calm down. You're upsetting Tamek. Can't you see she's as distressed as you are?"

The sudden flurry of energy had exhausted itself, and disappeared as quickly as it had come. Her strength faded rapidly from her body, and as she sank back against Menzin she heard herself pitifully whispering an apology. Whatever did she think she was doing? She must be mad.

"I am so sorry Tamek," she repeated, "Please forgive me."

Darkness rushed at her from all sides as the room began to violently tilt and spin, her arms felt strange sensations running up and down them, and her face felt as though there was some kind of energy pulsing through it. She remembered nothing else as she fell back into Menzin's arms.

Chapter 14

Quietness. Darkness... Fulmin!

Sahlin's eyelids flew open and she gazed wildly about. She was lying on her own bed, but had been covered by one of her father's ceremonial cloaks. She felt confined and claustrophobic in her wild panic, and her stomach lurched as she remembered the events that had led up to her senses failing and leaving her.

Fighting the dull beating inside her head, she pulled herself up into a sitting position, swept the cloak around her shoulders, and swung her feet to the floor.

Walking across to the window, she drew back the hangings and looked out. By the dim sunlight she knew that it was still early morning, but was relieved to see that the crowds had dispersed and left.

How could the sun still rise, and the day begin as normally and beautifully as ever when such a terrible thing had happened?

Panicking that she had lost several hours during which anything could have happened, she flew along the passageway to her father's study, where she could hear quiet voices from within. She knocked softly, and entered slowly. Her eyes immediately fell upon her father, who looked pale and drawn and had evidently not slept at all.

Menzin was seated in a high backed chair opposite Latnor, and he greeted her with a fleeting, polite smile as he rose to his feet. Although she guessed that he probably hadn't slept much either, youth was on his side, and he looked alert and fresher, ready for the trying times ahead.

"Good morning, Sahlin," he welcomed her in hushed tones. "Tea?"

"Father. Menzin. Yes please."

"I trust you feel a little better this morning, and have calmed down?" Latnor asked as he rose stiffly and briefly from his chair, acknowledging her presence.

"I'm so sorry, Father," she said solemnly, as she remembered how she had spoken to Tamek, "I don't know what happened to me." Menzin placed a cup of the green, herbal tea in her hand and fleetingly looked in her eyes before drawing up a chair for her between him and Latnor.

"It's alright, child. Tamek understands. She knows that you are upset. You have had a lot to deal with lately. Everyone has their limits." He turned his bowed head away and sank back down into his seat.

Still, Sahlin looked sheepishly at her feet. She sat down woodenly next to him, and instinctively grasped at his hand for moral support. Some of her tea spilled onto her lap but she didn't even notice. A weak smile from him gave a small amount of comfort, although she still flushed with embarrassment at what she looked upon as a failure of her responsibilities and position.

Many questions pounded against the walls of her head bursting to break free, but she held them inside, not wishing to appear as out of control as she had last night. She sat quietly for a few moments trying to sort them out into some kind of logical order.

Trying to portray calmness she didn't feel, she first asked whether there was any news on the disappearance or whereabouts of her brother. Of course, she knew the answer to that question, for they would hardly be sitting here if they had.

Latnor let out a deep sigh as he awkwardly rose once more to his feet, walked slowly to the door and stood facing it, almost as though he expected it to open. With head bowed, he too was trying to compose his thoughts and escape from the many voices in his mind all clamouring and jostling for answers he could not provide.

"At this moment, we have absolutely no idea where Fulmin is, why he was taken, or who has him."

Sahlin shot a worried look at Menzin. So, he hadn't told her father anything about Rusnan. Menzin shifted in his chair looking uncomfortable. It was clear he didn't like holding back on what they knew.

"Nor have we received any word from his captor," continued Latnor, oblivious to the sudden tense air in the room and the glances being exchanged between the pair.

"There are of course search parties out looking for him, or any clues, but I haven't heard anything from them yet, and it all seems rather hopeless."

Sahlin thought she could hear a slight break in his voice as he ended the last sentence, and she looked across in desperation towards Menzin, appealing for support.

"It isn't hopeless, Sir. With so many people out looking we are bound to hear some news soon."

"I hope so," he replied returning back to his chair. The pained expression on his tired face was too much for her to bear, and she looked down at her hands knotted together in her lap.

"The best we can do is sit and wait," he concluded.

Wait, thought Sahlin. That was something she could not do.

"Father, please tell me exactly what happened last night. I…I think I know who took Fulmin." There she had said it. She waited quietly for a response, and didn't know who looked more shocked out of the two men. Rarely had she seen her father, Ruler of Vantil, look so lost for words. His

195

look was one of complete astonishment. As for Menzin, he had clearly not expected her to reveal anything to Latnor just yet.

She felt slightly ashamed that she was accusing someone in her own mind without any facts, but who else could it be? Her thoughts were interrupted by Latnor striding across the room and seizing her arm a little more roughly than he had intended.

"What do you mean? How do you know? Do you know how long I have been sitting here agonising over who could do such a thing on Vantil? Do you?" he demanded, shaking her so that her teeth rattled.

"Father, calm down," she pleaded breaking free from his grasp, and sucking in air quickly.

"How can I calm down? Such an atrocity occurs, completely unheard of except in the chronicles of our ancestors, and you, a child, suddenly announce that you know who it is. I have been sitting here all night, trying to fathom out who could possibly do such a thing, inwardly accusing all my best friends, and questioning the loyalty of my people, and you say, "Calm down!""

He let go of her so suddenly that she fell backwards into her chair. She was completely stunned into silence by seeing her father react so, and for a moment she could not have uttered a single word even if she had known what to say next. Tears began to form in her eyes, and as they swelled, spilled quickly down her wan cheeks.

Eventually, the only response she could mutter was, "I am not a child."

His own reaction had also upset and shocked Latnor. Taking deep breaths to calm himself down, he shook his head in mortification. "What is happening to our planet? Is it my fault?"

"No Sir. No-one could question your ability as Ruler." Menzin felt as though he should step in to take the tension away between father and daughter.

Latnor raised a questioning eyebrow. "You think so? Never in our history has such a despicable thing happened. Never. We have all lived in the shadows of fear of what we have read happened on our ancestor's home planet, but have never before felt first-hand the terror of this kind of threat. Until now, under my leadership.

"When this planet was colonised, everything was so clear about how we should live to avoid a repeat of the tragedy on Zaren. We carefully followed the rules set by Parlon Dremun all those centuries ago; learning from their experience, and promising it would never happen again. And yet, it has. This could be the first small spark in a chain of events that could mean a war. A war! Here on Vantil. I despair. We have let Parlon Dremun down. We have let Zaren down. I have let Vantil down. If my ability as Ruler isn't being questioned, then it should be."

"No Sir. With respect, you are wrong," ventured Menzin. "You alone cannot be held responsible for another's actions."

"Yes I can. I am Ruler. I am supposed to set an example for others to follow. I nearly broke when Cameen died, and now this. Obviously, I am not fit to be setting examples to anyone."

"You have. That's the whole point! Don't you see?" By the puzzled look on his face, Menzin could see that he didn't. "You have carried on the traditions and rules set out exactly as they should have been. The people have always followed you, and the Rulers before you, unquestioningly."

"I still don't see."

"Why suspect one of your own innocent people?"

"One of my...innocent...?"

"Don't you see, daddy?" Sahlin implored, "It's not one of our own people."

"Rusnan! By the gods, I had completely forgotten about him since he went to live in the forest. But I haven't seen him for a long time. How do you...?"

"Sahlin has," Menzin tensely interjected.

"You! When?"

"With respect, that's not important now sir. What is important is that we stop questioning our own loyal people and do something to stop them doing the same. This is exactly what Rusnan wants to happen. To trigger off that chain of events you mentioned, that could lead to a war as it did on Zaren."

"But why would he do this?"

"I think I may have the answer, or part of it, from the ancient books," replied Sahlin excitedly, "But first I must find out exactly what happened last night before I commit myself to making any accusations." Casting a look at her future husband who was watching her proudly handling the situation so well, she shot a radiant smile at him that was immediately reciprocated. "Last night in the nursery, Tamek kept repeating that everything was her fault. What did she mean? Was she in the room when the kidnap took place? What did she see?"

"It was after Tamek had finished her meal, and settled Fulmin down in his crib. A noise outside disturbed her and she went to investigate. She found nothing, but when she returned, the door was open, and she heard Fulmin crying. She ran into the nursery to see someone bundling him into a sack." Here Latnor paused to control himself, trying not to think of his poor son being taken by force.

"A sack – how could he!" exclaimed Sahlin.

"In her fright," he continued, "she picked up the nearest object to hand which happened to be her platter, and tried to fend him off."

"Brave Tamek."

"Unfortunately, she was not quick enough, or strong enough, and Rus...the attacker flung her aside. She hit her head and has a rather nasty bump. The intruder did momentarily lose balance though, and Tamek feared he would fall forward and crush Fulmin. Fortunately though, I suppose, he regained his balance, snatched up the baby and ran, leaving a trail of his blood where Tamek had wounded him. She was knocked out by him as he left."

Sahlin closed her eyes as a huge wave of relief swept over her. So, at least the blood she had seen Tamek trying to clean up was not her brother's.

Smoothing the material of her father's cloak absently as she spoke, she asked, "So why does Tamek feel that it was her fault?"

Latnor sighed and replied, "Despite my numerous reassurances to the contrary, she believes that she shouldn't have left Fulmin alone in the first place, and also that she could have done more to prevent him from being taken."

"I see," Sahlin murmured dejectedly. She knew the strength of Tamek's unwavering loyalty, and although it was quite wrong, it would be the natural thing for her to assume responsibility for anything that happened. It hadn't helped, no doubt, that she herself had blamed her last night in her panic and confusion. That must be making her feel even worse. She cringed at the thought that she had contributed to her friend's current state of mind.

"Where is she now?"

"I sent her home to rest. A couple of her friends took her. There was nothing she could do here to help, and all the activity and people coming and going was only upsetting her more. Besides which, her head must be very sore this morning. I am told she remained deeply distressed throughout the night and did not rest at all. Now she is sleeping quietly at last in peace. She wanted to remain here of course but she was clearly unfit to do so."

"Then I must go and see her. She must tell me everything again, including every minute detail. There might be something that she overlooked mentioning to you that could give us the vital help that we need." She hesitated for a few moments until she finally added quietly, "And it will give me the opportunity to apologise for my bad behaviour."

Her thoughts drifted back to when she had wrongly accused Tamek in those terrible earlier hours which seemed like a very bad dream. Her train of thought then led her onto the trail of blood she had seen on the nursery floor, and she stared into empty space as she relived those moments when she feared the worst.

The space she was staring into seemed to completely entrance her until Menzin finally broke the spell by speaking.

"We will go together, but it's still early and Tamek needs to rest. You haven't eaten since yesterday, so we will have breakfast and you can get ready."

"Eaten? No, you're right, I haven't." She met his gaze with great affection. Here she was trying to handle everything calmly as she thought befitting for the Ruler's daughter, and here he was reminding her that she hadn't eaten.

Throughout this tumultuous turn of events he had repeatedly demonstrated just how deep his love and care for her really was. He was completely prepared to offer a quiet but firm hand of assistance despite his own recent problems, and yet remained in the background while she and her father adjusted to the continually changing events.

Within his eyes, she found her confidence, her calmness and her strength. She wondered why she had been blessed with the good fortune to meet him. Then it struck her, that it was when Rusnan had attacked her in the forest that Menzin had come to her rescue. Fate was extraordinary – the man that had threatened her, and who she was inwardly accusing of kidnapping her brother, was also the man responsible for bringing Menzin to her. If that day had never happened, it was unlikely they would have met. She and her father would not be getting his help, advice and calm reassurance and reasoning now. One thing was for sure, if it hadn't been for Menzin, she would not have been able to handle the situation half as well as she had so far. It was insane. All of this passed through her mind in a flash, and yet the thought of her encounter with Rusnan had unsettled her again and she visibly started at the thought of him.

Regaining her composure, she continued, "Yes, of course you're right. I shall take breakfast before I...we leave. Would you care to join me, Menzin? Father, you must too."

"No my child, I couldn't eat anything." Seeing her scolding look, he added firmly, "Really! I will eat later. I promise."

As the two teenagers stood to leave the room, Latnor suddenly clasped his daughter's hand. "I'm sorry that tempers have been a little frayed. I love you very much, and haven't cared for you recently in the way I should have. I'm very proud of the way you have handled everything. A lot of young ladies of your age would have given up a long time ago. Your mother would be proud too."

"I'm sure she is looking down on us giving us strength, and I know she would be proud of you too."

"Bless you for that."

"I love you father, very much. When this is all over I promise things will get back on track."

"Look after her," he told Menzin, embracing him, who nodded in response.

Her heart felt a little lighter as she walked along the passageway towards another day, arm in arm with Menzin. She felt as though she could cope with anything that came her way. Everything was going to work out just right. She would make sure it did, for her father's sake.

Chapter 15

During the walk to Tamek's house, Menzin and Sahlin at last had an opportunity to speak to one another freely. Although they had breakfasted together in peace, Sahlin had found it difficult to talk openly in the house where so much had turned sour lately. She felt as though the walls were listening to her every word.

Now at last outside in the open, enjoying the clean, fresh air, she relaxed and opened her heart to her companion. She explained how she felt she should not have told him about Rusnan when she found it difficult to tell her father, but that she felt he would deal with the situation much better as he had less personal involvement. She also believed that she had owed him an explanation as to why she was being attacked in the middle of nowhere! Whatever happened, she was glad that she had Menzin to confide in. Anyway, now Menzin had explained everything to Latnor about what had happened to her, after breakfast while she freshened up, he was now fully aware too.

She slipped her hand into his and gave it a light squeeze. Menzin stopped and turned to face her, smiling. As they looked at each other, words became unnescessary. He pulled her closer to him and gently kissed her. Sahlin felt the blood rising to her cheeks, and instinctively nestled closer to him, feeling completely protected from all harm. This seemed to be the moment to apologise for not mentioning their engagement this morning, and she drew slightly away.

"Menzin, I didn't think it was right to tell Father..." she began.

"It's all right," he interrupted, "I understand. We have forever in front of us. A few more days won't matter. We have a secret - a pleasant secret – and each other's happiness. You said you didn't want to tell him yet anyway."

Sahlin dropped the twig she had been toying with and absently brushed the dirt from her fingers onto her skirt. It seemed to her that every time she was nervous and dreaded relaying information, or confiding something, her nerves were totally unfounded. Here she was again, worried she may have upset him, and he completely understood.

"Thank you. I worried so much that you would be offended, and knew that by telling him now, he wouldn't show his happiness and approval to you as fully as he would under normal circumstances. Hmm, normal circumstances; we don't have many of those at the moment, do we?"

"Yes, there's been a lot to contend with recently. It seems awful that so much should happen to one family, and in such a short space of time. I think Latnor has shown great courage; and of course, so have you."

"You know how much I love you, and I want you to be so happy. I want you to feel like part of the family from the very beginning."

"I know. Everything will soon return to normal, you wait and see. Fulmin will soon be back home, your father will be able to resume his duties to the council's satisfaction once the weight of worry has been lifted, and then you and I can announce our engagement."

Sahlin let out a small sigh. "It has been dreadful to watch him in such torment; but somehow it was worse seeing him almost reprimanded by the councillors for the compassion he showed towards his family. That is what dulled his enthusiasm for his official duties. I know that will have upset him greatly, for his position as Ruler has always taken priority over everything; it had to – except family. But it just seems to have been one thing after another, and any man would have suffered. It feels almost as though they have penalised him for it."

Menzin thought she had suffered too, for her happy, carefree, beautiful face had once again become clouded with anguish.

"You needn't convince me," he chuckled, and at once she realised she had let her emotions out in a rambling, gushing overflow. She shot him an apologetic look, to which he let out an even louder laugh, and hugged her close again.

Under the cover of the trees, a dark form followed the lovers from a safe distance watching their every move. His blood boiled with the seething anger he felt, and his locked up frustration showed on his tight, drawn features. His fists bunched together in a ball, and he felt the uneven nails biting into the rough skin on his filthy hands. How dare they be so happy? How dare they?

What right had she to revel in the love of this man, while he existed in this awful place alone? How could she be so happy with her baby brother missing? She made him sick.

With a thousand angry voices crying in his head to be heard, the adrenalin began to pump again, filling his body with an energy that needed to be unleashed.

He had followed the couple closely up until the point they had exchanged kisses, and he had overheard their conversation. He waited like an animal in hiding, close to the trees so he could remain unseen, his heart beat seeming to become louder and louder. He fancied that the leaves on the tree he was pressed up against must be shaking through the vibration.

Carelessly, as he had edged forward he had trodden on a dried branch, and his weight had caused it to snap. With baited breath he had waited to be discovered, but no, the two on whom he spied were so caught up in their embrace they had hardly paid any attention. Sahlin had cast a fleeting glance in his direction, and for a moment he had feared the worst. But Menzin had cupped her chin in his hands and pulled her lips back to his. In a moment, the slight disturbance had been forgotten.

He wanted to follow them as they moved off once again, but he had other business to attend to. Still, it would not take long and he would soon catch up with them again. Yes, he would enjoy that. An evil smile spread across his lips, and he released his clenched fists. He winced as the nails pulled away from the indentations they left in his grubby palms. Looking down he saw traces of blood.

So, they were going to be married were they? Well, he would see about that.

* * *

The twin suns were crossing at their highest point as the pair made their way through the last wooded part of their trek. Hand in hand they walked up to the doorway of Tamek's house which was set on its own in a small clearing, and Sahlin called out softly that they had arrived. There was no reply to her call, and they made their way quietly inside.

All was still as Sahlin crept through the simply furnished but beautiful house to the room where Tamek slept. She carefully peeped inside, and there lay Tamek fast asleep, still dressed in the clothes that she had worn on the previous day, and uncovered by any bedclothes.

Poor thing, thought Sahlin. She must have been so weary

that she had literally just hauled herself on to the bed and stayed there, too exhausted to even cover herself. Gently, she pulled her own cloak over the sleeping form, and guessed by the tear stains on her face that she had only given into sleep after a fight. She sat for a while watching the steady rise and fall of her friends rhythmical breathing, wondering how much more they would have to endure before everything returned to the way it was. They had taken their peaceful existence too much for granted, and only hoped that it was not too late to see it return.

After a while, when she was convinced her friend was enjoying a deep comfortable sleep, she tip-toed out of the room and went to find Menzin. He was outside, busily drawing up water from the huge well.

"She's asleep. What are you doing?"

"Well, there was no water inside and none in the barrel outside, so I thought I would replenish the stocks."

"That's strange; normally Tamek is so efficient on keeping everything well stocked up."

"Well, my guess is, she hasn't had much opportunity lately. She has been over at your house a lot, and probably just hasn't had enough time to do her own chores."

"Poor Tamek. She should have said. I thought she was

tired because of last night, but it's not just that is it? That is so typical of her, not to say that she was falling behind with her own work, and I'm ashamed to admit that I never thought to ask her if she was coping ok."

"You've had a lot on your own mind, remember."

"Yes, but that's no excuse. I should still have remembered other people as well as myself. Maybe if I'd done that, Fulmin would still be at home."

"It's no use fretting now; it's done. But we can make up for it a little by helping her out while we are here. That's why I thought I would draw up plenty of water to keep her supplied for the next few days. Next I'll collect some wood, and then tidy the yard. There's a lot of debris that must have been blown in during those high winds the other day."

"What would I do without you?"

"Don't think about it. I'm not going anywhere!"

"Good, I'm pleased to hear it. I will make us something to eat. By the time I've made it, you will be hungry, and Tamek should be just about stirring. If not, I will wake her anyway. She needs to keep her strength up."

She lingered silently for a while longer, continuing to watch him furiously pumping his arms to bring up the water, completely absorbed in what he was doing. She smiled to herself, and turned to go back inside. Just for a second she paused, looking into the thickness of the surrounding trees. She was sure that someone was watching her. She shivered, and casting a glance back at Menzin still busy bringing up the water, went inside.

There, she too became engrossed with her work, and sang happily to herself as she prepared the Banil, a type of bread, and a vegetable stew. At least there was food in the house, though not much. She went to bring in some more vegetables from the store at the back of the house. It felt good to be doing something for her friend for once.

The food would all be ready soon, and she had to say, for one of her few attempts so far at cooking, it smelled very appetising. She only hoped it would to Menzin and Tamek too! As she took the bread away from the flames, so Menzin entered the kitchen. At first she didn't notice anything was wrong, as she was preoccupied with taking the newly baked bread to the table. But as he approached her, she saw blood pouring down his face.

"Menzin!" she cried, dropping the bread on the table and running to him. "Whatever has happened?" She led him round the side of the table and helped him sit down on a chair. Fetching a bowl of the freshly drawn water, she began to clean his injuries, taking great care every time he let out a moan or made a sudden jolt where she tried to wipe the cut. "Are you all right?" she demanded.

As he began to speak, she realised just how shocked he was, by the slowness and deliberateness of his words. His face was very pale.

"It sounds so silly," he mumbled.

"What does? Tell me."

"I was leaning over the well, drawing up the last bucket. I stretched out to haul it towards me, and began to pull when the cable holding it snapped. I was on tiptoe, and the weight of the water caught me off balance I suppose, and I fell over the edge."

"Into the well? Then what happened?"

"Well, that's the silly thing. I grabbed hold of the well ledge as I fell, and I should have just been able to pull myself back over onto my feet."

"But?"

"But suddenly, something really hard hit my hand, and I couldn't hang on any longer. I let go and fell down further, hitting my head as I went. For a while I couldn't see anything out of this eye at all." He indicated his left eye.

Seeing the worried look she was wearing, he assured her, "Its ok now, I can see properly again."

"Thank goodness for that. Then what did you do?"

"I instinctively reached out to grab hold of anything I could and managed to catch the cable. I hung on with everything I had, but I slid down it and it burnt my hand. Anyway, after that I had something to swing myself over to the wall, and I climbed back up to the top."

"Let me see your hand."

"It's nothing really."

"Let me see, I'll decide that."

Menzin looked rather shamefacedly at her as she saw the deep red burn marks across his palms. "Nothing to worry about; look at it! You must be in terrible pain!" she scolded.

"Well, not really, but I do have a mighty big headache!"

"Oh, you!" Crying with the fright she had felt for him but also laughing with relief that he appeared to be alright, she clutched him to her and cradled him in her arms.

"Ouch!" he protested, and as she pulled away in alarm thinking she had hurt him further, he grinned and said, "Just kidding!"

Playfully she pretended to hit his arm. "When your bruising has faded away, remind me to give you another one for frightening me like that!" She cuddled him even closer.

She was surprised that although he was trying to shrug off the events as though nothing had happened, she could still feel shivers running through his body. She lightly remarked that she didn't know out of the two of them, who was shaking more.

After he had calmed down a little, Sahlin said softly, "You know, that could have been Tamek out there?" He thought quietly for a moment without raising his head from her bosom.

She continued, "In her present state of mind, she could easily have been killed. I can't believe it." Still no reply from Menzin, and she felt his silence was keeping something from her. "It must have been a very old cable to have just snapped like that, and it's not like Tamek to be so careless..."

"Sahlin," he interrupted. "There's something I didn't tell you."

"What?" She pulled away, and looked down at him expectantly.

"The cable was new, and still well oiled."

"So it was faulty? That doesn't happen very often."

"It doesn't happen at all."

"I don't understand."

"I'm afraid to say the cable didn't snap because it was faulty, or anything like that, It snapped because it had been cut."

"Cut?" Her face echoed the disbelief that he himself had felt when he made the discovery.

"Whoever made the cuts did a very poor job at hiding the evidence. I could clearly see the marks where the knife used had slipped and made smaller scratches on the wire around the main cut."

Sahlin was staring open mouthed at him, as though she had just had a terrible thought.

"What is it?"

"I was just wondering; suppose the knife used was the one that Rusnan held at my throat?"

"The thought had crossed my mind."

"But why would he try to harm Tamek?"

"I don't know. Who knows how this maniac's mind works. I suppose he might think that she is a friend of the family and that is good enough reason. Or it could be that she could identify him from last night."

"No, Father said that when she was recalling the events, she said that Rus…the intruder wore a hood. But better to be safe than sorry, I suppose. And, if you think he did that because of last night that would mean he's close to us now."

"The only other thing I can think of…"

"Yes?"

"…Is that he knew we were coming here, and he laid a trap, waiting for us."

Sahlin was quite obviously startled at this, and she failed to look as though the thought didn't bother her. "But how would he know that we would come here?"

"Either he heard us before we left, which would be highly unlikely because that would mean he was in the house while we were, or someone told him, which is impossible, or…"

"He followed us," she finished the sentence for him. He caught her hand as she gasped in fright."

"He could have heard where we were going, and gone ahead to lay a surprise for us. It's alright, he didn't succeed. And I'm going to make sure that he doesn't get another chance."

"What if he's still outside? You don't think he's *inside*?"

"Take it easy. No I don't, but we'll go round systematically checking every room together. Each room we check, we'll fasten the shutters at the windows, then lock the doors as we leave. I don't think he would be foolish enough to still be around, but it won't hurt for us to check all the same. Come on."

Carefully, they methodically went through each room, Menzin ahead holding Sahlin's hand as she followed, checking in cupboards, under beds and behind furniture, securing all entrances. The last room they checked was Tamek's.

"You go in and wake her up. I'm going outside to check around out there. Lock the door behind me and only open it if you know it's definitely me."

"Please don't go outside."

"I honestly think it's okay. He wouldn't stick around, not with three of us here. If one of us had fallen for his little trick, excuse the pun, then I think we might have had something to worry about." Sahlin at last relaxed a little, and giggled at his joke.

"That's better. Now, remember what I said? Only open the door if it's definitely me, okay?"

"Yes."

"Good."

"Menzin, please be careful all the same."

He squeezed her hand affectionately, and made his way

along the hallway to the door. Sahlin followed and bolted it firmly behind him. She realised that this was the first time they had ever had need to use the door locks for anything other than security against the weather they experienced. Putting all bad thoughts out of her mind, she entered Tamek's room amazed she still slept, and gently began to wake her.

Chapter 16

Outside, the activities had been observed from a safe distance. Twitching hands nervously played with the greasy hair now hanging across his dirty face. Short, stubby, sweaty fingers lingeringly stroked his moustache. "Come on," Rusnan urged, "Draw some water from the well. Go on."

As though his thoughts had been strong enough to stir Menzin into action, so he walked to the well and began to lower the pail.

"Yes!" he hissed triumphantly. The shaking hands knotted together in eager anticipation at the prospect of succeeding in a well laid trap. He couldn't wait to see Menzin go hurtling down into the depths to his death; a cracked skull, a broken neck, or drowned, he wondered. Any of those would do, or all three would be better still. Once he was out of the way, Sahlin would be almost helpless inside...That pleased him very much. Tamek would be no match for him, but she was different. For a young girl she had a lot of spirit and had coped well with the dilemmas she had faced. If he didn't hate her so much, he could almost admire her.

His heart had almost stopped when he saw the hapless Menzin lose his balance as the cable snapped, and fall over the side of the huge well. He couldn't believe his luck; his plan was working. Edging his way nearer, he had cursed under his breath when he saw the youth hanging on to the ledge with one hand.

Making sure that he was not being observed from inside, he ran to the well and seized a large stone. Summoning all his strength, he raised it high above his head, and brought it down with all his might. Luckily, the stone had not hit Menzin's hand squarely, or it would have broken most of the bones. However, the blow was enough to send an agonising pain shooting through his hand and up his arm. Crying out, he had no choice but to release his precarious grip on the well edge.

Assuming the job was finished, Rusnan had run off back into the shelter of the trees while he thought out the next part of his plan. He had waited so long that he wanted to be sure that everything ran smoothly and properly, down to the very last detail. How he was going to enjoy the next few hours. Once the two women were out of the way, he would be able to move from his shelter in the woods into Tamek's house and be properly warm and secure. Nobody would suspect a thing.

But wait! What was that he could see? No, it couldn't be. Pulling himself to his feet once more, and straining his eyes into the sun, his suspicions were confirmed. How could it be? How could he possibly have survived the fall? Watching Menzin haul himself painfully back over onto solid ground, Rusnan realised that he must have caught the cable as he dropped down. That wasn't something he had bargained on. Instinctively he pulled his knife from his boot, and held it ready. Maybe he would have to finish him off in a different way. Curse them all! This was not what was supposed to happen. He had not suspected that things were going to be nearly as difficult.

Muttering and swearing to himself, he knew he had no chance today of executing his plan, and strode back up the hill, rethinking and carefully plotting his next move. In abject annoyance, he tossed aside his knife, and it landed half hidden beneath the fallen leaves on the ground. He was far away by the time Menzin had ventured outside to check everything was fine.

* * *

Inside, a rather dazed and bemused Tamek had been roused from her exhausted sleep, and hastily and briefly filled in on the details of the day's events. Sahlin waited anxiously for Menzin to return, helping Tamek to come to terms with the latest twist of their ever changing story to pass the time.

Although she had waited for the rap on the door to signal his return, when it did come she nearly jumped through the ceiling. She raced to the door and almost unbolted it without checking first. Trembling fingers poised, she shouted out, "Who's there?"

"Me, Menzin, it's okay to open up Sahlin."

"I'm so glad you're back. You were so long. Where did you go? Did you see anything? Are you all right?"

"Slow down! So many questions in one breath, I have been all around the outskirts of the property and grounds, and quite a way up into the trees. I circled round a large area and found no-one." He wasn't sure if the look on Sahlin's face was one of disappointment or relief. "However, I did find this."

"What is it? Let me see."

Menzin produced a knife from his pocket, and Sahlin gasped. "Where was it?"

"Discarded or dropped up in the trees. I would say that this was the knife used to sever the cable in the well."

"That's definitely not the one he threatened me with. It's very different." She stared at it wide-eyed as though looking at it would make it disappear, and with it, the awful events that seemed to follow one another.

Her tranced was interrupted by Menzin snatching the knife away suddenly, and pacing up and down in annoyance. She was completely amazed at the dark, agitated expression which occupied his features. Obviously the shock of his "accident" earlier had broken and his reaction was now one of anger.

"I really can't understand why he's doing this. What does

he hope to gain from all of it? Kidnap is one thing, but attempted murder? Why?"

He had temporarily lost his dispassionate, calm attitude, and was now marching about furiously. He had checked the cable countless times, hoping he had been completely wrong, and the dreadful fall that he had endured was the result purely of an awful accident.

Sahlin looked on, and could not help feeling as though she were in the presence of a younger version of her father, watching yet another bout of his endless pacing.

Each step seemed to beat a word as he said, "There has to be a reason for all of this. What?" He kicked the chair as he walked past it, and then suddenly halted as though an invisible barrier had been placed in his path. He stared at Sahlin, for she was wearing that look again; the look which suggested to him that she may know more than she was telling him. Crossing over to her, he took her arm and led her firmly but gently outside, aware that they may be disturbing Tamek who was washing and dressing.

Once out in the sunshine filled yard, he sat her down on a wooden stool. "If you have discovered why he is doing this, then I really think that now would be a good time to tell me. You told Latnor before we left that you had an idea. It's getting too dangerous now to take lightly as some sort of adventure."

"How dare you!" she cried angrily, rising from the stool

as though something had catapulted her up. "I have not treated any of this as "an adventure" as you put it. If you think for one minute that I have enjoyed any of this in some sick way, then you are not the man that I thought you were." Turning her back on him she stood biting her lip to stop more words that she might regret later coming out. Huge tears fell down her red, angry face. She felt a light touch on her shoulder but ignored it.

"Don't touch me," she spat.

"I'm sorry, Sahlin. That was a very poor choice of words, and I think you know I didn't mean it the way it sounded. It's just I've been trying to stay strong for your sake, but this business with the cable being cut has really got to me. I was scared, but not just for myself. I was scared that if I let go and fell, that I would have let you down."

"Me?"

"Yes. If I hadn't made it, you would have been alone against this maniac. And what would my father do, he…"He didn't get to finish the sentence.

"Oh, Menzin," she cried, whirling around and flinging herself into his arms. "Don't say that you could have died."

"Relax. I told you, you can't get rid of me that easily!"

She looked up into his face, trying to smile, and he saw

the traces of tears on her cheeks. "What's this, I made you cry? I'm sorry."

"It's not your fault. I suppose it's a mixture of relief that you came back, fright over the accident, all mixed with the other emotions that I have whirling around inside. It's driving me crazy."

"Yes, you've had a lot, haven't you? I forget you are still so young when you act so grown up all the time. It's the first time I've seen you cry like this."

"I thought pretending I was all right would make everything else alright. Rather a naïve perspective, isn't it?"

"No, don't be so silly. We all face things differently, but I do wish that you hadn't kept everything bottled up inside. Please don't shut me out, I want to share in every part of you, whatever you are feeling. Promise?"

"Yes. And you?"

He nodded and held her close.

"By the way, I don't know for certain what the reason is behind all of this. I just had an idea from some of the old books I was reading, that's all; to do with the war between Zaren and Spilon. And a clue from the badge that Rusnan wears -"

"Ahem, I believe lunch is ready," a soft voice broke in

from behind them. Turning, they saw Tamek at the doorway, looking rather tired and dark eyed, but smiling at the pair locked in their loving embrace.

"I'll tell you later, Menzin."

"Okay."

Sahlin left his side and went in with her friend who was very anxious about Menzin's cuts and grazes. Sahlin reassured her several times they were superficial and looked worse than they actually were, on the way to the kitchen.

"I'll call you when it's on the table," Sahlin told Menzin, meaning she wanted some time on her own with her friend. He understood the tone and look, and set about chores outside.

"Tamek. I cannot be excused for what I said to you last night, and the way I behaved. I'm so ashamed. All I can ask is, can you forgive me? I don't know what happened."

"It's all right, everyone was in such a state, and to be honest, I don't remember a lot of what you said, I was in shock myself and I felt like I was cocooned in a dream, or more like a nightmare. I still can't believe what's happened. Your poor father...and of course you, and dear little Fulmin. Oh dear..." Tears began to come again, and the two women held each other in silence.

Sahlin whispered, "You do know, don't you, that it isn't your fault? Please don't torture yourself for something that you aren't to blame for. If I had stayed behind last night, as I should have done, it would still have happened, but it would be me nursing a sore head, not you! Menzin has taught me a lot about putting things in perspective, and you need to do that too." Tamek nodded.

They broke apart, and fetched the dishes from the cupboard.

"You know, it reminds me of when I was younger," Tamek said as the pair shared out the food.

"What does?"

"Seeing you and Menzin together. When I was about your age, I had a boyfriend. Actually, we were going to be married." Her eyes took on a soft look and Sahlin knew that she was remembering.

"I didn't know."

"What?"

"That you were married once."

"I wasn't."

"But you just said...I'm sorry, it's none of my business."

"That's all right. Not many people did know; except your parents and mine. His name was Arubek." She said the name so softly and tenderly, Sahlin knew she still loved him.

"What happened…If you want to talk about it?"

"I was young," Tamek sighed, "and I thought I knew everything." She looked at Sahlin who took the hint, and fidgeted with the cutlery in her hands.

She continued, "I was very headstrong too, and had everything for my life all mapped out. I was young, ambitious; full of unbreakable spirit. Father owned a large farm, and I worked with him in the fields experimenting with new crops to grow. It was only temporary in my eyes, before I left to see what the rest of the world had to offer me. It upset father. He wanted me to carry on at the farm and take it over. I was good with the crops, and we were making progress, but I wanted more. We were doing so well, and using more and more land space for the experiments, that we had to take on extra help during the peak months, and to harvest as much food as possible before The Period of Bleakness came.

"One of the young lads that came to help was Arubek. He was shy and quiet; I liked him straight away. In fact, it was I who asked him to come out with me! We secretly spent a lot of time together. Sometimes we could only get a few minutes, sometimes it was hours and hours. But it was never long enough."

"Father would never have approved of me seeing him. I was too young he would have said, and besides, he saw just the farm and my future in it. There was no room for what I wanted or how I felt. He didn't find out for a long time, and when he did it was from someone else who had seen us together. He was livid. He said I was incorrigible, and had embarrassed the family by secretly seeing someone. He thought Arubek would soon be leaving and I would be broken hearted. He didn't know I had planned on going with him. We argued such a lot, and mother was devastated, but father told her he was in charge and things were to be done his way. It was all such a mess. In the end, he was so angry, that he gave me an ultimatum that either I told the village I was leaving of my own free will, or he would publicly disown me and send me away. He preferred the first; people knew I wanted to travel about on my own and that way the family would be spared the shame."

"Tamek, I had no idea," Sahlin breathed, "That's so awful."

"Oh, it gets worse! It wasn't really my father's fault; I don't blame him for what he said and did. Of course, I did at the time. But as I grew older I realised just how much I had hurt him."

"But how?"

"He only found out about Arubek and me after three months, a long time after most of our people. I suppose he was just so busy, he didn't see it. Or just didn't want to; I don't know. Back then, it was almost unheard of for a girl to ask out a boy, and the most terrible thing not to have your parents' permission to go out."

Sahlin began to feel a little uncomfortable, thinking about not asking Latnor about Menzin, and now keeping their own future plans secret.

Tamek continued, "The last straw was when the news came from someone else. Father thought I was deceitful, and I suppose I was."

"What did you decide on? About leaving I mean."

"What could I do? Arubek had been sent away without anyone apart from my father knowing where. If I had allowed him to publicly denounce me, not only would I have been disgraced, but it would have hurt and shamed him even more. It would have been intolerable for me and my mother in that atmosphere, so I left."

"Where did you go?"

"I spent a long time looking for Arubek, but of course I never found him. I don't know what my father had said to him, but it was obviously very harsh. He just seemed to disappear off the face of Vantil. Nobody had seen him, or knew where he had gone. Wherever father had sent

231

him, it was a lot further than I could travel on my own. I happened upon this village about six months later. My parents had known yours a long time ago, and had been good friends."

Menzin appeared at the door to see where the lunch had got to, but reading the ladies expressions, left again without uttering a word.

"Your parents took me in, gave me somewhere of my own to live after a while and really looked after me without judging. They tried to heal the rift with my parents, but told me they had found out that not long after I left, my father died in an accident in the fields, and mother died soon after of a broken heart. So even if I had gone back, there was nobody to go back to."

"What about the farm?"

"They had left instructions it was to be shared among the community. I was completely cut out. Your parents helped me out a lot, and I did live with them for a long time. They were so kind. Then they helped me move here, and I helped them out whenever I could. At first it was to repay them for their kindness, but soon it came to be just because I was a friend and had grown to love them dearly. I suppose they filled the gap my own parents left, and they were more accepting than mine ever were."

"And you never met anyone else?"

"Yes, I did. But it wasn't the same. My heart belonged to, and always will belong, to Arubek. So I chose to live alone."

"I see. I'm so sorry."

"Don't be. That's life sometimes. Anyway," said Tamek pulling herself out of her dreams, "I don't know why all that came out! Come on; let's eat before lunch gets cold."

Deciding it was safe to go outside, they carried everything out and called Menzin over from repairing the well cable. He looked better now Sahlin was relieved to see; the blood had dried up and been cleaned away but the cut still looked nasty. She couldn't help thinking though that even if he was left with a scar, it would suit his features. He had more colour and he seemed more his normal self as he came over and greeted Tamek.

"How are you feeling today?" he asked as he sat down beside her, wiping the sweat from his face.

"Better than you by the look of it," she replied with a grin. "No, thank you," she continued, "I'm much better now. Everything seems like such a long time ago, it's hard to believe it all only happened last night." Menzin judged by the faraway, unblinking stare, that she was yet again reliving everything from the previous evening. At last, she blinked, wiping away the images, and started as she came back to the present moment.

233

While they ate, Tamek recounted the entire evening's events to them, trying to include absolutely every detail she could remember. She knew how important the information that she gave them could be.

When she had finished, Menzin ran through the traumas of their time in detail since they had arrived earlier. She looked worried but not very surprised; almost as though she had expected something of that nature to happen eventually.

Perhaps she was growing used to these awful occurrences, or simply that she had taken her fill and could take no more, thought Sahlin. What she had confided to her this morning had given her a whole new insight into her friend, and she realised she had totally misjudged her, never dreaming anything of her past could have been so awful and hard.

She felt so sad herself, as she went over Tamek's story in her own mind while Menzin was finishing his update. One could never tell from someone's appearance what they had been through in their life she decided.

She felt deflated as she realised they were no better off for information from Tamek about the previous evening. She had hoped she would provide more detail than Latnor had, but then she hadn't really expected her to. She rested her chin on her hands, and let out a long, deep sigh, and then mentally chided herself as she realised how much of a habit that was becoming with her lately.

Taking note of what the other two were conversing about, she heard Menzin asking Tamek if she could provide a description of the man in the nursery once more.

"Why bother," she cut in, "We know who it is."

"Correction; we think we know who it is."

The look of astonishment on her features was very apparent, and she was aware that her mouth had dropped open. Woodenly she closed it, and heard her teeth crack together.

"We may think we know who it is, but remember, we don't really have any conclusive evidence. We have to prove to other people beyond doubt that it was Rusnan. After all, we might be accusing a completely innocent man, while whoever is to blame could be running about free."

"Okay, so we were all absolutely fine until Rusnan appeared and it's all completely coincidental that at the same time he showed up and started verbally and physically threatening me, that my brother was kidnapped, Tamek was attacked and someone decided to sabotage the well cable and try to kill you. Not to mention, there's some crazy person throwing knives around in the forest. He dresses in black, the kidnapper wore black, but we are looking for someone else entirely. Makes sense."

"Okay, okay, so I know that we all know it's Rusnan, but we still have to find out why and prove it. Only then can we stop him."

"Yes I know, but it's all so frustrating. Time is ticking away, and meanwhile, poor Fulmin could be going through who knows what. I'm desperate to get him back. I doubt that wherever he is, he's being very well looked after." She gasped, adding, "What if he's still in that sack; he could suffocate, or maybe he already..."

"You musn't think like that. We'll get him back, don't worry. Rusnan has nothing to gain by killing him. If he wanted to do that, he would have done it there and then last night in the nursery. No, he wants him for his little game he's playing, except we don't know the rules. That's exactly why we have to go through all of this first. If we systematically work through it, we may just find the clue we need. Then we can find Rusnan and save Fulmin. If we do it properly, we may save time and Fulmin, instead of clutching at straws that will waste time and not help anyone."

"Yes, I know," Sahlin conceded as she laid her head on his arm. "As always, you are right."

"Right, let's go through it again. Height?"

"Taller than me," Tamek said slowly, "but not much."

"Build?"

"About your build Menzin, but difficult to be sure because of the heavy clothing he wore. I think he was less muscular than you, but bigger if you know what I mean."

"Fatter," Sahlin interpreted.

"Features?"

"I can't tell you anything about his features; they were completely covered by a hood."

In exasperation, Menzin questioned, "Well, what was he wearing apart from a hood?"

Tamek didn't answer instantly, and instead sat for a moment with tightly closed eyes, as she fought inwardly to recall any little detail that would provide the missing link that they were so desperately searching for.

What had he been wearing? It all happened so quickly. She remembered the hood, and the gloved hand that sent her crashing to the ground. Instinctively her hand reached up and rubbed the bruise on her head. She could not quite picture what else he wore. Going over it so many times in her mind made her unsure whether she was recalling him accurately or not. She had been sure; well, she thought she had. Her face took on a drained, pained expression as she struggled to prompt her memory to recollect everything accurately once more. Just once more...

"It's no use," she wailed, covering her face with her hands.

"Ssh, ssh, it's all right," cooed Sahlin, placing a comforting arm around her, "It's all right."

Her inward feelings betrayed her reassuring words, and she glanced up at Menzin, guessing he felt the same. He shrugged, stood up and walked away deep in thought.

"What have you been thinking about," he asked Tamek sweeping back over to her.

"I would have thought that was fairly obvious."

"No, no. I mean, from what point have you been trying to remember? From the moment you found the intruder or before that?"

"When I saw Fulmin being bundled into a sack."

"Right. So now go back further in your mind."

Sahlin was now sitting perched on the edge of a rock with hands twisted together, suddenly optimistic at the look on Tamek's face. Menzin seemed to be putting her in a trance, and it looked as though she were remembering everything more clearly.

"What are you doing?" she whispered to him.

"Ssh!"

"Sorry!"

"Now," he addressed Tamek calmly, "Where are you?"

"I'm sitting in the nursery and go across to comfort Fulmin. I lift him up, and sing and talk to him. Eventually he quietens down, I lay him back down in his crib, and he goes to sleep. I am about to clear away the supper things, when I hear a noise outside. Thinking it's Sahlin returning, I call out, but there's no reply. Checking on Fulmin, I go outside, closing the door behind me to investigate. At first I find nothing, and then I discover a Sonx.

"Relieved that's all it is, and reproving myself for being so silly, I walk back and find the entrance open. I panic and rush inside, hearing Fulmin scream as I run. I enter the nursery, and find a man...I can see him! He's holding Fulmin and trying to push him into a sack."

She began to cry as she spoke, and Menzin gently encouraged her to continue. "What happened next, Tamek? Take it slowly."

"He turns around and sees me."

"Can you see him clearly?" urged Sahlin.

"Ssh!" Menzin reprimanded her. She looked on slightly amused as he asked, "Can you see him clearly?" and she tried to stifle a grin.

"Yes, he's all in black. Black coat, black gloves, boots and hood, except..."

"Yes?" prompted Menzin as he and Sahlin edged closer to her to hear her fading words.

"Got it!" she shrieked as her eyelids sprang apart and she jumped to her feet, nearly knocking both her companions over in their fright.

"What?" they both cried together in delighted unison.

"Sometimes when I concentrate on something, little obscure things flash into my head that are not really anything to do with what I should be thinking about."

Menzin and Sahlin exchanged puzzled glances, and Tamek frowned. "Sorry, I'll try to be clearer. I remember thinking at the time, despite everything else that was happening, what an unusual badge he was wearing. It was shining in the moonlight through the window."

"Badge?" snapped Sahlin, her full attention once more on her friend, "What badge?"

Tamek's face drained of its grin at her delight of remembering, as she saw Sahlin's pale face looking numb and hearing the edge in her voice.

"Can you describe it?"

"A silvery coloured brooch or badge of a crescent moon

with a lightning flash through it; about this big." She indicated with her hands. "There was a piece missing."

"Where?"

"The top of it was snapped off. A shame really, it would have been so pretty. Why? Have I remembered something which means anything to you?"

She could see by Sahlin's reaction that the question was completely unnecessary, but she wanted to know what she had uncovered. Tamek's enquiring eyes and the intensity showing on Menzin's face shot a terrible feeling through her body, and her stomach lurched.

"I have seen that badge before," she shuddered, remembering the first time Rusnan had come to her by the river, and once again she felt his rough hands on her skin and smelled his vile breath.

"Where? Whose is it? Tell me!" Tamek demanded in exasperation.

"Yes, I have seen it too," interrupted Menzin, "In the forest, the day we met."

"Someone please tell me what is going on!"

"I first saw it when I was by the river one evening alone. A man came, and threatened me, and he was wearing that badge."

"Threaten you...you've never said anything of this to me young lady!"

Sahlin bowed her head, and looked down. "I couldn't. At the time I didn't really think he meant anything by his threats; that he just wanted to frighten me. And then after that, everything happened so quickly, and I didn't really have chance to tell anyone. Well, except Menzin. And that was only because he saved me the day I was lost in the forest when Rusnan held me at knifepoint." It all came gushing out in one breath.

"Saved you...lost in the forest...knifepoint? Whatever has been going on that you've kept so quiet?"

"Please don't be angry."

"I'll have time to be angry later. At the moment I'm just very confused. So who came to see you at the river — Rusnan?"

Sahlin nodded.

"And it's his badge?"

"Yes, it is."

"I see."

"I can confirm that," interjected Menzin. "I saw it when you were fighting with him. The sunlight had caught it, and it was almost blinding as I ran towards you."

Sahlin couldn't help squirming as Tamek watched open mouthed. "Fighting with him...dear me!"

The embarrassed couple knew that they had some explaining to do, for her bewilderment could not be ignored. Besides which, Sahlin was quite relieved to have someone else to confide in; especially a woman.

"I think it's about time we told you everything that's been going on."

"I think you could be right young lady. From the beginning; and don't miss anything out."

The pair settled themselves down and began their long narrative, whilst Tamek listened in complete astonishment. They were careful to be completely honest and not miss anything out. Things had gone too far to try to spare her feelings; she had to know everything in order to understand just how much danger they were in.

The discovery had been made, and now they prayed for the courage to follow this through to the end, whatever that might be. Beyond doubt now, Rusnan was their man. They needed to find him, and Fulmin, and put an end to this terrible saga.

As their story unfolded, dark clouds rolled across the sky as if casting their opinion, and both the suns disappeared. Large raindrops spattered onto the dry, dusty ground; slowly at first, and then faster as they gathered momentum. Thunder rumbled in the distance, and Sahlin realised that the tension she felt had been added to by the awful, stifling heat that none of them had noticed while submerged in the thoughts that shrouded them all.

Perhaps the gods were showing their disapproval she wondered, gazing up at the startling bright flashes of lightning that were now tearing the sky apart.

Hurriedly, the three ran inside to shelter from the elements, glad for the brief break away from such dark and foreboding images of the fight still to come.

Chapter 17

Long after the pair had finished their story, nothing could be heard except for the distant rumbles of thunder as it rolled away over the hills, grumbling and moaning as it went.

The three friends were trapped in the house; there was no going out in this weather. They sat staring at each other, or at the floor, each locked in their private inner thoughts, debating what the next move should be, and each looking up hopefully at any slight move from the others, hoping that they had found the magic solution they sought.

How tired Menzin looked, thought Sahlin, noticing the dark circles around his eyes; and how much older too. It was hard to believe that he wasn't much older than her. But then, she hadn't looked in a mirror lately either, so he probably had the same ideas about her. She looked at his burnt palms as he stretched and rubbed them, and the marks and cuts on his face. They were probably so sore, yet he didn't mention them once. If it hadn't been for her, then his face would probably still be unblemished.

She wondered how his father would react if he knew what his son was dealing with. She vowed she would go and see him as soon as she could when this was all over with. She would tell him how incredibly brave, caring, kind and thoughtful his son was.

Then she thought of Latnor, and how he had aged too. It was as though when Cameen died, something inside of him died with her. She wondered if he would ever recover from his grief. She thought of Fulmin, and then realised she couldn't bear to dwell on it; it was too painful to think about what had happened to him, or what he was going through right at this moment. Thank goodness he was too small to understand the danger he was in. Her thoughts then turned to Tamek. She struggled to believe everything that had happened to her quiet, unassuming friend in her youth. If it weren't for this current situation, she would probably never have found out about it. She had even more respect for her now.

Then she remembered her dear, sweet mother. How much she missed her, her smile, her laugh. The way the room always felt alive when she entered it, her natural beauty and elegance, the way she laughed. She remembered that her perfume always smelled of the freshest, sweetest flowers. The way she fiddled with her hair when she was nervous. The way she always laid her cutlery out a different way to everybody else's; she smiled to herself as she remembered the teasing she provoked about it. Little things, but they were so special.

Then she thought about Rusnan, and her smile vanished. She wondered how a person could be so bitter and angry at everyone. Did he have any idea how much he had touched so many people's lives? She doubted that no matter what the outcome ahead was, that none of them would ever be the same again, not really.

Menzin was thinking about his father and wondering how he would cope on his own in this atrocious weather. The house was fine; it was good and strong, but how would he feel being alone? He was sorry that his father was probably worrying about him, where he was and if he was safe. He probably could make it there to check on him, but other than the storm there was no threat to him. He daren't risk leaving the women alone. They were scared enough as it was without him disappearing. He would be home soon enough, he hoped. What was he going to say to Latnor when he next saw him? "Despite your wife dying, your son being kidnapped and the trauma you have been through, I would like to marry your daughter who is really young but we know we are meant to be together". Hmm, that didn't sound like that was going to be a fun conversation. He wondered if his mother would have been happy for him, and then questioned he had even thought that; of course she would have been happy. She was an amazing woman who was always only ever really concerned with what made "her boys" happy. If they were happy, she was happy, she used to say. He still missed her, and knew he always would.

Tamek's thoughts as always lay with everyone else apart from herself. She had always had an inner stubbornness that her father rebuked, but that she had found had come in handy on more than one occasion. She felt not duty bound to Sahlin's family, but out of pure love and devotion wanted to see everything turned out right. She had nobody else in her life, they were all she had.

As the lightning split the sky yet again, so Tamek's words split Sahlin and Menzin's thoughts as she absently remarked, "It's not over you know."

"No, there is much yet to do."

"No, I mean the storm. It's not over. I can feel it. It will return soon."

"Well, we should really start out now Sahlin," Menzin's quiet tones sounded stern and ominous.

"Yes, father will be worried."

"No, I don't mean home. I mean to look for the wreckage of Rusnan's shuttle – if there is any."

"You mustn't go out yet, not until after the storm. It's not safe," Tamek repeated.

"We will be fine. Rain and a flash of lightning don't frighten us. We'll be okay."

"No! Stop being flippant! Please, you mustn't go."

The urgency in her voice stopped them both in their

tracks as they were standing up. Questioning looks from the two of them prompted her to continue.

"A storm like this one has not occurred for a long time, not in your lifetime. What we have just sat through was only the beginning. Mark my words; you would not want to be out in the next one."

"How do you know? You've experienced a bad one yourself?"

"Yes, a long time before you were born. It started as this one, and after a while, sounded as though it were fading away. Many people ventured out to carry on with their work, and children fetched their friends to play in the puddles and mud.

"The animals were released back into the fields, and nobody understood why they behaved so strangely. They ran about, jumping in the air and calling, or stood huddled together looking miserable and afraid. The young cried though they were right beside their mothers. We assumed they were just frightened from the noise the thunder had made. We thought that had been violent but worse was to come.

"A few hours passed, and the suns had not reappeared from behind the banks of swirling black cloud and it was as dark as night time. We thought it was exciting, in our naivety. All had been still and quiet, not a breath of wind or warning of any kind from the distant hills.

"It came quicker than anything any of us had ever witnessed, but unfortunately it didn't pass as quickly. From nowhere, strong winds blew, whipping up the straw and hay, making it impossible to see. We couldn't find the children, or they us. Many of our homes were flattened with the people still in them. Those that survived had terrible injuries. We had no chance to gather any of the animals back in, and many perished. Trees came crashing down like they were stalks of corn. And the sound of the storm – it was terrifying. It sounded like the sky was screaming and howling at us; like we had committed some unpardonable sin against it and it was wreaking its revenge. All we could do was huddle together where we were as the animals had, behind any kind of shelter we could find, hoping we would survive.

"Eventually the winds eased, the rain died down and we were left to pick up the pieces; literally. The suns finally reappeared, and the sky cleared. Then we were faced with the devastation of finding the children's bodies, buried in the mud, and the carcasses of the animals lying with their young. Practically all the homes were destroyed and the crops in the fields either flooded or ripped up by their roots and smashed down on the ground. It took days to assess how many people lost their lives and to account for their bodies."

Sahlin found that she was crying as she listened to the terrible words, seeing it in her own mind as Tamek spoke and knowing that she could never really imagine just how awful it must have been. Casting a glance at Menzin, she could see that he too was visibly moved by what he had heard.

Sensing she had not quite finished her tale, Sahlin gently enquired, "What else Tamek? There is something else you haven't told us yet, isn't there?

"No, of course not," she said defensively, wiping her eyes dry.

"Tamek, please tell us. It might help if you shared it."

"You may as well know it all. Remember what I told you before," she sighed, "about my parents and when I left?"

Menzin looked at Sahlin with raised eyebrows, but the look he received back told him to stay quiet and listen.

"Yes, go on."

"Well, the main reason I chose to leave was because, well because...I was pregnant." The second half of the sentence came out so quickly, and then stopped so suddenly, that her words hung on the air for a few moments without being fully comprehended.

"Pregnant?" The awkward silence was broken by Menzin, and Sahlin instantly glared at him, again telling him to be quiet. He was getting quite good at deciphering her looks, he decided.

"So, how does that fit in with the storm?" she tentatively enquired, realising as she said it exactly how it must fit in and added, "Oh, I see."

Menzin couldn't interpret that meaning and was completely baffled, not helped by missing out on everything Tamek had explained earlier.

She continued, "I left home pregnant and alone; and very scared. Latnor and Cameen were very kind to me and offered me shelter with them, as I said earlier. After a while, they decided it was better for me to move to a larger village where I would meet more people who didn't know me and my background, and would just accept me. They said I wouldn't be judged, and constantly be asked about the baby's father. They were right; nobody asked. I didn't offer an explanation and they didn't pry. I guess they thought maybe he was dead, and I never lied; I just didn't offer them the truth. I settled in and was very happy. It seemed the perfect place to bring up my son, Famen."

"You said before that you moved here after you left my parents."

"Yes, I know, and for that I am truly sorry. I didn't know then that I would tell you about this. But I've had enough of keeping secrets, and there is a reason why I tell you now. I moved here after the storm, from the village I moved to after Famen was born."

"Go on."

"Everything seemed perfect. Famen was beautiful and full of energy and looked so much like Arubek; it was like he was still with me. I loved him dearly. He was two when the storm came. I had helped the village with my knowledge of crops and farming them from home, and we had been able to pass that information on to neighbouring villages. We were all busy in the fields that day. When the first storm moved away, we didn't know that was just a foretaste of what was to come; we thought that was it. Famen went out to play where I could keep an eye on him and continue working. I told you how the storm returned with a terrible vengeance, almost like it had wanted to lure us all out into the open with the taster, where we were so vulnerable to its power.

"Well, his body was missing for two days, and I carried the hopes that he was still safe somewhere, frightened but alive, waiting for me and crying. But I never heard his voice again."

"You poor thing; I had no idea, if only you had confided in me before."

"There seemed no point, making someone else sad over something that was a long time ago and couldn't be changed. Your parents were more helpful and supportive than I could have ever dreamed, when I needed it most, back then."

"What about now? How do you cope?"

"Oh, the pain is still there, sometimes as great as it was all those years ago. But I had to get used to the fact then that there was nothing I could do about it. Everyone said that as time passed the pain would subside and it would grow easier to cope with, but it never has.

"That's why I don't want you both going outside yet, not until the storm is finished. Don't be fooled that it's over. It's so easy to lose something very precious you take for granted, and life can be a very long time to regret decisions."

"But the storm could take a long time to pass."

"Please. I failed to keep Famen inside, and I lost him. I don't want to lose either or both of you, too.

Sahlin was too upset to speak by what she had heard, and Menzin looked equally distressed as he struggled to make a decision.

Silence reigned once more, and the three weren't sure if the pressing heaviness they felt was due to the presence of the storm, or whether it was the stress that emanated from all of them.

Sahlin realised how dark it had become outside, and felt her eyes straining to make her companions faces out in the dimness. In her own heart she felt she still wanted to go and find Rusnan that instant, but knew Tamek was already distressed, and if they left now after what she had said, wasn't sure how she would cope. Hating herself for doing so, she opted to leave the decision to Menzin.

* * *

Once Sahlin and Menzin had left, Latnor had sat alone for a while thinking over events and trying to work out how to carry on with his day. There was no point going to his rooms; he had no wife to talk to. There was no reason to go to the nursery; there was no baby to hold. Sahlin was gone, so there was not one family member for him to find solace in. He sank deep into his chair as though it would be able to hug him tight and comfort him, and as he did so, he wept uncontrollably.

After a few moments, he felt a gentle hand on his shoulder. He turned to see Gabney, one of his councillors, and close friend. He smiled tenderly at Latnor, tears in his own eyes.

"My friend, you must come and eat something. Try, please."

"No, I couldn't."

"You must. Come. Come Latnor," he started to gently coax Latnor from his seat. The Ruler sighed and knew Gabney was very persuasive. Slowly he rose to his feet, patted his friend affectionately on the arm, smiled weakly and walked beside him to the door. Gabney stood aside out of respect to let Latnor pass through first. Latnor paused and said in a barely audible whisper, "I'm so sorry I have not conducted myself or council matters very well."

Gabney knew better than to try to convince his elder to the contrary, and smiled reassuringly instead. Latnor wobbled slightly on his feet, and instantly his friend supported him.

"Food first, apologies later," he grinned.

They walked to the lighter, brighter rooms and while food was being brought in, Latnor looked at his wife's empty chair, and thought about his son's empty crib along the passageway. He sighed again, but then his eyes fell upon Sahlin's books lying across the table.

Sahlin; she was such a bright and curious child. Not so much a child now, he corrected himself. He paused; what had he been thinking? He may have lost his wife, and his son may be missing, but he still had a daughter. She needed him more than ever. It was as though an electric shock went through his heart, and jolted him to life. She must have been feeling so hurt and rejected.

The books that held him captivated suddenly moved out of the way, as his friend made way for the food dishes. Latnor suddenly felt energised, alert and ready for action. He sat down at the table but instead of slouching in silence, he sat straight and tall, and picked up a fork straight away.

"Mmm, smells delicious. Can't wait," he said.

Gabney, somewhat taken aback by the change in spirits, replied, "I'm glad. I hope you enjoy it. It's spiced vegetable casserole."

"Cameen's favourite," Latnor commented quietly.

Gabney instantly froze, inwardly kicking himself for making such a glaring error, and waited for tears to start again from old friend's eyes.

"I'm looking forward to it. I didn't realise how hungry I was. Pass the salt please."

Gabney recognised his normal, authoritative voice issue a request. Momentarily he stared at him, and then kicked into action, passing him the condiments.

"After this, I want a full report on all urgent council matters, and an update on any news concerning my son as it comes in - immediately. Summon the council for a meeting this afternoon. Inform Sahlin where I am upon her return." He paused for a moment as he chewed on his first forkful of food.

"This is very good," he smiled pointing at the food, with a twinkle back in his eyes.

"Yes, it is," Gabney's response had a different meaning. They understood each other and smiled.

* * *

In the thick of the woods, Rusnan struggled up the hill to his hiding place; a ramshackle hut that he had literally thrown together himself in a day. It was made of small tree trunks, branches, stones and mud. He should have been warm and dry in Tamek's home by now. If only his plan had worked.

He pulled at some dead wood he had gathered, enough to keep a small fire going until the weather cleared, and hurled it under the small lean-to, panting from his exertions. It had been no easy task to drag the branches up the slippery slope, trying in vain to remain standing up, let alone walk.

His coat was even more filthy than normal from falling down repeatedly, and his hands were frozen from the rain soaking them and the chill wind blowing on them. They were sore, red and chafed.

Glancing up at the small patch of dark grey sky that was just visible through the dense canopy above, he pulled up the collar of his heavy coat roughly about his neck, and swearing as he went, entered the hut.

Still cursing at his bad luck from earlier, and now on top of that becoming drenched in the downpour, he pulled off his mud-caked boots with an effort and stared first at the thick brown muck covering his hands, and then at the hole in the sole of his left boot. That was the final straw. He propelled them across the hut and they thudded into the wall, and then dropped heavily to the floor.

The sudden noise from the far corner startled him at first, and then he remembered. Wiping his hands on his trousers, he strode over to the heap of untidy blankets.

Bending down he growled, "Hungry, eh? Well there is nothing here except some milk that I have to eke out for you, and a few scraps, and I'm not going hungry for you. So keep quiet, and let me eat in peace."

A tiny pair of hungry, frightened eyes looked back up into the stranger's face. Fulmin opened his mouth and began to cry.

Chapter 18

"I hope we've done the right thing."

"Hmm."

"What does that mean?"

"It means I don't know either."

"Oh."

The young couple had painfully decided against Tamek's advice and left her to look for Rusnan's wrecked craft. It had been so hard to go against Tamek's advice, but she did understand time was passing by rapidly. They only had a rough idea which direction to head in, based on something Rusnan had said to the council when he had arrived. Sahlin could only hope she had remembered the vague directions correctly.

She was sure they had said he had crashed north of the river on a hill at the top of the Great Forest. Even if she had remembered it right, there was no guarantee that they would find anything, for the area was huge. Nobody had bothered to go looking because he had told them there was nothing to salvage, and as it was a fair distance, they had just trusted him.

"I expect she'll get over it."

"What? Who?"

"Tamek, I expect she'll get over us leaving even though she told us not to."

"Oh. Yes, I hope so, but she didn't look as though she would."

"She'll be all right. It's just that at the moment things seem so black that she's over anxious and pessimistic about everything. You tend to always think the worst when things aren't running well."

"You know, you amaze me sometimes."

"Why?" Menzin paused from his striding through the undergrowth to rest a moment. Sahlin had struggled to keep up with him for most of the journey so far, but hadn't said anything for fear that they would lose valuable ground. She couldn't imagine how fast they would be travelling if he hadn't been injured at the well. Time was pressing on, and she either wanted to be home when it grew dark, or under good shelter, and there wasn't much of that around here; just trees, nothing solid. She remembered what her parents had said when she was little about never staying under trees in a storm. If the storm struck again as bad as Tamek had predicted...

Brushing the hair from across her eyes and pretending that she really wasn't as out of breath as she sounded, she replied, "Well, you always seem to say these wise things that make everything seem bearable, or hopeful."

"Do I?"

"Yes, you do. For someone so young you have such a wise head."

"Shall I take that as a compliment?"

Trying not to sound breathless again, she puffed out that he should, and wondered why on earth he didn't even look tired yet, as though they had just been for one of their casual strolls along the river. The only trace of exertion that she could see was a thin line of perspiration on his brow.

Her own cheeks were burning, and she felt very uncomfortable. She knew for a fact she was sweating more than he was. What a mess she must look she thought, and it actually crossed her mind that he might be ashamed of her. As though he could see right through her and knew she was tired, he suddenly said, "Let's have a proper rest for a while."

"No, no it's all right, let's keep going," she said gathering her skirts determinedly, and wishing that she had thought to put something more practical on before she left. So intent was she on not showing her weakness, that she hadn't noticed that Menzin had stopped dead in front of her and was regarding her with a rather bemused expression on his face. She walked straight into him, and the impact knocked her over backwards into a heap of muddy leaves.

He couldn't help laughing at her as she tried unsuccessfully to get up, and at first this heightened her embarrassment. Then she realised she was taking herself way too seriously, and realising what a sight she must look for a Ruler's daughter, she began to laugh too.

Menzin tried to help her to her feet, but he was laughing so much that he ended up falling down into the heap of leaves beside her. She picked up a handful and draped them in his hair, to which he immediately retaliated by doing the same. She then scooped up a handful of mud and propelled it at him hitting him squarely on the jaw.

There the two sat, in the middle of nowhere covered in mud and dirty, wet leaves, with tears of laughter rolling down their faces.

Eventually exhausted, they both sat with legs splayed out, hair a muddy mass, and heads down, inspecting what they had done to each other.

"Don't ever change," Menzin said through the last sputtering laughs that were escaping him.

"I won't if you don't." Looking towards him, she suddenly burst into laughter again.

Not understanding why this simple request would

provoke such a response he looked quizzically at her. She leaned across and pulled away a leaf on a long stalk poking out of his hair. "It looked like a headdress," she explained.

"I wonder about you sometimes," he teased, pulling her dirty but happy face up close to his.

Both held each other's gaze intently, falling silent, all traces of smiles vanishing as the two felt an immense energy surge between them, almost as though an electrical charge had leaped from one to the other.

"Perhaps we should move on now," she said, not moving away from him

"I stopped so that you could rest, and look what happened!"

She was glad Menzin was trying to defuse the atmosphere but knew her feelings were reciprocated, and too strong to ignore. She tried to fight them, but wasn't sure if she wanted to.

"So I could rest! I only stopped because of you," she retorted in mock sarcasm.

"Oh, you! I love you!" he shouted out loud pulling her back down into the leaves.

She screeched with laughter as she landed back where she had started, and this time just lay there too out of breath to retaliate.

Stroking away the mud from her face and absently removing leaves from her hair, their feelings began to take over as he kissed her, slowly and gently.

At first her instinct was to pull away, but her heart was overcoming her head, and she didn't want to resist. She felt herself responding to his passion, and realised how deep her feelings for him really were. Her hands caressed his neck, and she pulled him closer. Strange sensations she had never felt before began to dominate her body, and closing her eyes, she felt herself conceding to them.

"I love you so much," he whispered as his lips left hers, and travelled around her throat and ear.

"I love you too." She was trying to ignore the feeling of guilt that was beginning to nag at her. She shouldn't be doing this. She should be looking for Fulmin. This was not how she should be behaving.

Feeling her hesitance, Menzin moved slightly away and asked what was wrong. She looked into his eyes and saw such deep love for her there, but this wasn't right. Her mind was filled with two voices competing for attention, but demanding different things.

Menzin suddenly realised he too was running away with his emotions and brought himself back to the reality of their situation. He was meant to be protecting Sahlin and here he was acting irresponsibly and immaturely.

They sat up looking sheepish as they both arrived at the same conclusion simultaneously.

*   *   *

Further up the hillside in the thicker protection of the trees, Rusnan was pacing to and fro in the shack, sick of listening to Fulmin's cries.

"Will you shut up!" he stormed as his patience finally snapped, picking up a cup and flinging it violently across the hut in his anger. It exploded against the wall and a thousand tiny splinters flew about the room.

The sudden noise had startled the baby and he stopped crying for a moment. Then, once again, his mouth opened and he began his ceaseless screaming.

Snatching up his soaking coat, Rusnan had intended to go out for some peace and quiet, but realising his coat was still too wet from the downpour, threw it back down on the floor in abject disgust; his feet squelching in his patched up boots. He ran his fingers through his hair, wondering what he could do to stop the child's noise. He had nothing he could give him to play with, and certainly didn't want to hold him and comfort him. He had no idea how to occupy children and he was beginning to wonder if he had done the right thing snatching him in the first place.

Of course he had, he reassured himself. He was just tired, hungry, cold and lonely. The whole point of his coming to this stupid, inferior planet was to wreak havoc and revenge. He had a lot to do to make up for the way his ancestors had been treated, and he fully intended to carry on with whatever was necessary to re-balance the score for his people and their suffering of years gone by.

Of course, things were different universally centuries ago, but that wasn't the point. He wanted to show his objection to the way his people's planet had been slowly destroyed because of Vantil's ancestor's plots, plans and rebellion. Things could have been so different without the meddling do-gooders like Parlon Dremun. His people could have achieved unrivalled power, dominating all the minor planets, and who knows, maybe even one or two major ones by now.

If they had just known their place, bowed down to Spilon and surrendered. Yes there were many thousands killed, but they had to be taught a lesson about who was in control. Show them how things were going to be so they didn't rebel and fight back, so that they became subservient and knew their place was to serve. They weren't doing anything decent with the planet anyway. Spilon could have done such a lot to it and with it.

But no, Zaren had to employ the services of interfering busy bodies who wouldn't give up as the Spilons had predicted and counted on. Didn't they understand and accept the supremacy of Spilon? Because of their interference and rebellion, they had lost their chance of taking over Zaren, and because of that, they had then lost the fear of, and power over, planets they wanted to dominate.

He saw it as a chance to take revenge, show their ancestors that time had made no difference to the contempt the few remaining Spilon's held towards Zaren's spawn. If only he wasn't the only one to think like that. None of his comrades had the backbone that he had to come and prove his point; they were all content existing, managing and getting by. He wanted to show them their error and prove that conquering weaker worlds and aspiring to greater power, was what they were now lacking and needed to return to. They had given up; become lazy and seemingly incapable of tapping into that strength they once had. He wanted to show them that even one Spilon on their own could still move in on an unsuspecting weak planet, and take it for their own. Their time was not over; it was coming back, and he would show them how.

It had become an obsession with him to study the old history books and dream of what might have been for his people if things had been left to run their natural course.

He ran his fingers absently over the brooch on his lapel; a replica of the ones the Spilon soldiers, or Greedmen as they had become known, had worn centuries ago.

Years before, he had spent many months tracing his

family history back and had discovered that he was directly related to the great Thalez, Leader of The Greedmen. Only he recognised what a hero Thalez really was. Everyone else falsely accused him of cowardice and betrayal, and could not see the strength the man had; the vision and determination. He was so much more than he was given credit for; he had been made a scapegoat, when it was really the Zarenian's who had been lucky against all the odds. He would redress their reputation - singlehandedly it would seem. But one day he would be seen as a hero and then he could tell his people he was descended from Thalez, and how much they really owed him, and how unfairly he had been misjudged and maligned. He would get the history books rewritten accurately; he would make sure Thalez was now only talked about respectfully, not as though he were vermin.

His life could have been so different if Thalez and his men had succeeded in their plans, and their power could have been, and should have been, passed down from generation to generation, until it reached him.

Instead, Parlon Dremun and men called Opposers who were a group set up to combat the efforts of the Spilons, had hatched an escape plan, commandeered a shuttle, and escaped to Vantil. Even that should not have worked, but against all the odds, it had.

Here on Vantil, a new generation established a population that had thrived and grown, becoming richer as time passed, though they didn't even realise it themselves. Happiness and peace reigned throughout, and it sickened him to the stomach. When he thought about what had become of his people...his mind was again reading the pages of the journal that Thalez had written, and were etched in his memory. The journal had been recovered during a reconnaissance mission and been kept as a historical artefact and example of bad conduct and cowardice, but when Rusnan had uncovered his family connection he had asked for it to be presented to his family. The request had been rejected; it was deemed too important to be given away. So Rusnan had stolen it instead and run away. It was now where it belonged. He would make sure Thalez was remembered in the way he should be, and he himself would be revered for uncovering the truth and steering Spilon back on its path to recovery; he himself would be a great leader. He would be a hero. He would at last be proud of his ancestry, and no longer ridiculed, mocked and ostracized. He had worth, he had potential - and he would have the power one day that was rightfully his...

His hands flew to his head; it hurt so much. It was as though each memory, each thought, and each dream caused a pain to dart through it. He longed to be rid of this agony. He knew he wouldn't know peace until he achieved what he had come here to do. He must be strong, ignore the pain and carry on.

His fury had completely overtaken him, and snapping out of the jumble of images, thoughts and voices that had completely dominated him for the past few minutes, became aware once again that the baby was still crying loudly.

He sank to his knees, his head resting on the floor, buried between his arms, trying to make everything go away and be quiet. He cried, he pleaded, he howled in agony.

The craziness began to pass and he waited, panting for breath until he could stand. How many more times would he torture himself with the awful nagging feelings of failure that he couldn't change? Well, he may not be able to change everything about the past, but he could certainly do something to change things as they stood now.

He would give the Vantilians a little something to worry about; cause some upset and fear. Maybe cause a panic, and start a fight. Once that happened he had no reason to stay any longer. He could leave in his craft that he had lied about being badly damaged anytime he wanted. Stupid Vantilians; they were so gullible and naïve – they didn't even check his story out. How pathetic was that? They made it so easy to take advantage of them. They hadn't even worked out the planet he said he came from of Lospin, was actually an anagram of Spilon! He could soon go back to his poor, poverty stricken, fallen world, knowing that once he left, a war on Vantil would be imminent. That would be his satisfaction and reward.

After that..? He didn't care what happened to him once

he got home. He just wanted an end to the relentless mental torment and to do something good for his people.

 He would pick his time very carefully, he was good at that. It was a proven formula; start a fight, put a few unsettling fears into people's heads, spread rumours, get a few dissenters on your side, panic followed, fear grew, once united people divided into sides, men assumed leaderships, and before you knew it, a full scale war broke out. They even did most of the dirty work for you! He loved it when people were so afraid they wouldn't listen, they just blindly acted.

He slapped his balled fist in to the palm of his other hand, grinning from ear to ear, sweat glistening on his brow, a maniacal glint in his eyes. That was precisely what he wanted to happen on Vantil. He would teach them that peace could never completely reign unbroken. There were no perfect worlds, not even theirs. It was going to go his way this time, not like Thalez and his broken dreams. Even if it took the murder of the Ruler's son to provoke the response he wanted.

He advanced towards Fulmin, strangely now happy and content and smiling up at Rusnan. He picked the baby up. As if sensing danger, the baby's smile disappeared, and he stopped gurgling.

"That's right, you're going to shush now aren't you?" He jiggled him about and then put him back down again, repulsed at the smell. "You'll have to stay like that 'til I find something to clean you with. You can't stay in here with me, smelling like that. Though I suppose you could always go outside...Well, I know you're hungry, but I have some work to do. I'll give you some of that feed when I get back," he said as though Fulmin could understand what he was saying, pointing at the small amount of milk he had brought from the nursery. "After that, depending on if they're sensible or not, you'll either be returned to your father, or...well, you just won't be needing food anymore."

Laughing, he kicked his stool out of the way as he left the shack. Baby or no baby, he was hungry too and needed to get some food, regardless of whether the sky still looked unsettled and ominous.

On Spilon, storms were very rare, but when they did occur, they were over in a short space of time. He didn't even think that Vantil might be any different. Perhaps the climate here just took a little longer to get back to normal he had thought.

Pulling the collar of his shirt close around his neck, he glanced up at the still dark sky, sneered and marched off into the woods to hunt for prey. A bird maybe, or even a Sonx would do.

Disappearing into the thick copse, he missed the first flash of lightning and the first few drops of rain hitting the ground.

Chapter 19

Tamek had watched the great heavy storm clouds rolling back in across the hills, and her face reflected the darkness of them.

Since Sahlin and Menzin had left over an hour ago, she had not been able to concentrate on anything and had wandered aimlessly from room to room. Picking random objects up and putting them down somewhere else without even realising it, pacing like a caged animal fretting for its freedom, she kept sighing and tutting to herself. She had decided it was safe to open the window shutters up, as to her it felt more eerie not having any daylight in her home. She could also keep an eye on anything going on outside. Her hands clutched together in a tight ball and she crossed the room and looked out across the valley to the hills for the hundredth time, wondering if this time she would see anything different; of course not. Nothing changed, except for the cloud formations which now looked so heavy and low that she felt she could reach out and touch them, and the light which was fading rapidly and had a yellow hue about it. An awful ache wrenched inside her stomach as well as her head. She realised that she was so tense with worry that she wasn't breathing properly, and made a conscious effort to take deeper, slower breaths than the shallow, short ones she took at present. Perhaps then she would calm down a little.

Crossing the room yet again, she sat woodenly down on a chair and closed her eyes. In her mind she could see her son and remembered that day long ago, when he had pulled at her skirts until she let him go out to play with friends.

She hated herself as she recalled how she had not even considered properly whether it was safe. Instead, she had leaned down and stroked his hair as she chatted to a neighbour concerned about the animals, and told him it was ok to go with his friends and their mother. She hadn't even looked down at him as she said it; she was too preoccupied, and just gently pushed him off in the direction of the door.

Faintly she remembered him giggling as she called over her shoulder, "Don't be too long." She never saw him again.

Her eyes sprang open. Why was she still tormenting herself; it was done. Nothing she could do now would ever bring him back. Trying to change what she had said and going over her reactions inside her memory were going to make no difference at all.

So why was she going over that day in her head, over and over again? Because of the storm? The past echoing back to haunt her? No it was more than that. It was because she had never forgiven herself for not listening to what her son was saying, and not thinking to stop him from going outside. She had sent him to his death. She was responsible. That was it - she was terrified the same thing would happen to Menzin and Sahlin; only this time, she had warned them but they hadn't listened to her. But it was still down to her that they had left.

"Stop it!" a voice in her head cried.

"I tried to warn them," another shouted defensively.

"Well, you didn't try hard enough. They still left."

She began to cry as she stood slowly, and again walked to the window looking out in the direction that the two youngsters had left, wondering how far up into the hills they had reached.

She remembered how she had spoken to Fulmin before he had been kidnapped, telling him how special he was. She loved that baby. Mostly it was because his parents and Sahlin were so dear to her, but partly it was because of how he reminded her of Famen, especially when he smiled. Even the name sounded similar.

He too, was out there somewhere; poor little frightened child. If she had gone to look for Famen sooner, maybe he would still be alive. She wondered what he would have looked like now, whether he would be tall and strong like Menzin, or shorter and more delicate, like she was. Would his hair have changed colour as he grew. What would his laugh have sounded like? She snapped out of her mental torture and snatched up a wrap.

She ran from the house in the direction the others had gone. Maybe she could make all the difference between the child living or dying, instead of harping on about the past and waiting for it to repeat itself. Either way, she wouldn't find out sitting alone at home. Fear must not hold her back.

Casting an apprehensive eye at the sky, she wondered whether she had become insane; leaving after telling the others how unsafe it was to do so. If there was one thing she had never done, it was to turn her back when someone was in trouble. She supposed that was due to the way her parents had treated her, and then how Cameen and Latnor had stepped in and offered her shelter and help.

Right now, Fulmin needed her. Who knows, maybe even Sahlin and Menzin could use her help.

Pulling the wrap determinedly about her shoulders, she marched off into the hills.

*   *   *

 "We should hurry now." Menzin was standing, looking up at the fast moving clouds heading towards them.

"I'm just coming." Sahlin's heart was nearly bursting with happiness as she tried her best to look half way decent considering that her already dishevelled clothes were now completely covered in mud. Straightening her skirt, she joined Menzin and put an arm around him. She felt no response in return, just rigidness. Looking up at his face in concern, she saw the lines of worry there.

"What is it?"

"Look." He gestured upwards, and her eyes travelled in the direction in which his finger was pointing. She gasped as she too saw the terrific speed and colours of the advancing clouds.

Turning towards her, his crestfallen face made her happiness disappear instantly. He apologised, "I should never have permitted what just happened between us." Seeing her stunned face, he added, "I should have hurried us on instead of dawdling around, and found shelter. I'm so sorry."

"Now who is always apologising?" she chided.

"Look at that sky!" he again gesticulated, finding he was fascinated by the swirling masses that came together, divided and pulled back in bigger than before. "I think the very least you deserve is an apology, and that won't help, will it?"

"Don't worry. How long do you think we have before the storm hits us?"

"I don't know. Not long by the look of it. I haven't any experience of anything quite like this." "Me neither; but according to Tamek, it's going to get a lot worse."

"Well, I just hope that she's safely inside and has protected herself from it as much as she can..."

Chapter 20

Rusnan was not a very happy man. This was the second time in one day he had been caught out in a storm, and he didn't much care for it. To make matters worse, he hadn't had much luck hunting either.

"You'd think that as nothing is hunted for food here that the animals would be easy prey," he muttered to himself. Perhaps they were sensitive to the weather conditions and sensed something bad, he thought.

Stopping dead in his tracks, he listened intently to a faraway sound, trying to identify it; a low roaring sound, growing louder by the second.

"What the...?" He didn't have time to finish the sentence before a huge gust of wind came from nowhere directly at him. As it increased in velocity, so the terrible howling it made, grew louder. Rusnan could only stand and stare in amazement as it burst through the clearing and hit him with such force that he felt he had just run into a stone wall at high speed.

Letting out a cry that was completely stifled by the wind, he was literally swept off his feet, carried along a few feet, and dumped heavily on his back, winded. He lay there for a few moments trying to get his breath back, each gulp of air filling him with terrible agony.

"What on Spilon was that?" he thought as he tried to get

up. Feeling stunned by this new experience, and the sudden stillness and quietness, he stood panting, looking around, as though he expected to see some visible source to answer what had just occurred. How could it be so violent and then so still? He remained standing, anxiously looking about and listening intently for any hint or clue of a further gust such as he had just experienced. He wanted to be prepared for the next one, although he doubted there was anything he could do. No wonder the animals were all hiding. Evidently, they weren't stupid.

Perhaps, he reflected, there would be no repeat, for there wasn't even a breeze now, nothing at all. Maybe it was just a one off. But then, the gust had come from nowhere before, and there was no reason to believe it couldn't do that again. He felt uneasy in a way he seldom did. He didn't like surprises; no, not at all. He needed to find shelter here quickly, or get back to the shack – if it was still there.

Standing still for a minute more, he gathered his bearings and estimated how far away from his shuttle he was compared to the walk back to the shack. The baby though...well that would be one less thing to have to deal with if anything had happened to him.

He decided it would be quicker for him to go to the shuttle, rest, get some of his food supply and wait for a couple of hours, to see what happened. When it looked safe to do so, he would go back to the hut.

Heaving an impatient sigh, he once again set off, cursing all the bad luck he had experienced in just one day. Surely nothing else could go wrong?

* * *

"What was that?" cried Sahlin in fright as something roared above their heads, shaking the trees as though they were sticks, and breaking off massive limbs, flinging them to the ground.

"Get down!" yelled Menzin as he threw her down, and shielded her with his body.

For a while they could not speak and be heard because of the tremendous noise, and the pair lay as still as they could, wondering how long this would last. Despite being flat on the ground, it took all of Menzin's effort to hold him and Sahlin where they were, and not be swept along the ground.

Finally, the noise and force began to abate, and as it did so, a snapping noise could be heard directly from above, and Sahlin felt the impact through Menzin's body as a branch torn from the top of a tree fell down landing across his legs. She heard his muffled cry of agony but could do nothing, as the force of the wind was still strong enough to keep them pinned to the spot where they lay.

Then suddenly, as though nothing had occurred at all, the wind dropped, and nothing could be heard in the eerie silence that ensued.

"Menzin, are you alright?" There was no reply and she tried frantically to move from beneath his weight, causing him to cry out in pain.

"I'm sorry." she cried, partially relieved that at least making a noise meant he was alive. "Where are you hurt?"

"My legs," he moaned.

She tried not to sound frantic as she said, "I'll have to move you so that I can get out. Can you shift any weight at all?"

"I think so. I'll push myself up onto my arms, and you'll have to roll out."

"All right. Are you ready?" No reply. "Menzin, are you ready?"

"Yes."

"Good. After three. Ready? One...two...three."

She hated herself as she heard Menzin's strangled cry of pain as he fought hard to bend his back, shifting his weight to his arms so she could wriggle free.

"I'm out!"

Rolling over, she felt sick as she saw the size of the branch across his legs.

"Is anything broken do you think?" she demanded.

"I don't know."

"Okay. Don't worry, I'll get you out as soon as I can," she said, not sure how she was going to do it, but trying to sound positive and in control. "It's not too big," she lied. She tried with all her strength to pull at the branch, and then push at it, but nothing she did would make it budge.

Her eyes quickly scanned around her, waiting for inspiration to strike. What could she do? There must be something she could use to help...

Menzin remained quiet apart from the odd murmur and groan. Seeing a longer thinner branch also flung to the ground, she rushed over to it and with a determined tug, lifted one end. "I'm going to try to lever it off. Stay still."

Menzin must be in pain; he didn't answer with one of his quick quips, like "I'm not going anywhere," or "Right, that's hilarious!"

Realising the branch was too heavy for her to drag, she staggered a few paces still holding one end cupped in her hands, until it laid parallel to Menzin. Then she let the end drop once more to the ground.

Menzin felt the vibration travel along the ground

beneath him as she did so. He hoped that whatever she had in mind was going to work.

Standing up straight for a few moments to get her breath back after her exertions, Sahlin stood with hands on hips surveying the scenery around her.

It was devastated. The tops of the trees looked as though an enormous blunt knife had lopped them all off untidily, and everywhere she looked she could see scattered branches. Some trees remained standing, but were leaning up against others as though they were resting up against old friends.

She felt uneasy that the same thing would happen again before she was able to get Menzin free, and hurriedly she dropped to the ground. Pushing with all her strength, she began to roll it towards where he lay.

At first she thought her efforts were in vain, for she could feel no movement beneath her, save her feet sliding in the mud. Then a small fleeting smile appeared on her lips, as she felt it begin to give. Not daring to stop in case she lost the momentum, she carried on pushing until she was level with the offending limb.

Trying to ignore the pain in her back, legs, hands and arms, she then ran to the other end and repeated the manoeuvre until it occupied the space by Menzin's legs. She pushed and pulled until she had the tip in the space next to his legs.

Her breath came now in rasps as she ran backwards and forwards, getting just the right position. When she was happy it was just about where it should be, she took a few quick, deep breaths, and bent down.

"Please work!" she muttered as she saw in her mind's eye that as she lifted the other end, the branch should rise up from Menzin's legs, hopefully enough that he could drag himself out to freedom. She took her position carefully, knowing this was not going to be easy, and exerted all her remaining strength into trying to lift the end up.

She felt it beginning to come up, and looking anxiously along the length of it, could see a tiny space beginning to appear by Menzin's knees as her "lever" pushed up.

"It's working!" he cried triumphantly, as the weight mercifully lifted from his lower body. Unfortunately, the victory was only to be momentary, as the weight became too much for her, and despite all her efforts to the contrary, she lost her hold, dropping her branch, and the other fell back into its original place.

Tears streamed down her face as Menzin screamed out in pain again, but she knew she had to keep trying. There was no alternative. Without a word, she again struggled to pick up her end, and began to prise the other up with it.

She refused to give in, and her arms began to shake

uncontrollably with the strain of the weight. Seeing a space begin to appear again, she called through clenched teeth to Menzin, "Start to pull yourself out. Slowly; be careful."

He shifted the weight onto his arms again, and the moment he could feel the space above his legs and feel no weight on them, he dragged himself a few feet on his clawing hands.

"You're clear!" she yelled, letting her end drop with an almighty thud. She rushed to his side. "How bad is it?" she demanded.

"I don't know. I can't feel anything though."

"It could just be numbness from the weight of the branch?" she asked optimistically.

"I hope so, otherwise we're stuck."

"We'll be fine, don't worry."

"Have I told you how amazing you are?" he managed to smile at her.

"Yes!" she replied, inwardly worried about pale he seemed.

"Well, let me tell you again...You are amazing!"

She wanted nothing more than to put her arms lovingly

around him, but found she could do nothing; her nerves had not recovered from the strain of the weight she had had to bear, and her arms were weak and shaky.

As the pair sat recovering and getting their breath back, so Sahlin suddenly felt drops of rain on her face. At first, it was one or two, and they fell slowly and intermittently. Then the pace seemed to quicken and the drops became bigger, heavier and harder.

"Here it comes," she said under her breath, and then turning agitatedly to Menzin, "Can you walk?"

"I think so. Help me to my feet."

She was very concerned at the amount of effort it took for him to stand, and even when he was not standing erect but bent over, each shuffling step seemed to take him an eternity and much concentration. She knew that at this rate, they would never make it under cover before the storm really started, and she dreaded to think what might happen this time. In an open space such as this, with no protection from the elements, and not even suitable clothing, they were very vulnerable.

Steeling her face against the stinging raindrops she looked upwards and saw that the boughs on the trees were beginning to wave back and forth as the breeze picked up into a light wind, and then grew stronger by the second. She wondered if any more isolated gusts like the first were going to take them by surprise again. She hoped not.

Putting her arm even more firmly around Menzin's waist to support him, she tried to hurry him on a little, beginning to wonder if they were ever going to make it out of this alive. They should have listened to Tamek, and waited until after the storm. Her friend was right; she was just a teenager who thought she knew everything and how to handle any situation. They would have been more help to Fulmin trying to save him later, than to be killed in their haste and nobody left to save him at all.

Tamek...

Chapter 21

Even though she had lived through it before, Tamek was still as stunned as the others had been at the force and ferocity of the wind.

She had been much further down the hillside when it struck, and so was more protected than the others from its wrath. Even so, as it had raged overhead and she watched its effect on the trees and landscape, she had become over-awed, and could only stand and watch in a mixture of fright and fascination.

Knowing she should find cover, she had instead stood rooted to the spot as it howled over her head like a gigantic invisible bird with huge wingspan, the noise taking her back to the day she lost Famen. "Remember," said her heart, "Run!" said her head.

Eventually she pulled herself out of it, and ran through the leaves and dust in the dry areas that had been whipped up around her, and skidding through muddy patches where the rain had reached. It was exhausting coping with trying to move at pace through different conditions. She made her way over to a safe looking spot near some fallen trunks. She hid in a space beneath them until the terrible noise ceased, with her hands covering her ears.

When she had presumed it safe to continue, she carried

on away from the path, taking a shorter, less worn route to the hill top. She doubted Menzin and Sahlin had taken this path as they wouldn't have known of its existence. If they had stumbled across it, they would probably have ignored it, fearing it would lead them in the wrong direction.

Once she had reached the crest she would be able to see around for miles, and get an idea from seeing so much sky area of what the weather was likely to do.

Puffing and blowing, she hauled herself up the hill, wondering what she was doing up here alone. At least Sahlin and Menzin had each other for company. She should be at home, safely locked inside, listening to the storm within the safety of the four strong, sturdy walls. What was she doing instead? She was out here in the middle of it, alone, unprotected, and afraid. Nobody knew where she was, she reminded herself. If anything happened to her, who would know where to come looking for her?

"What are you saying?" she sternly addressed herself out loud. "You're supposed to be giving yourself encouragement, not frightening yourself to death!"

She shook her head, buried her chin determinedly into her chest, and took great strides up the hill. All the while she had friends out here that needed help, she was going to continue. "Anyway, what are you?" she questioned herself irritably, "A woman or a Sonx?"

Onwards she trudged, weary and worried, but resolute to carry on with her journey. She could hardly believe it when suddenly, the incline under her hot, tired feet, levelled out into even ground. Surprised, she looked up and saw she had at last reached the top. "Yes!" she shrieked at the top of her voice, punching the air with a balled fist, "Yes!" Then turning and seeing the colour of the sky, "Uh-oh!"

It seemed terrible and frightening, yet at the same time, beautiful, wonderful and mysterious. She watched open-mouthed as black spirals of cloud winged their way towards her, casting large shadows across the earth as though it were being devoured. As the land grew black as it passed overhead, it reminded her of a sheet being pulled over a dead body. She shuddered. She could make out the trails hanging in drapes beneath what she knew was the rain falling in torrents. It looked as though a knife had cut open the belly of the sky, and it was spilling its contents unashamedly.

It crossed her mind that she might not live long enough to see anything quite so magnificent ever again. In all her years this was only the second time she had witnessed it, and although she was scared standing there watching it advance, its beauty seemed to engulf her, mesmerise her, freeze her.

She must seek lower ground again, and find a safe place to shelter. It wouldn't be long before the full force of the storm hit, and she didn't want to be standing on top of a hill when it happened, regardless of how beautiful it might be to watch.

Making her way down the other side of the hill as fast but as carefully as she could, she wondered about the others that were out here somewhere, hoping they had found a safe place to hide during the brief gale. Maybe they had turned back, and returned home, realising the mistake they had made she thought. Then she considered, if that was the case, it was completely pointless her being out here...One day she hoped they would see better communication links and devices on Vantil. If they had them now, it would be so much easier to work out what to do, which way to go, and find out what had happened to the others. At the moment, it was all guess work. If she was them, which way would she have gone...?

She was completely enveloped in her thoughts, when she suddenly thought she heard someone talking.

"No, you may be lonely, but don't start imagining voices," she told herself. But wait, there it was again; and there was a second voice; and it sounded like...

"Sahlin!" she screeched, running off in the direction the voices were coming from, "Menzin, where are you?"

Darting through the trees into a clearing, she stopped and looked wildly about for her friends as she became soaked through to her skin. There appeared to be no-one about anywhere. She must have imagined it after all. She could have sworn…

"Tamek?" Sahlin cried incredulously, running out from behind some gorse bushes towards her. "I can't believe it!" she exclaimed after the two had embraced. The rain was lashing down, and felt like knife points stabbing into their exposed skin.

"I know what I said, but I decided that I would be more help out here with you," Tamek explained, "Besides which, I was fretting myself silly just sitting at home!"

"Well, I can't pretend it isn't wonderful to see you," Sahlin admitted as the two embraced once more. "Let's get out of this rain," she tried to compete with the noise the falling drops were making.

"Where's Menzin?" Tamek shouted. She had been anxiously looking about all the while they exchanged greetings.

"He…he had an accident."

"An accident? What accident? Where is he? Is he all right?"

From beside her, she saw movement out of her peripheral vision, and straining to see through what was now like a waterfall of water falling from the sky, saw Menzin finally appear from the place Sahlin had previously. He was obviously experiencing difficulty remaining upright, and yet was trying to appear as though nothing was wrong.

"Menzin," she cried flying into his arms, "What happened?"

"I'll tell you as we go along, Tamek. Time is important, especially now that I'm going to hold us up. We must get on our way – now!" he hollered above the rainfall.

The three hastily exchanged their news as they made their way through knee high undergrowth; Menzin finally acknowledging that he needed help, and supported either side by the two women.

"I can't believe that I caught you up so quickly," Tamek commented as they rested Menzin up against a tree for a minute or two, and then couldn't understand why the pair exchanged a sheepish glance at one another.

"We, er, we made one or two unscheduled stops," explained Menzin, seeing by Sahlin's hot, flushed face that she would offer no explanation.

"Oh?"

At that precise moment, Sahlin suddenly crashed to the ground in a jumble of skirts and tried unsuccessfully to untangle herself. Menzin couldn't be sure if it was coincidence, or just plain convenient.

"That's why!" He breathed a sigh of relief. Planned or

not, he was grateful to Sahlin for the well timed distraction. He didn't really want to lie to Tamek, but he couldn't exactly tell her the truth either.

He tugged Sahlin to her feet, and then saw just how annoyed she actually really was at being slowed down by her attire. It was hard enough that she had to help him, but the weight of her wet, long skirts must have been interminable all this time. Yet typically of her nature, she had not complained.

"I think it's about time that we gave you a change of outfit."

"I suppose you brought a spare one with you," she grumbled tetchily, and then instantly regretted it. "I'm sorry, it's just I'm fed up with this stupid skirt. I wish I had thought to change before I left. I just don't think sometimes."

"Don't be silly; you were just too caught up trying to leave quickly to get this over with."

"Stop trying to make me feel better."

"Do you really mean that?"

"No!" she laughed.

"Come on, come over here." Menzin hobbled over to a tree that offered a small amount of shelter from the rain bullets, and the wind that was again whipping up, and beckoned her to follow.

"Why"

"Stop asking questions and come here."

She did as she was told, and he motioned to her to sit down. He pulled Rusnan's knife out from his shirt, and held it up.

"I don't think I'll be able to create anything sophisticated enough for the Ruler's daughter, but I can do something that's more practical for you now. Do you trust me?"

"Of course I do," she nodded.

With a few quick flicks of the blade, he had cut off the bottom of her skirt all the way round, and he then made a slit at the front, from about the middle downwards.

"Stand up," he told her, and in her bewilderment she did not question him, but obeyed. She heard the knife as it made an identical slit down the back. He appeared in front of her again, holding the strip that he had cut off from the bottom. This he cut in half, and told her to tie one piece around each leg around the flapping strips of cloth.

"There," he said proudly as she stood up straight. "Not exactly the latest fashion, but they will serve as a reasonable pair of trousers until we get back."

"If we get back," Tamek muttered inaudibly beneath her breath.

Sahlin walked up and down, looking at her legs. At first, she was a little unsure about what he had done, but then realising how much more freedom of movement she had, flung her arms around him and kissed him.

"Well, I think they're great!"

"Come on then, on we go."

*   *   *

"I just don't believe this," cried Rusnan in anger, "What is going on today?"

He stood surveying the remains of the sack in which he had hoarded a supply of food in his shuttlecraft. During his last visit up here, he must have neglected to secure the hatch properly, and a hungry Sonx or some suchlike small rodent must have decided to take advantage.

Not very much was left at all, and what there was, he really didn't fancy after the animals had been at it. He stooped down and picked up the remains; perhaps he could at least salvage something to feed Fulmin with. Could a baby eat something like that, if he made it into a fine pulp and mixed it with some of the remaining milk? Ah well, what would a baby know anyway? It was food. Plus he wouldn't know what had happened to it first.

Besides which, it wouldn't be long before it was passed back through the other end, he mused.

Tucking a few odd pieces in his pocket, he pulled the hatch fully shut behind him making sure it was secured properly to keep him warm and dry, and walked round the small ship, checking everything was in proper working order. When the time came, he wanted to be sure that he could leave this planet as quickly as possible. He made the various standard checks and found that everything was in order. Surprising, he thought, considering the Sonx had chewed through some of the wires. Just a few small repairs and minor tweaks, and everything would be fine again. At least that had been in his favour today.

"No major repairs. Good."

Running his fingers across all the controls just to make doubly sure that everything was fine, he mentally ticked off each light that was showing, indicating that all was functioning normally.

The shuttle wasn't very big, and been designed especially for one man to travel in alone. In fact, part of the reason that he had been able to secure its loan, was the pretence that he didn't mind volunteering to "test" it. He was careful to avoid telling anyone where he was going or what he intended to do once he got there, for although Spilon could still be barbaric at times, a lot had changed since the years of The Greedmen's notoriety, and he would never have been permitted to leave if his reasons had been discovered.

When he had left, he'd wondered what problems he would encounter with the shuttles maiden flight; but there had been none.

Landing on Vantil, he had felt almost guilty radioing back to Spilon advising them that an engineering fault had forced him to land on an unknown planet for repairs; especially as the designer had been a personal friend who thought Rusnan was doing him a favour.

He couldn't help sneering though, as he thought what anguish he would be experiencing; for although Malix was very talented, he knew it, and Rusnan was intensely jealous since they had taken the same design courses and only one of them had passed.

Still gloating at the prospect of his friend losing face over his new "perfect in every way" design, he walked to the back of the craft to check the fuel supply.

*   *   *

The trio of friends were near exhaustion now, but were fully aware that they had to keep going for as long as possible. The clouds were even darker and heavier, the wind was howling, and the change in the air was very noticeable. Practically every second it seemed to be growing cooler. The rain now felt like it was skewering them, and they grimaced as they battled on despite that, shivering as their soaked clothes and hair clung to them. The icy wind felt like it was gradually freezing the water on their heads and bodies into burning ice. Despite the effort of assisting Menzin, their body temperatures were rapidly falling.

Sahlin was mainly concerned for Menzin, although she tried not to show it. His limp seemed more acute, and his grimaces of pain were more frequent. She saw how pale his face still was. It was bad enough being out in this weather, but suffering physically with injuries and shock was not a good thing at all. Tamek also happened to look across from the other side of Menzin at the same time, and the two realised they were sharing the same thoughts simultaneously, as they caught sight of each other's expressions.

Deciding to make it look as though the onus was on her, Sahlin stopped in her tracks and said, "I'm sorry, but I really must rest."

"We can't," mumbled Menzin almost inaudibly, "We have to go on."

"No, we must rest," insisted Tamek. "I wasn't going to say anything, but I too feel I must rest a little while."

Sahlin mouthed a silent "Thankyou" at her, and helped Menzin to sit down on a rock.

"All right. But not for long, okay?"

It upset the women to see him trying to put such a brave face on his situation, for it was all too clear that he had gone just about as far as he could.

"Whatever you say." Her reassurance didn't sound as it should have done, but Menzin didn't seem to notice. His eyes were closed and his breaths were shallow and rasping now.

"Can I have some water?" he asked.

"Of course. Tamek," she called, "Could you pass the water?"

"There isn't any," she said quietly.

"What? How can there be no water with the rain we've had?"

"Menzin drank the last of it a while back, and I guess we forgot to fill the bottle up again," she replied apologetically.

Looking back at Menzin, Sahlin realised she needed to get him water, and quickly.

"Menzin," she spoke gently but loud enough that she could be heard, "I have to go and collect some more water from the stream."

"What str...?" Tamek was about to interrupt, but stopped abruptly as Sahlin glared at her, motioning to her to be quiet.

"There's water just on the other side of those trees." Her hands gesticulated vaguely to her right, and Menzin's eyes opened momentarily to see where she pointed.

"All right, but be careful, and don't be long. Take Latnor with you."

"Latnor? You mean Tam...? Menzin, are you all right?"

"I'm fine. Slip of the tongue, that's all." His head began lolling about.

"No, Tamek needs to stay here and look after you. I can't risk leaving you alone. I won't be long, I promise."

In the few moments it took her to stand, she noticed Menzin had dropped into a deep sleep. She watched his chest rising and falling steadily for a few moments to check he was breathing without problems, and then crept a few steps away, motioning to Tamek to follow.

"Are you insane?" Tamek whispered. "You don't know if there's water on the other side of those trees or not."

"Well, there might be," she faltered, trying to avoid looking into her friend's concerned eyes. "If I don't go, I won't know."

"Yes, but what if there isn't any?"

"All I know is that Menzin is ill and he needs water. Despite the cold, his skin feels like he's burning up. If that means I have to go a little out of our way to find it, then so be it. But I'm not standing here wasting precious time with who knows what the storm is going to unleash yet, when I could be on my way."

Consciously lowering her tone which she knew had become raised as she spoke, she added, "The sooner I leave, the sooner I return."

Her friend still appeared distraught, and she placed her hand gently on her arm. "I have to go, Tamek, for Menzin's sake."

"Of course, I know you're right. I'm just worried about us getting split up."

"I know. It's not ideal. I'll go now, and I promise not to wander far. If I can't find water, I'll come back and we'll all have to try to move on a bit farther before I search again."

"I don't think the worst of the storm is far off now."

"Well, maybe I can find somewhere for us to shelter while I'm gone, as well."

"I have to tell you, you are one very determined young lady!"

"I know! Takes one to know one!"

The two hugged, and then parted company, Sahlin telling Tamek as she left to see if she could find any branches that had reasonably dry foliage on she could place over Menzin to keep him a bit warmer. As she walked off, she heaved a sigh of relief that she hadn't given away how loathe she was to leave the others.

Tamek busied herself with anything she could find to do while Menzin slept. She knew she should rest, but was too unsettled. Sahlin was now wandering around in these wild conditions, and Menzin was sleeping so deeply she wondered if he was ever going to wake up again. She wiped his brow, checked his pulse and his breathing, and did indeed manage to find a few dryer branches that served as an imperfect but still much needed blanket. She gathered any dry leaves she could find, and packed them in under the branch, and discovered they actually made quite a good insulation. Then she sat, shivering herself from cold and worry, counting out the remaining provisions, and then tidily replacing them in the little bag Sahlin had given her to look after. She had done anything she could think of to avoid watching Sahlin walk off into the trees and disappear, wondering where and how she was.

She huddled up closely next to Menzin to try and share body warmth, and tucked herself under the branch alongside him. It was definitely a bit better than being completely exposed. She looked up at the sky which seemed to be growing darker in its fury with every minute. The wind seemed to scream as it flew over their heads. Was it a willing party to the storm she wondered, or was it too trying to run away from its violent outbursts? Lightning began to zigzag across the sky; first alone, then after a few minutes, the rumbles of thunder began to join in. When the lightning blazed from above, Tamek had to close her eyes against its brightness. Then, there was not just one flash at a time, but two or three simultaneously dancing about them. The thunder crashed about, growing in ferocity until Tamek could hear nothing else, not even the wind and the rain. She was a grown woman, but found herself wanting to cry. Was it possible that this storm could be worse than the one she remembered all those years ago?

Either they had underestimated nature, or nature had overestimated them.

The light was changing from its yellow hues to a dirty orange colour. How much more rain could there be in the sky, she wondered? The treetops bent backwards and forwards, forced to the limits of their flexibility.

Thoughts of her mortality passed through her mind. At the moment, death seemed undecided in which way to court her; either through exposure to the cold, burnt by lightning, drowned in the rain, or crushed beneath falling trees; and that's if she wasn't blown away first. Well, at least she still had her sense of humour. Her eyes strained against the failing light until she gave up looking for

Sahlin amongst all the imagined shapes her mind seemed to be tricking her with.

How Menzin could possibly be sleeping in this, she had no idea. As though her very thoughts had roused him, he began to stir a moment or two later, breaking her concentration.

"Is she back yet?" he asked drowsily.

"No."

"I should go and look for her," he said trying to rise to his feet but yelping in pain.

"No Menzin, she hasn't been gone very long. You have only been asleep for a short while." She hated herself for lying but wanted to keep him calm, warm and resting for as long as possible.

"I'm no fool, you know."

His words surprised her and she stayed silent. How did he know how long she had been gone?

"I know there's no water where she went."

Tamek's breath exploded out in one long exhalation of relief. "Oh, I see. We don't know for sure that there isn't."

"Apart from the rain I haven't heard any running water,

have you?"

"Well I doubt you'd hear anything over that; but there might be a little stream," she said doubtfully.

Menzin smiled weakly at her, "You are indeed a good friend."

"I think not, or I would never have let you leave my home."

"No, but despite everything you told us, you still came out after us to make sure we were safe."

"That's true, but whether I shall succeed in keeping you safe is another matter." Grimly she looked up once more into the black sky.

"You will. Thanks dad." Tamek's surprise and worry was lost on Menzin as he fell asleep again.

"Please hurry Sahlin," she thought, "Hurry back."

* * *

Once on the other side of the trees, Sahlin had not been very surprised to find that there was no stream, even though she had uttered a little prayer asking that by some good fortune there might be drinkable water of some description she could collect in her bottle. Heaving a sigh, she decided to look around a little further before turning back, and continued in an upwards direction.

A few moments later, she found herself on the verge of a clearing and there on the other side, was a stream. If she wasn't so exhausted, she could have jumped for joy. Looking skywards she cried, "Thank you!"

In reply, the rain suddenly ceased. It did not lessen gradually until it stopped, it merely ceased all at once. The sudden cessation of noise made her feel as though she had lost her hearing, and she shook her head about from side to side.

As she was about to run across the sodden grass to the stream, she suddenly spied something jutting out from behind the rocks, and she remained still.

"A shuttle?" She thought she must be dreaming, and then it hit her; it must be Rusnan's. She had stumbled across it completely accidentally! She felt the colour draining from her frozen cheeks. This meant he might be quite near, and if he was, then they had succeeded in their quest. The trouble was that she didn't particularly want to face him alone.

She looked keenly about, wondering if Fulmin was here somewhere, or whether he was being kept elsewhere. Supposing Rusnan had killed him? "No, she told herself, you mustn't think like that."

Her ears strained for any sounds in the unfamiliar silence, and in the back of her mind, niggling worries prompted her to think that if this really was Rusnan's shuttle, then his story about crashing here could be true, and they would have come all this way for nothing. He might be completely innocent after all.

A voice of reason interrupted telling her that wasn't very likely. To begin with, there really couldn't be anyone else on Vantil that could do such a thing. Rusnan had threatened her more than once; and look at the shuttle – from the little she could see, it didn't look that damaged at all. If it had crashed in the way he said it had, then there would have been debris everywhere; of course, there was none. It was also rather convenient she thought that he had crashed very neatly behind the rocks. No, this vessel had been purposefully and carefully set down.

Whatever had she been thinking? She was trying to make out he was innocent and had nothing to do with the terrible events that had taken place. Why? This awful man had kidnapped her brother, threatened her, attempted to kill Tamek which could have resulted in killing Menzin instead, and thrown the people into terrible turmoil; not to mention the stress it had caused her father. No, he was the guilty one; there was no doubt about that.

Suddenly she gasped and started, as she unexpectedly saw Rusnan. It hadn't crossed her mind that he might actually be here. She had assumed that he would be in hiding somewhere with Fulmin. Perhaps the baby was here too.

She began to advance slowly from her cover, but then it struck her that he might have an accomplice. Just because they had never seen anyone else, didn't mean there wasn't someone up here hiding with him. Maybe even more than one other person, though the vessel didn't look big enough, she decided.

She shrank back into the bushes as quietly as she could and tried to think calmly and rationally about what she should do.

Her heart pounded as she watched the man she feared and loathed so much, walking around the vessel, and thought she would die when he suddenly stopped and looked in her direction. It must have been a coincidence, surely? He couldn't possibly have seen her from there, could he? She held her breath until she thought she would faint, not daring to move a muscle. It burst from her lungs as he turned back the other way and continued with whatever he was doing.

"Come on Sahlin, pull yourself together." She hoped that telling herself these words would give her the confidence to think of something one way or another.

Her mind grappled with a number of suggestions her brain was making all at the same time. Trying to sort them into a logical order and dismiss the preposterous ones, she decided on circling around the shuttle, keeping herself hidden in the bushes and trees. She would then be able to find out whether Rusnan was alone, and whether Fulmin was nearby.

If she found that her brother wasn't here, she would creep back to the others, and they would come back together to follow Rusnan to his hideout. It couldn't be far away surely, so even if they lost him, they still had a good idea that he would be within a close radius of this area. She must hurry back to Menzin and Tamek with water, that was for sure, so despite her fears, she needed to press on.

Carefully she made her way around the clearing, making sure that she kept herself well out of sight.

Once or twice, she couldn't help making a small noise that drew Rusnan's attention to the surrounding trees, but thankfully he seemed so intent on what he was doing that he didn't really pay proper attention. Typically, she thought, it would have been ideal if her movements had been masked by the sound the rain had made earlier, but when she needed help, it had turned very quiet.

At last, Sahlin reached a good observation point, and eagerly looked out. There was no sign of anyone else and apparently no baby either. She wasn't sure whether to be relieved about that or not. At least if she had heard him crying it would mean that he was still alive.

She debated whether to tackle him alone now after all, or return to the others to get help. It seemed too good an opportunity to ignore the fact that he was right under her nose, but at the same time, she knew it was extremely dangerous, and if anything should happen to her, then the others would be more vulnerable; especially as Menzin was injured and becoming mentally confused too.

Where had Rusnan got to, she wondered? He had walked behind the shuttle then vanished. She assumed he was checking something out of her sight, and continued contemplating what to do next. Eventually she reminded herself of Menzins predicament, and decided her head must overrule her heart, and she must return to the others.

A scream escaped her as she turned and found herself face to face with Rusnan. As she yelped with surprise and fright, her sub-conscious was telling her how calm his face looked, but how angry his eyes were.

He had been sitting as still as a Sonx but now suddenly darted forward and grabbed her. A rough hand clasped itself tightly around her mouth, trying to stifle her yells.

She felt herself land backwards on the sodden grass with a jolt that knocked the wind from her body, and trapped her arm beneath her. Through her fear, she felt the pins and needles running up and down the length of it. That was the least of her worries.

She felt the weight of Rusnan's body holding her down on the ground, and she stared mutely into the wild eyes that held her gaze.

"This is becoming a habit," he sneered through clenched teeth. The smell of his breath made her want to vomit, and she fought to turn her face away.

Immediately forcing her to look back at him again, he continued, "You really think you could hide here without me realising? You must think me stupid."

As she was wondering why she had an incredible urge to laugh at that statement, she was aware something white was drifting down around them; great flakes of something that was very cold as it touched her already freezing skin. This was new. It was like snow, but much larger and shaped like huge feathers. Well at least she wasn't going to get soaked anymore. Her heart was pounding as she turned her attention back to Rusnan, who had also cast a glance at this latest phenomenon. She knew the urge to laugh was because she was so afraid of him. She had come to learn recently, that that was how she dealt with being so frightened. Her head turned wildly about, trying to break free of his hand so she could scream again, but he was too strong for her.

"Lie still," he commanded. The fury in his voice halted her efforts for a brief moment, but then she squirmed and wriggled all the harder, resolving that whatever he was going to do to her, she wouldn't let him do it without a fight.

His hand let go of her mouth for a second, and as she seized the chance to take a gulp of air and cry out, so it flew back at her face with great force. She felt the sting of its intensity before she heard the slap.

Stunned, her resistance ceased, and she lay quietly beneath him, like a dazed animal beneath its predator, frightened of what he would do next. His other hand had slowly moved down her body, over her hips, and she felt herself pushing down into the ground, as though she might be able to press herself so far down that she could escape him that way. She closed her eyes to hide from the grin across those awful, thin, cruel lips, but found she still pictured them in her mind. His hand was lingering on her lower body, and she wished she could just die now.

"Are you alone?"

She heard his voice, but it seemed strangely distant, even though his face was pressed as close to hers as it could be without touching. His wet tongue flicked around his lips, saliva coating his teeth. Her body trembled, and she knew that he was delighting in the terror she felt. As her mind raced trying to decide what answer to give, she looked past his ear at the white icy feathers that were now not floating down but dropping with purpose. If she told him she was alone, the others might still stand a chance, but then she risked him killing her. If she told him there were others with her, then he might leave her alone; but what were chances that he wouldn't go after Tamek and Menzin.

"Are you alone?" This time his question demanded a response, and she faintly mumbled an answer beneath his hand.

"What?" He removed the pressure from her lips, and she took a breath to answer him. As her lips began to form the words of her response, they were both suddenly interrupted by a tremendous gust of wind which, as it had done previously, came without any prior warning; this time not even a distant noise growing louder; it simply just materialised seemingly from nowhere. Sahlin's words were snatched away before they reached his ears, and for a moment neither of them knew what to do.

The force of the wind held them both down on the ground, but Sahlin knew she had to take advantage of this one chance she had unexpectedly been given. Seizing the moment of astonishment that had frozen Rusnan, she reached out with her free hand and clutched frantically at a large stick lying next to her. Before he had chance to realise what was happening, she had struck him over the head.

Unfortunately, because of her awkward position, the blow she succeeded in delivering to his head was not as effective as she had hoped it would be. It stunned him, but not much else. She drew her legs up under him as far as she could, and together with her arm pushing against his shoulders, managed to tip him slightly to one side.

It would be impossible to get up and run in the strength of this wind, but she must try to get away from him. As she withdrew her legs and began to pull herself aside, she found that her left arm had been pinioned for so long that she had no feeling in it, and it hung limply by her side.

Just as she thought that she had pulled herself a safe distance away, so she felt a hand seize her leg. She fell flat on the ground and immediately began pulling and kicking, desperate to escape this evil man. She was facing into the wind, and was having difficulty even drawing breath as it blew with such force directly into her face. It was like suffocating. Why couldn't she feel her arm yet, she panicked, scared her life was going to end here.

The hold on her leg was firmer now and she could feel herself being dragged back to where she had just crawled from. She was not going to give in. Swinging herself over so that she was sitting up, she kicked hard against Rusnan, and caught him a mighty blow in his face with her foot.

He instantly let go and clasped his hands to his face in pain. His eyes were already streaming from trying to keep them open against the wind and the frozen flakes blowing into them. Now it was impossible for him to see.

She was free of him – it had worked. Now she needed to make sure that it stayed that way. She worked hard, leaning into the wind, and pulled herself to her feet; her

317

left arm still hanging uselessly at her side.

With her right hand spread out protectively in front of her eyes, she staggered towards the opening in the trees where she had come from, but found she began choking on the white flakes that were now falling down in small ball shapes and blowing directly into her mouth and nose.

The only chance she had was to turn so that she was running with the wind, instead of against it. That meant going back past Rusnan, who was still lying on the ground, writhing about and clutching his eyes.

Once she had turned to assess her situation though, she had little choice in her movements, for the wind pushed her very quickly nearer to Rusnan and there was nothing she could do to stop it.

Suddenly, the light grew simultaneously darker again, and the small balls of white falling down were now jagged shards of ice. They were small at first and fell intermittently, then rapidly grew bigger and fell faster. They stung her face and her clothes offered no protection at all. It was like being pelted with sharp stones or pieces of crystal. She cried out in pain as one after another the icy spears pricked her skin, drawing blood in several places. Her head was completely unprotected and she had no idea what to do. A confusion of thoughts crowded her mind, but she really had no choice in the matter; the elements were deciding all the rules in this unknown game. Still, she could hear Tamek's words before they left her home, warning them of what to expect. Even after her description had appalled and terrified her, she still could not have expected anything as harsh and as brutal as this. Little did she know that Tamek was at the same time in the same conditions, wondering how she had failed to think a storm could be worse than the one she had previously experienced? Sahlin could only hope they were more protected than she was, or that perhaps these ice spikes were not falling where they were.

The next thing Sahlin knew was that something hard struck her back; she had no idea what, but found herself flung against a tree. She did not fall down to the earth however. Instead, she remained pinned against it as she stood, as though she had been fastened there. If the situation hadn't been deadly serious, she could have found it amusing. As it was, she found she could do nothing but stand and wait for as long as the wind wanted her there, and then she was just going to run and run, until she was far away from this place, and from Rusnan.

She found she still couldn't see as the wind and ice combined with the soaking hair plastered to her face. Her body was completely numbed now as the ice lowered her body temperature even further, but at least, she thought, she didn't feel the stinging pellets as much.

She became aware that her feet were beginning to slide

from underneath her in the mud at the base of the tree, and her dead hands gripped the bark to try to keep her balance. Her ears were full of the screaming of the wind, the leaves and debris being blown about, the boughs swaying, creaking and breaking, and the sound of the huge ice shards hitting the ground.

A crack of thunder opened the sky further and unbelievably the ice lumps fell even harder. She felt like she was standing beneath a waterfall of ice, and found she again had time to worry that Tamek had managed to provide Menzin and herself with some form of shelter.

As though a barrier had suddenly been placed across the tops of the trees, the weather stopped its assault. Again, it did not gradually lessen and fade away; just simply ceased.

Drawing great gulps of air into her lungs, Sahlin automatically looked back at Rusnan who remained still on the ground, face down in the mud. She hoped he had suffocated in it.

Her whole body felt heavy and weak, her limbs demanding she collapse, but instead fighting to stay upright. Everything around her looked completely different than a few minutes before. The ground alternated between patches of slimy, slippery masses of moving mud, and areas frozen like lakes with jagged icicles sticking up from them. It took all her remaining strength to make her way across the small distance between herself and Rusnan.

He appeared not to be breathing, and she gave a half-hearted kick at him. His body moved only at the shove it received. She would go to the stream in case Tamek had not managed to collect sufficient rain water, and then would find something to tie Rusnan up with while she fetched the others.

She realised he wasn't dead; his breathing just shallow. In a way she was relieved, for now he would have to tell them where Fulmin was. It would probably have been impossible for them to have found him for themselves in time to save him.

Woodenly she began to cross over to the stream which had now swollen into a river. White water was gushing down its length, desperate to dispel the fallen rain, and the noise it made blocked out all other. It was ironic, she thought, that with the amount of water that had fallen from the sky, here she was collecting some for her thirsty companions from the stream. Wearily she bent down and began to fill her bottle, cursing her arm for still being of so little use to her.

The sound of the water immersed her thoughts and she wasn't aware of any sound behind her, or she might just have been able to move out of the way in time. Instead, she was taken by surprise as a hand gripped her hair and tugged it with such force that she lost her balance and toppled over backwards. She cried out not only with the fright and the pain of her hair being pulled, but also because she had once again landed on her numb arm.

Twisting around quickly, she couldn't believe her eyes when she saw her enemy standing there.

"Did you think that was the end of it?" he snarled.

"Just what is wrong with you, Rusnan? Why do you do all of this? What is the point? You could at least explain."

"Do you really want to know?" he asked, keeping his distance Sahlin noticed thankfully.

"Yes, I do. If I knew why you were doing this, I could try to understand and help. It's not too late for that, you know."

Rusnan realised just how weary he was too; he was tired of this game. He had had his fill of being on this planet; he was sick of being alone, and exhausted by the constant hate and anger he felt. The storm had emptied him even of what his purpose was; and its fury had nullified his own.

"Here we go again!" he mocked, "All this drivel about how you want to help me. Why do you lie all the time?"

"I'm not lying; I really do want to help you, contrary to what you think. Tell me so I can understand, at least. You must see from the amount of time you have been here that we are a patient, tolerant and caring society."

Bargaining was all she had.

"If I told you, do you really think I could be forgiven for what I've done; everything that's happened since I arrived?"

Sahlin noticed the change in the tone of his voice; now reasonable, not angry. Was this another trick?

"I said understand, not forgive. There's a difference, but yes, in time I will try to forgive. Providing you stop all of this nonsense now, tell me where my brother is, and let me return him home to my father."

"Just like that? I'm supposed to believe you?"

Sahlin heaved a deep sigh. As frightened as she was of him, he really tried her patience. "I could say the same thing."

His raised eyebrow prompted her to continue. "The day I was lost in the forest, and we had our little... encounter. I trusted you then and you deceived me. You actually wanted to take my life. If it hadn't been for Menzin..."

"Huh, him," he interrupted.

"Yes, him; if it wasn't for him, I wouldn't be here today giving you the benefit of the doubt – again."

"You have courage girl. Then you really will listen to me?"

"Yes," and inwardly added, "Against my better judgement."

"All right. If it's really that important to you."

"Of course it's important to me. Whatever your reasons are they are holding my brother captive somewhere and tearing my people's security to shreds."

"That's the idea."

"What is?"

"To rip your miserable planet apart." He answered with such vehemence that she was completely taken aback and unable to answer. "Like my planet was, all those years ago,"

"Spilon?" she ventured. He regarded her with equal surprise.

"How did you know?"

"I was reading the old books, and I had an idea it was to do with that," she explained; "I recognised the badge on your lapel. I had seen it in a picture – it is the same as the Spilon soldiers wore on their uniforms. And Lispon is an anagram of Spilon."

"Something else you can congratulate yourself you are so clever for," he hissed.

"Don't patronise me. I was making an effort to find out what was going on, as you chose not to enlighten us yourself."

"Well, if you read about Spilon in your books, then you should know what all of this is about."

"I can guess, but I'd rather you told me."

"Spilon was once a great and powerful planet, until Zaren interfered."

"As I understand it, it was the other way round." Rusnan glared at her and she carried on, "Spilon sent men to Zaren to take it over. The resulting war happened only because they defended themselves."

"They should have given up; surrendered to us, as they were supposed to."

"Why? If a neighbouring planet had tried to take over Spilon, would you have just "given it up"?"

"That is different. Spilon is a powerful planet; was a powerful planet," he corrected himself.

"What happened?"

He looked incredulously at her. "You don't know? Or is it another of your lies?"

"I have never lied to you, but you must think whatever

you want to. If you don't continue, I won't be able to help. Our books obviously only tell of the events leading up to my ancestors sending a party here to colonize and start again. We couldn't contact them after we left. We didn't know how to, so we have no knowledge of events after. We have never wanted to know; we preferred not to."

"I see." Rusnan actually looked as though he was listening and digesting the information. How different his face looked now he was calm.

"What happened? Tell me; I want to know now."

"After the chosen few left in the shuttle, disease spread everywhere on the planet surface, and was uncontrollable. The last of the serum had been smuggled to The Opposers by disloyal Greedmen, and no cure was ever found.

"Thalez, who I am directly descended from, was the leader of The Greedmen as they were known. During an interrogation of one of the rebel prisoners named Parlon Dremun, he contracted the disease, and after agonising suffering, killed himself. The Greedmen could not contact Spilon; all communications had been severed, and chaos broke out. There was no obvious leader amongst those men that were left, and they began to fight among themselves."

Sahlin noticed that as he told his story, his face was

expressionless; as though in a trance and living through every moment he described.

"Those that did not die of the disease were killed by their own men. A few remained alive and waited for the day that Spilon might make contact with them and take them home. But when they did eventually re-establish communications and found out what had happened, they refused to send a rescue party and they left them there to die.

"A soldier found the journal that Thalez had written during his final days. A dying Zarenian had told him under torture about Vantil thinking that nobody would live to divulge the secret. But the soldier wrote it in Thalez's journal when he came across his body, and when The Spilons eventually came back to look around after the disease had died out, they found the journal among the skeletons of the Spilon soldiers that had died in agony."

"That's terrible." Sahlin felt genuine remorse at what had happened to the Spilons as well as the Zarenians, no matter whose fault it had been.

As though it was some dreadful atrocity for them both to be agreeing on something, Rusnan suddenly snapped out of the past and his reminiscing, changing his tone and expression. "I don't want your pity."

"I am not giving it. I am merely empathising with what must have been a terrible situation. But you must remember that it was not only the Greedmen who died of that awful disease. And it was their fault that it actually started."

"I should have known I couldn't trust you. You tricked me into believing you were interested."

"What are you talking about? No-one has "tricked" you; I am just stating the facts of what happened."

Rusnan was pacing furiously up and down, his clenched hands stiffly at his sides, reminding Sahlin of her own arm.

She rubbed at it automatically, and instantly wished that she hadn't; for Rusnan immediately honed in on it.

"What's the matter with your arm?"

As she was about to open her mouth, she realised it would be a big mistake to tell him anything that might give him the edge over her. Yet, she could call his bluff if she dared. Although it was true that she did want to help him, she saw from the look in his eyes that he was beyond that. He lived in the past, and thought he could single-handedly change the reputation Spilon had of being a world of cowards.

She knew that he would not rest until he had avenged those dark days centuries ago, and it appeared he felt the best way to do that was to destroy Vantil and its peace.

For Vantil was the product of what had happened on Zaren. They were the descendants of the Opposers, and they had put an end to the barbaric ways of the Spilons.

If she really tried, she could understand why Rusnan hated them so. He lived in those days inside his head. For him, the war still raged and he believed he could make a difference.

"My arm?" she faltered, "I think it broke when I fell on it."

"Broken?" She saw the little smile appear at the edges of his mouth and pretended she had not seen it there. She didn't trust him one little bit.

"How long did you plan this for Rusnan?"

He didn't seem to hear her at first and she knew that in his mind he was still reliving past events, but probably portraying them as he thought they should have ended, with the Spilons victorious, and Zaren butchered.

"What?"

"I said, how long did it take you to plan all this?"

"Oh, not long."

"I see." She continued to look at him, prompting him to tell her more and stalling for time.

"I had a friend at the academy. He designed this shuttle," he gestured with a sweep of his hand. "I told him I would test it for him, but what he didn't know was that I planned to steal it for my purposes from the very beginning."

Sahlin was about to comment, "Some friend," but then thought better of it.

"He thinks that because of that design fault, I am stranded in an unknown destination, unable to get back until I have completed repairs."

"Meaning, I take it, that you "borrow" this shuttle, come here, pretend to crash and carry out your little scheme until its conclusion. Then I suppose you miraculously manage to repair the ship, and then head off home."

"Precisely." His whole face was lit up with the genius, or what he thought was the genius, of his plan.

"Hasn't it crossed your mind that all this happened such a long time ago, and it would be best if you just forgot about it?" As soon as the words were out, she realised she had made a mistake.

"Forgot? Forgot?" The outrage and madness on his face made her skin crawl.

"Poor choice of words. What I meant was that it is all over. Instead of living in the past and reeking revenge on innocent people…"

"Innocent?"

"Yes, innocent. You are talking about something that happened centuries ago. It is our history, Rusnan. None of us were alive then; you weren't alive then. How can you seek revenge now on something that happened then? You don't even know for sure what happened. You are acting on your feelings, based on what you have read in books. How do you know it's all accurate?"

"It wouldn't have been written if it were not accurate. What would be the point of writing lies as you lay dying? And you do have something to do with it. It was your ancestors who caused our demise."

"I'm growing tired of this; you just aren't listening, and keep going round in circles. I have just explained that we cannot be held accountable or responsible for the actions of our ancestors. But we have tried to learn from the mistakes made by them. The whole idea of colonising Vantil was to start again; to live in peace the way it should always have been. That is what you should be doing with your energy – trying to plan for a better future."

"That is precisely what I'm doing."

Sahlin heaved a great sigh and as she did so looked up to the sky. "Uh-oh," she thought as she watched the ominous black clouds gathering again.

The breeze was once again beginning to pick up and she could feel the electricity in the atmosphere. Or was it because of the fear she felt as she looked back at Rusnan and saw the maniacal glint in his eye? A shiver ran down her spine. Now what was he thinking about?

"Rusnan, what are you doing?"

"I'm going to do what I should have done a long time ago."

Somehow she knew what that was, but still found herself asking, ""Which is?"

"Get rid of you."

"I'm trying to help you."

"Huh! You have pursued me, interfered and irritated me. Now I am going to dispose of you."

"You can't!" she shrieked, realising any plans she had of trying to give a calm performance had completely flown away.

"Oh, can't I?"

"Where's Fulmin? What will you do with him?"

Advancing slowly with each word, Rusnan sneered, "I will

dispose of him too. I don't know why I took him; it wasn't part of the plan. I suppose I thought it would be fun."

"Fun? You're sick, Rusnan, sick!"

"Thank you."

He was now right in front of her, and she had that familiar sinking feeling that she had been in this situation before and knew what was going to happen next. As if her thoughts were his cue, he darted out a hand to seize her disabled arm, thinking it was broken,

Nimbly she dashed out of the way and stood meeting his gaze, ready to match anything he did. She had to; her life, and that of her brothers, depended on it.

"Come along Sahlin. Why don't you just give in now? I promise I will make it quick and painless...almost."

Sahlin felt the panic rising in her. He continued, "Your father will then have lost his wife, his son and his daughter. He won't cope. He will be forced to resign for incompetence to fulfil his duty. Oh the shame of it... I will leave false tracks, spread lies, and who knows where that distrust and suspicion will lead?"

That was the spark she needed.

"I am never going to give into you Rusnan. Never! Do you hear? Remember, each time we have met, I have defeated you. Perhaps it is you who should give into me?"

She had pushed him too far and he let out an almighty roar as he rushed at her, his face contorted in terrible rage.

At the same time a bolt of orange lightning unexpectedly leapt from the sky and struck a tree directly behind Rusnan.

Sahlin dived for cover behind a large boulder as he turned to see what was happening. As he did so, a second flash like a huge trident tore through the air and struck his lapel pin, and he fell screaming to the ground, his clothes smouldering and his face blackened.

Sahlin stared at him for seconds after the lightning had faded, the sight of his contorted face lit up by the flash stamped in her memory She was torn from her shock by a terrific crash of thunder that shook the ground. She covered her ears against the crackling as it ricocheted around the clearing, and tucked her head down to her chest. When she looked back, she saw Rusnan staggering away down the hill, his dark shape lit up by the constant streaks of yellow and gold flashes of light from the sky.

He stopped momentarily and looked back. Despite the distance between them Sahlin still gasped at the horror of seeing his burnt face. She dropped to the ground and vomited, thinking of the irony of the lightning symbol on the brooch he wore.

Breathing deeply she tried to calm herself down and she drew hungrily at the air feeling as though she was submerged under water and drowning.

The wind had picked up and began blowing harder and harder, whistling then screaming, raging over the tree tops and through the valleys sweeping away everything in its path. She had to break free from her state of shock or she would not survive. She peered over the rocks back at where the terrible sight of Rusnan had been and saw no-one. He had completely disappeared.

"No!" she shouted angrily. "Where is he?" She could not believe she had lost sight of him. Now how would they find Fulmin? By the time she reached the others, and then they doubled back, Rusnan would have had time to dispose of the baby and flee. Unless the storm had killed him first...

Perhaps she should try to disable the shuttle. Battling against the elements, she gradually struggled towards it straining every fibre of her being. Being next to the metal craft in lightning was dangerous she knew, but she had to do this. She deliberately blocked out the memory of Rusnan's injuries. At least if lightning struck her now, she hoped it would be over quickly. It seemed to toy with her as it danced all around her, singeing and smouldering the ground. Where it had struck the path ahead of her, she felt the warmth through her boots as she moved forwards, and she tried to keep to where it had hit the ground, hoping it wouldn't fall in exactly the same place twice. Every time the thunder boomed she jumped, thinking she had finally been hit.

At last she had made it to the craft. She tugged at the hood which covered the area where the pilot sat. Nothing happened. She pulled harder. Still nothing. "Come on!" she yelled, cross that everything seemed to be against her. The wind forced her away, yet still she fought back and clung desperately to the hood. She banged her fist down in frustration and then noticed where her hand rested that there was a key code panel.

That was it then, she had no hope of doing anything. The best thing now would be to try to return to the others, get the water back to Menzin, and just hope they could find Rusnan's hideout before it was too late. As she contemplated all of this, she didn't notice a form slowly making its way up behind her, silenced by the sound of the hysterical wind.

A hand reached up and touched her shoulder and she screamed as she jumped round, fearing the worst.

"Ssh! It's only me!"

"Tamek! I thought it was Rusnan." Their voices were stolen away by the wind and it was hard to draw breath to form new words.

"Ssh!" Tamek screeched; the irony of what she said and what she was doing lost on them both, "He could be anywhere."

"He's been here already."

"What?"

"Never mind that now." Sahlin gestured to two big boulders resting against one another and they struggled over to its shelter. The rain bounced off the ground again, the wind shrilled, and the light totally disappeared. Though still quite open inside the rocks, it afforded them at least a little refuge from the elements, and they felt they weren't at peril from the lightning so much. "Where's Menzin? Why did you leave him?"

"We became worried when you didn't return; you were gone so long, and we decided to come after you. Then the wind and rain came and these really sharp shards of ice started falling down, and I had to get Menzin to decent shelter. He's over there in a small crevice in the rocks we found, like a tiny cave almost." She pointed to show where she meant. "Look at you; you are drenched child."

"That's the least of my worries. I had another little encounter with Rusnan. Listen, I have to go after him. He's going to kill Fulmin," shouted Sahlin.

A crack of thunder obliterated the last sentence and Tamek leaned nearer to Sahlin struggling to hear the words.

"What?"

"I said, he's going to kill Fulmin. He told me."

"I can't hear you." Tamek shrugged in frustration as the rain determined to prove it's superiority in loudness.

"Never mind," she muttered under her breath, "There's no time to explain." Then louder and pointing to make herself understood, she yelled in as few words as possible "Just stay here. Look after Menzin. Water over there."

She gave the container to Tamek and looking towards the spot where she had last seen Rusnan and remembering his face, shivered.

She must put her fears well behind her and think of her brother; the future Ruler of Vantil. As the wind swept her hair back as though it were brushed out horizontally behind her and the rain continued to beat down, she struggled off.

Chapter 22

"Where's Sahlin?" asked Menzin as Tamek returned alone and knelt down by him. She undid the top of the container and gave the water to him.

"I think she went after Rusnan. Drink this."

"What? You let her go alone?" he snapped pushing the water away.

"Well she told me to stay here with you and what with the wind, I couldn't really hear her properly anyway."

"Well what did you hear?" he demanded.

"That she had seen Rusnan and had some sort of confrontation with him, and I think she said something about…" she held back not wanting to alarm him in case she had misheard, "…he was going to kill Fulmin; but I'm not sure."

"Oh no.! I have to go after her," he yelled, struggling to get to his feet.

"No wait. We don't know where she's going and you obviously are in no state to go on; and look at how bad the storm is."

"Precisely. I can't leave her on her own in this. Confronting Rusnan is bad enough, but to have to face him alone in this is madness. I can't leave her; I must go."

"Yes but look at you. You can hardly walk yourself. If you go out in this I doubt you will survive it. Think about it – what are your chances? Trees are being blown down, the rain is making the ground hazardous, and the river is so swollen it's about to burst its banks, and the thunder and lightning is..." Tamek stopped in mid-sentence. For she realised by the look in his eyes that instead of dissuading him, her words had only succeeded in making him more determined to go after the woman he loved. She sighed. "I didn't do that very well, did I?"

He smiled at her and put his hand on her arm. "Tamek I know what you're trying to do and any other time I would listen and take heed. But this is about my future wife and I must go after her. I couldn't live with myself if something happened to her and I knew I hadn't been there to help."

He noticed Tamek looking at him with an open mouth. "What is it?"

"Future wife?"

"Ah!" He looked down at the floor, slightly embarrassed. "Yes, Sahlin has accepted my marriage proposal but we haven't told anyone yet. We decided not to until after this is all over. It just didn't seem right."

The whole of his explanation had come rushing out in

one breath, and when he looked up at Tamek's face he saw a broad smile across it, replacing the surprise he had seen there before.

"I am so pleased for you both," she said. "I knew that it would happen eventually; I just didn't think it would be yet."

"So you see I have to go to her. I truly feel better now."

"I understand my child. I will come and do everything I can to help."

"No. Stay here in this cave, and we will come back for you. And if we don't," he added grimly, "You know how to find your way back from here?"

"I am coming with you and that is an end to it. You need me to help you walk; otherwise you will never make it in time."

Menzin saw the light outside growing brighter again, but for how long?

"There's no point trying to talk you out of it?"

"None whatsoever! And anyway there isn't time for arguing!"

"No, you're right. Let's go then."

*   *   *

Rusnan was in terrible agony. The shock had worn away, and now he felt the hot, searing pain of the burns on his face. He felt sick and shaky but knew he had to get back to his shack for fear that that interfering wretch of a girl would ruin his plans altogether.

He had to remain strong in his mind to keep his body functioning. Blind in one eye and the other weeping puss, he stumbled on through the forest, trying not to make any noise that would betray his position even though he wanted to scream at the top of his voice to vent some of the pain he felt.

The wind that seemed to blow relentlessly was making his face even sorer and made it harder for him to half walk and half crawl. At least the rain and that cursed lightning seemed to have stopped for the time being. Though, if he made any noise it probably wouldn't be heard over the sounds of the thunder that still growled and roared overhead. Thankfully he didn't have far to go now and then he would show them what he could really do. He was going to finish what he had started even if it killed him – and that was precisely what he was going to do with the baby. Kill it.

Perhaps if that girl had not constantly hounded him, and kept lying to him, then maybe he would have spared the child's life. After all, what did a baby know of the struggle his people had faced during the last few centuries? How did he understand that had happened on Zaren and the repercussions that had been felt ever since?

He clutched at a hanging branch trying to remain on his feet as another exceptionally strong gust nearly knocked him over, his feet slipping around in the mud. What was he thinking of? Was he going soft? He came to do a job and he was going to finish it. So what the baby was innocent? What about all the countless babies back on Spilon that had never had the chance to grow up? And those that did survive in the terrible hardships now cast upon them by the Zarenians? They did not live the days of their lives as their ancestors had, carefree in their continuous, victorious conquests of the weaker planets that were too cowardly to stand up and fight.

Rusnan felt the war taking place in his head. The angry, loud voices that spoke of what should have been; the rightful position he would have occupied if things had been left alone.

Then he heard a single small voice that had until now been obscured by the others in their rage; the quiet voice that told him that that was what this was really all about. It told him that for once in their history, instead of rushing in and trying to dominate a planet which had surrendered to them immediately, a whole world had stood up to them and ultimately defeated them. Not just defeated them, but completely brought about their downfall. The other worlds had followed in their revolt against their pursuers after hearing of the Zarenians triumph and Spilon had lost all control over all the planets they dominated.

All the time they had mocked, "Stand up and fight, you cowards," knowing that most worlds lived a peaceful existence and were not likely to retaliate or resist.

Then one little insignificant world had stood up to them and done exactly what they had been provoked and goaded to do, and suddenly the Spilons did not like it; especially as they had succeeded in bringing Spilon down - for good.

The little voice held Rusnan captivated for a moment as he actually pondered that he could possibly have gone through all of this for totally the wrong reasons. Perhaps he had been a little hasty in his actions. He could make no difference alone either to what had happened on Spilon all those years ago, or the state and chaos it lived in today. It was revenge that was all. Pure revenge.

"No!" he cried, breaking loose before he was sunk in these cowardly thoughts and lost. He was not going to give up now. He would show that at least one Spilon had the courage to carry his convictions through, and try to make a difference to the way his people were thought of. He had come for the right reasons, which were that these people of Vantil were descended from those that had destroyed his, and he was going to set things straight, once and for all.

He felt ashamed that he had even temporarily thought that he might be wrong, and he brushed away the stinging tears from his cheek angrily. Blaming his momentary weakness on his injuries, he battled once more against the elements, confident in what he must do.

 "Which way now?" thought Sahlin, as she held grimly onto a tree trunk for support as the wind raged on and on about her. On top of all the obstacles and difficulties placed in front of her, now there was another; it was beginning to get dark. Not just the temporary loss of light that kept happening in the storm, but night time was closing in at last. The prospect of being out here alone at night with Rusnan on the loose somewhere and trying to cope with the storm terrified her. At least the rain had stopped.

She wished Menzin was here, just to hold her for a few seconds. At least feeling him holding her would give her the strength and determination to continue when she was so very tired.

As it was, she held her aching arms around her body, trying to comfort herself, shivering with fright, hunger and cold. Her clothes were soaked but she had long since noticed them, and the trousers that had once been her skirt, were now hanging loosely about her in strands.

Suddenly she could see marks in the mud, and struggling to bend down a little without falling over completely, examined them. They looked like they could be footprints but she wasn't entirely convinced.

What did she have to lose? There appeared to be more

of the marks, whatever they were and she had no other leads to follow.

Hoping that this ordeal would soon be over one way or another, she put her head resolutely down and pressed on down the hill.

*   *   *

"How much more rain can there be?" asked Menzin in dismay. Trying to walk was difficult anyway but as he was hurt, it was practically impossible.

Tamek was near collapse trying to pick her own way through the sludge, and having to help Menzin as well in such terrible conditions was just about as much as she could bear. Her arms ached from holding him up, her back hurt from being bent over, and her legs were shaking from sliding about under her in all directions. All around her the sounds of the storm raged, playing its dramatic symphony, and she battled to hear what Menzin had just said.

"I can't hear you," she yelled for the umpteenth time.

"Never mind," he shouted back. He didn't mean to complain. After all, he knew if it was difficult for him, it must be nearly impossible for her. He just felt such a burden and he was extremely worried about Sahlin. She was strong willed, and obstinate sometimes, but at the end of the day she was only a teenage girl on the brink of womanhood and no match for a brute like Rusnan. It was beginning to get dark and the idea of that unsettled him.

The rain stopped. It was a relief, but no surprise; they had grown used to the extreme conditions turning on and off instantly. But just the sudden cessation of that noise, and one less thing to contend with, was an instant boost.

"I hope we are going the right way," yelled Tamek, and then found she didn't need to because the wind also suddenly turned off. "I don't really know if this is right or not."

"The last tracks were quite a while back. I haven't seen any more, but there's not really anywhere else for them to go other than this way. Apart from in the undergrowth. That would be a stupid move to make in these conditions.

Straining his eyes into the distance to see whether anything new was looming on the horizon, and then looking back to Tamek, he realised just how dark it was becoming. A flash of lightning briefly lit up her face, and he saw the lines of tiredness and worry etched there. He knew that she was pre-occupied with thoughts of the tragedy that happened to her son, and wished that he had not complained so much. She had been very patient to listen to him and not to shout back angrily in retaliation over her own concerns. But then she was like that, and always had been; more concerned with everyone else's problems than her own.

Mulling these thoughts over, he didn't see a large root sticking up out of the ground, and tripped and fell heavily down, taking Tamek down on top of him.

"I'm sorry Tamek. I wasn't paying attention."

"It's all right, don't fret. We will soon be back up on our feet again."

"Look!" Menzin frenziedly grabbed her arm, and pointed onto the track a few inches in front of them.

"What is it?" Pulling herself free from the pool of thick mud she was sitting in, she crawled over to where Menzin was pointing.

A piece of material was jutting up, and as she lifted it, so more revealed itself from underneath the slime that had settled on top of it. It didn't seem to mean anything to her, but Menzin seemed very agitated and she passed it to his anxious fingers stretching out to touch it.

"What is it?"

"It's Sahlin's. I cut it from her skirt to help make the trousers."

"Oh yes, I see!" She clasped her hands to her face. "We must be on the right trail after all."

She bent down to Menzin and hugged him lightly; for he was holding the material to him as though it were Sahlin herself and his eyes were occupied with a troubled look.

"Come on, let's find her."

With renewed determination it seemed to take him less of an effort to get to his feet, and his strides were easier, larger and more confident.

"It's going to be all right," he shouted as another clap of thunder shook the ground, "I know it is."

*   *   *

Sahlin was stumbling along as best she could, trying hard to shake the memories of Rusnan's burnt face from inside her head. But every time the lightning flashed, there it was again in front of her eyes. She had no idea where she was going or if she was even heading in remotely the right direction.

She was hungry and yet felt sick. She was feeling desperately alone, and yet glad no-one was with her. She was afraid, and yet confident that this would all be over soon.

She had no idea how her legs were managing to keep carrying her, for she no longer felt as though she were making any effort to move them at all. She just seemed to be walking automatically. Numbness occupied her entire body which had been continually soaked, frozen and cut from falls and the icy spears that had fallen from the heavens. Now she no longer felt the cold gnawing at her. She had passed that.

The thunder and lightning didn't bother her now. She was unmoved by its ferocity and speed, and she had an overall feeling that she didn't care what happened now. An inner voice spoke to her, willing her to continue; her quest would not be in vain. She felt almost as though the lightning dare not harm her now; not after everything she had already been through.

She would save her brother now, and that was all that mattered. Whether she survived was of no consequence; she merely wanted to deliver Fulmin back into safe hands, and then she didn't care what happened to her. If she died from the prolonged exposure to the cold, the rain and everything else, so be it.

What she didn't realise was that this was the exhaustion speaking, and that the voice compelling her to move on and save her brother was still her own inner voice of determination.

All she knew was that somehow her feet dragged on step after step, monotonously. They knew where to go, even if she did not.

She wished she had some kind of feeling; whether it was terror, anger, or sadness. But there was nothing. She was void and empty, and she didn't care.

"Please let me find him soon," she murmured to thin air, "Please."

Not realising her plea was soon to be answered, she trudged onwards looking either dead ahead, or down at the dirty lumps at the end of her legs that were her feet. When she looked up again, what she saw made her stop in her tracks. Her mouth dropped open, and she stood staring.

Realising she could easily be seen, she jumped to the side of the track, and crouching down, looked gingerly out. She couldn't believe that right in front of her was a shack. It had to be Rusnan's; no-one else would live up this far, so isolated. Besides which, it certainly wasn't constructed anything like the way in which Vantilians made their homes. This looked as though it had just been thrown together, and unbeknown to her was exactly how it had been built. How could it possibly have stayed standing up in the winds they had had? But, that must mean there was still a chance Fulmin was alive.

Well she had found what she wanted, whether she believed it or not. The question was, what should she do now? Looking around she tried to find something, anything, which would serve as a weapon. It had to be heavy and solid; for Rusnan was not just going to let her walk right in and take Fulmin away. There was going to be a fight at the very least, and she knew that the outcome would probably cost one or more of them their lives.

There was nothing sturdy enough – she would have to trust that there would be something inside she could use and the element of surprise would work in her favour. She wished she had brought the knife with her they had found. She almost thought it funny that she would have then used Rusnan's own weapon against him.

She tried to swallow, but her mouth was so dry through thirst and fear that she couldn't. Opening her mouth, she tilted her head back and let some rain water trickle down some bush leaves onto her tongue. The relief was immediate. It seemed so sweet and pure. That would have to serve as refreshment for now. Closing her eyes tightly, she asked her god for the strength to go ahead with what she knew she must do, and wondered if he would approve of this at all. There was no alternative she tried to convince herself. Rusnan was past any kind of help she could have given him, and it had been his own actions that had forced her into this predicament.

"Come on Sahlin. You have come this far, do not back out now. Fulmin needs you."

Inwardly she answered herself, "Yes, but supposing he is already dead?"

"Then you have to go in and find out for sure."

She crept from her hiding place, wishing the wind would ease up, even if it was just while she went through with this. If anything it was getting worse again. "Don't complain," she mumbled, "at least it's not still raining."

It seemed it was only by luck in choosing the place Rusnan had erected his hut that it remained standing. It seemed to be just in the right place to miss the wind as it howled up the valley, protected by a bend in the hillside.

The light was almost gone. Her hands out in front of her, her eyes closed against the wind trying to strip the skin from her bones, she felt the wood of the shack suddenly touch her hands. She gasped in surprise and her eyes sprang open instantly. The shack provided a shield against the wind for a while, and carefully she set about trying to find an opening she could peer through.

At last she came across quite a large gap in the wood and pressed her face tightly up against it. At first she could see nothing, but by moving her head to a slightly different angle, she caught sight of a shape moving about. She gasped, realising this was it. She was here, and Rusnan was inside. She had to do something now. Watching him for a few moments while she tried to think clearly, she saw him walk to the back of the shack, and bend over a pile of material on the floor.

He stooped down, picked something up, and turned round. First of all, she again saw his face and immediately wanted to be sick again, but then she saw what he was clutching, and her nausea disappeared. "Fulmin," she breathed. He was still alive. Her heart began to surge with relief and at last she felt some emotion within her.

The sight of him proved she was not too late. She could still do something to save him.

Rusnan cast a glance towards the gap, and although she knew he couldn't possibly see her, her instinct was to drop to the ground.

Carefully on all fours, she made her way through the sludge to the doorway, and sat on her haunches, psyching herself up to burst through the doorway into the madness beyond. She found to her dismay however, that she didn't want to move. How could she go in knowing that either she would have to take another human life, or, her own and that of her brother's, would inevitably be lost?

The spur she needed arrived. She heard Fulmin's plaintive cry. He sounded so afraid and must be so hungry. Without any further thought, she jumped up and put her hand on the door. Taking a deep breath, she burst in.

The moment that she stepped over the boundary from outside, she paused in horror as she saw Rusnan holding Fulmin in one hand, and the other poised above a knife lying on the makeshift table.

Rusnan froze in surprise, not moving a muscle as he took in who was bursting through the door with only one seeing eye.

Realising it was Sahlin, his hand dipped down and seized the knife. He held it directly at Fulmin's chest, and Sahlin's heart missed a beat as he wriggled in the unloving grasp of the stranger, the blade moving perilously close to the skin. For a split second, her eyes moved from her brother to her enemy, and once again she recoiled at the horrific injuries to his face and neck. She could actually smell the burnt flesh and she felt dizzy and nauseous. He had behaved like a monster, and now he looked like one. Thank goodness that Fulmin was too young to realise what was going on.

"Rusnan, no!" she screamed, and then seeing the start she gave him and realising what the consequences of a slip of hand could mean, she whispered his name as calmly as she could.

"Rusnan, please let Fulmin go. What possible harm can he have done to you?"

"Look at me! Look at my face! See what your meddling has done." His voice was slow and deliberate, his mouth twisted and deformed, his blackened lips struggling to form words.

"Rusnan, please..."

"Why should I? See how it feels to have something precious taken away from you. How would you react?"

"Put him down and then we can talk."

"Like we talked before? Do not toy with me. Each time we talk you lie to me."

"No, I...I know it must seem that way, but you are wrong."

"Of course I'm wrong," he slurred, "That's what you keep telling me. Everything is so perfectly clear to you, isn't it?"

"Rusnan, I beg you, please don't do this. If this is retaliation and revenge because of the way you think I have treated you, then please let Fulmin go. You can do whatever you want to me, but let him go."

"Oh, I intend to kill you both. Only, before you die, I want you to suffer the loss of someone close to you so that you know what it's like. Then it will be your turn."

"I do know what it's like to lose someone. I lost my mother, remember? I know exactly what it's like."

"Well, now you are going to lose your brother as well. Then this world will really know what loss is. The outrage of two murders, including that of the future Ruler, will hopefully achieve what I set out to put into action. Then they will all know what it's like to lose something. Your people will lose respect for each other and that will be my reward. My work will be completed, whether I live to see it or not. Of one thing I am absolutely certain; although it will be a pity, you will certainly not live to see it."

"You are mad. Completely mad."

"Am I? My actions have been brave. I have stood up for what I believe and to try to restore the respect my planet once had many years ago"

"Your actions have been cowardly," Sahlin cried. "All of this could have been prevented if you had chosen to talk to us first; to communicate. And I will not stand here and listen to you telling me your planet once commanded respect. Spilon was never respected by anyone. Everything it ever gained was by pure greed, and for all the wrong reasons. All they ever did was take what wasn't theirs."

"No, stop!" Rusnan tried to scream out and saliva ran from the corners of his charred mouth. "How dare you!" He whirled round in anger and brought his fist holding the knife down hard against the wall of the shack.

At least it was away from Fulmin's chest breathed Sahlin with relief, but she had foolishly made matters worse by enraging him further.

"I will not listen to this. You lie again, Sahlin."

The blade of the knife partially reflected a flash of lightning from outside the open door, and Sahlin anxiously eyed it as Rusnan waved it about in the air precariously.

Trying to stall him for more time, hoping that at least would give her the chance to think of something positive, she continued talking to him to keep him focused away from Fulmin.

"So what happens afterwards? When we are dead? What will you do then?"

"Leave this cowardly place and return triumphantly home."

Sahlin noticed the difficulty in speaking for him was worsening, and wondered sub-consciously why she still felt sorry for him.

"How?"

"You know how. You know my story of my shuttle being damaged was a lie. It is ready and waiting, as you saw earlier."

"No it isn't." That got his attention. "I tampered with it after we fought before. I think you will find it won't be taking you anywhere in a hurry."

For a moment Rusnan seemed perplexed and didn't say anything, and then once again raged, "Liar!"

Sahlin still resented lying, even to Rusnan, but since he kept accusing her of it, she saw no reason why she shouldn't. Especially if it gave her time.

"Yes, I managed to get inside and disconnected a few wires, and pulled some quite important looking…things, out and disposed of them." She could get quite good at this.

She felt the roar building up inside of him before she heard it. It seemed louder than the storm, and very, very angry.

Realising that he still didn't know the others were with her, and that at least for now they would be safe, she continued her bluff.

"I should think it will take some time for you to repair it. Let Fulmin go, and I will see it is mended and you may go free. Think about it."

"I don't need your help. Your people haven't even got decent communications – how could you help? I am quite capable of mending any minor damage you think you may have caused."

"I agree that we are not technically minded people, but I would say the damage done is not minor."

Rusnan laughed, which was not the reaction she wanted to see; he obviously didn't believe her. Her bluff was failing.

"So what damage do you think you have done?" he

questioned her sarcastically as Fulmin continued wiggling.

"Why should I tell you? It will only help you escape faster."

"Because if you don't, I'll kill the baby right now."

Demonstrating that he meant what he said, he placed the blade directly by Fulmin's throat.

"All right," she cried panicking. "I...tampered with some of the switches on the control panel. I don't know what they do." Remembering the bank of lights she had seen, she continued, "Some of the lights came on and went out again."

Rusnan appeared to be digesting this information for a moment and his next question was delivered very quietly.

"How did you get in the shuttle?"

"I prised it open. It took ages but I managed it eventually."

He stayed quiet and studied her face which she was sure must be scarlet. She tried to keep any expression hidden, for she couldn't afford to give anything away. Too much was at stake.

As he neared her, despite the smell and appearance of

his face, she had a strong urge to laugh again, but didn't know why. Perhaps it was all the stress, and fear of how this was going to play out, but she had to force the corners of her mouth from rising.

He was suddenly rushing across the room away from her, announcing he had had enough; startling her and leaving her reeling in surprise. Now what was he doing?

He picked up some of the material that the baby had been lying on as a bed and tucked it under one arm, all the while keeping his eye on Sahlin to make sure she made no sudden movements.

"What are you doing?" She felt very uneasy now, and sensed that whatever he was going to do, it was to happen now. She quickly scanned around the room looking for anything at all she could use to defend herself and her brother. But there was nothing; it was only a temporary shelter for him while he carried out his plans, and there was nothing here except wood for a fire, and blankets to sleep on.

"I've listened to your lame excuses for too long. I am tired of them and you bore me Sahlin. Enough is enough."

She hardly knew how her legs were keeping her up, they shook so much, but now, in what appeared to be her final seconds of life, she was adamant that she would show no fear of him. At least he would not succeed in that.

"Outside," he ordered, and at first she did not move; could not move.

"NOW!" he yelled again with such fury, that her legs automatically began moving her body towards the door. Silently she eased past him and out of the door back into the throes of the storm, and yet strangely was not even aware the rain was once again lashing down as the wind beat about her cold, numb, defeated body.

"Stop!" he growled, and her feet ceased their steps. As though it were the most difficult thing she had ever done in her life, she edged her way round inch by inch until she faced him.

"Why the blankets?" she asked in a hollow voice, betraying no emotion.

"So I am not soaked in this coward's blood, or yours."

"How can you call an innocent baby a coward?" she questioned him mechanically. "He has no idea what this is all about."

"No, and he never will."

Relishing the pain he knew she must be feeling, even if she didn't show it, he lingered on every small movement he made with the knife, teasing her.

"Say goodbye, Sahlin." He mocked.

"No!" she finally shrieked and ran at him with as much force as her body could muster; her legs fighting hard to pump round in the mud and against the wind and rain.

Knowing she wouldn't reach him by just running at him, she dived the final few feet at him, knocking him to the ground still clutching Fulmin in his arms. He landed flat on his back with the baby and Sahlin on top of him.

She had jumped at an angle and crashed on top of his legs. Both of them let out a howl of pain simultaneously, and lay still, contemplating what they should do next while regaining their breath.

Rusnan was the first to show signs of movement, and Sahlin felt him squirm about beneath her body.

Wrenching her arms free from the mud that she was bogged down in, she pushed herself up onto her hands and then to her feet. Groggily she tried tugging Fulmin free from Rusnan's grip. But despite being winded and surprised, his reaction was to hold the baby even closer and Sahlin only succeeded in losing her balance again, dropping to her knees.

Rusnan's hand darted up unexpectedly and seized her hair, pulling it so roughly that her head was forced painfully back.

She could feel his weight shifting about, and then felt his head next to hers. Her hand reached out and instinctively scooped up some of the thick mud off the ground, and she flung it in his face.

It landed on top of the open wounds, and the howl of excruciating pain that he let out was as much as she could bear. He immediately relinquished his grasp on Fulmin who dropped into the mud beside her face down. Instantly Sahlin seized him, dragging him free, quickly wiping the offending substance away from his nose and mouth.

Dragging herself to her feet once more, she leaned into the wind and fought every step in the darkness to some nearby rocks, and laid Fulmin down into a covered crevice between the two large stones. At least he would be safe from the cruel elements until this battle was concluded. He seemed very quiet but otherwise uninjured, as far as she could tell.

Swinging back around she saw Rusnan climbing groggily to his feet, trying to see through one eye in the dark where she was. She picked up a few small stones that were lying about and began to hurl them at him. A few were lucky shots and struck him, but didn't succeed in stopping him from slowly advancing on her. Whatever happened, she was not moving out from between him and Fulmin. Only her death would move her away from shielding him.

Rusnan was still gaining ground and the knife was clenched firmly in his hand. It would be a hard task to take it from him.

"I had intended to kill that miserable, snivelling infant first, and take a great deal of time and satisfaction over your death. But now you leave me no choice; he can stay there and starve and freeze to death, and you must prepare to die now."

"You can try Rusnan, but it will not be as easy as you imagine," she shouted back triumphantly over the raging tempest.

She saw his black, burnt lips snarl back into mocking laughter but the sounds he made were obliterated and carried away to some far off place on the back of the wind.

Her words were empty, she knew that. Now when she needed her strength most, it was failing her, and she could feel her legs beginning to buckle beneath her, easing her in slow motion to the ground. The rain still pelted down on her so hard that she felt even the elements wanted her to fail in her efforts, and were pushing her down to meet her defeat.

Strangely though, she felt no panic or fright now. Calm seemed to engulf her and she knew she was giving in. After all she had been through, she was finally conceding.

"What about Fulmin?" she heard a voice frantically calling inside.

"I have done all I can. There is nothing left I can do. My strength is spent."

"Don't give up," it urged, "Fight!"

"I can't. I have nothing left to give."

It seemed that the wind blew silently, and the rain was not wet or cold anymore. All was quiet, and even Rusnan's mouth was moving without making any sound.

"My body is preparing for death," she thought. She felt so calm and serene, as though she didn't mind and it was natural to feel this way. "I make peace with my past thoughts, actions and deeds," she told her inner self.

Rusnan was now directly in front of her and she looked slowly up at his form from where she now lay, her eyes travelling from his feet, slowly up his body to his face. She saw no features there now, just a black shape. Whether it was due to the small amount of light behind him from the shack, and his face was in shadow, or because of the burns, or because her senses were failing, she didn't know. She didn't care.

Every move exaggerated, she watched in fascination as the knife blade moved back away from her, and then began to sweep down towards her. How pretty it looked when the light reflected in it. She could never have guessed, centuries ago on their home planet of Zaren, that a brave rebel against Spilon's intruders had also been mesmerised by the means of his execution.

As she was about to close her eyes and prepare to feel the blade tear into her flesh, the knife seemed to halt, and waver in mid-air.

Then quite inexplicably, Rusnan seemed to be falling down onto her. Not bearing down on her to thrust the knife into her; just falling.

She tried to instruct her body to move out of the way, but it did not comply. As he landed, the knife caught a glancing blow to her left shoulder, and she felt the serrated edges biting into her flesh. She winced as she felt hot, searing pain spread through her shoulder, like hot liquid pouring onto it.

Instinctively, her right arm reached up to hold the wound, but his form lay across her in the way. She waited for him to retrieve the knife and send it forcefully back into her body to end her life.

Instead, he lay perfectly still and she wondered what tricks he was up to now. Not that he needed any; she was right where he wanted her, helpless and unarmed, just waiting for him to send her to the entrance to eternity.

She craned her head around and saw another knife protruding from his back, between the shoulder blades. Dazed and confused, she lifted her head and looked around.

Like a vision, she saw a form rapidly advancing from the trees as she had once before, but this time in the darkness.

"Menzin," she breathed, and her head fell back to the ground in her exhaustion.

Within moments she felt the heavy body pinning her down being dragged away from her, and felt the air rushing back into her lungs as her chest rose and fell easily, greedy for the air it had been starved of.

Then she felt comforting but strong arms around her hugging her close and gently rocking her to and fro. She was so relieved to feel Menzin again. A different face peered into hers anxiously, and she dimly recollected seeing it before.

"Tamek?" she whispered, "Is that you?" The face smiled back at her, and she felt the arms move away from her, as they scooped her up and carried her towards the shack.

She tried to point to the crevice where she had laid Fulmin, trying to make them understand. Words wouldn't form in her dry mouth, but finally she muttered his name, and Tamek left her side straight away.

At last she could feel some warmth returning to her body as she was hugged tightly and protectively in those big, yet gentle, loving arms. Not arms that were unfriendly and trying to seize her and restrict her, but arms that wanted to shield and look after her.

Aware that they were now inside the shack despite Menzin still struggling with his injuries, she was being lowered now gently onto the floor, and rested upon blankets.

As he tried to examine her wound, she heard the sound of her brother's cries as Tamek joined them. He must be hungry, and very scared, yet the cry was wonderful to her ears; it meant he was still alive. She wanted to cry too but tears could not even form in her eyes. She heard him, but nothing else, and didn't understand why.

As she looked away from him, she saw the face fully in front of her that she never thought she would see again, and tried to make her hands reach out to touch him. There was no feeling however, and therefore no response, except for a very slight movement.

His mouth was moving but apart from Fulmin's cry, she still lived in a silent world and could hear nothing. Something moving from behind Menzin caught her eye, and she stared in disbelief towards the doorway as a blood soaked ghost from the dead world staggered in, and came lunging at him.

The look of horror on her face at once alerted him that something was wrong, and he turned in time to see Rusnan advancing.

Sidestepping his attacker who fell to the floor, Menzin at once pulled the knife he had thrown into him before from between his shoulder blades, and in rapid succession plunged it four or five times into his back again.

Tamek was looking on in mute horror; unable to comprehend they had been so careless not to check Rusnan was dead.

This time, Menzin was feeling for a pulse and found none. Sahlin watched his lips form the words, "He's dead," and an overwhelming sense of relief swept across her entire body. As though that was what she had been waiting for, she could suddenly hear again, and her thoughts were immediately for her brother again.

"Is Fulmin all right?" she croaked anxiously.

"Yes, look, he's right here. See?"

"Oh Fulmin," she whispered, and at last the tears came as Tamek laid him close to her, trying not to think of what he must have endured. Menzin was stemming the flow of blood from her shoulder with pieces of ripped blanket and forming a sling for her to wear.

"Fulmin," she sobbed again.

"I will take care of him, don't worry," Tamek cooed. Gently she removed him from beside her and placed more blankets over her. "Rest now," she gently said. As though they were the magic words she had been waiting for, Sahlin rested her head back and sank into peaceful oblivion.

Chapter 24

It was light, she knew that much. The storm had ended too, and all sounded quiet and peaceful.

Raising her head to look about, Sahlin winced at the ache in her shoulder and the stiffness all over her body. It appeared that she was on her own, and for a moment she forgot that Rusnan was dead, and looked about wildly.

One by one, each event that had passed yesterday ran through her memory and she felt the tears welling up in her eyes. The door to the shack opened and as she looked around, so she saw Menzin enter carrying Fulmin, who appeared to be in fine health and quite happy.

Menzin paused as he saw her open eyes and then said, "Good afternoon Sahlin."

"Afternoon? I've slept all night and all morning?" she asked incredulously.

"You've been through a lot. Or are you going to dismiss everything that's happened?"

"Well, what did happen? I mean I remember most of it, but where did you come from?"

"We were following your trail, or trying to. Tamek told me you had gone after Rusnan, and we came after you.

We had no way of knowing for sure if we were on the right track or not. I think it was sheer luck that we happened to be on the right path."

"I'm glad you came. I really thought I was going to die." Great tears began to fall down her cheeks and Menzin hurriedly laid Fulmin down and knelt beside her, cradling her closely to him.

"It's all right now, ssh."

"I thought I had let father down, and Fulmin; and I thought I would never see you again."

"I had doubts myself," he confided, "but I had to keep believing to give me the strength to carry on. Without Tamek's help, I don't think I would have got here in time."

A shiver ran though his body, that Sahlin felt travel through hers too.

"Is Tamek okay?"

"Yes, she's been great, but as usual has shrugged it off as nothing!" He laughed, "She reminds me of you!"

For the first time in many a long hour, she actually laughed, and once she had begun, couldn't stop. It seemed infectious, for Menzin joined in, and shortly afterwards Tamek came to see what was happening. At the sight of the two lovers laughing, she too in her relief that the ordeal was over, also began to laugh.

When she had exhausted herself, and her cheeks were wet with her tears, she asked, "What are we laughing at?" which sent the other two into great guffaws once more.

Eventually, they gained control of their emotions and Sahlin's face grew stern as she said, "Seriously, I thank you both for all your help. Without it, both my brother and I wouldn't be here now."

Instantly, the atmosphere changed, and all was stony silent as the three each sat looking at the patch of floor by their feet.

"What happens now?" Tamek asked, sensing the others didn't know what to say.

"Well, bury Rusnan I suppose; then see about the shuttle and head home. There was a little milk left for Fulmin, but he certainly must be hungry. We need to get him back as fast as we can all travel."

Sahlin had looked up sharply. "Bury Rusnan?"

"Yes, we thought that..." Menzin didn't know how to word his feelings and was grateful Tamek interjected.

"We thought after everything he had put you through, you might like to see him laid to rest."

Seeing her puzzled look, she added, "It might disperse any nightmares you have that he could still be alive."

"I see."

Her worried expression caused Menzin to interpose, "You don't have to if you don't want to."

"No. It's all right, I will. I want to."

"We can do it now if you want."

She nodded and the three moved slowly and silently out into the sunlight, Tamek carrying Fulmin, and Sahlin gazing up in wonder at the clear blue sky.

"I can't believe we had that terrible storm when it's like this."

"Until you look at the devastation." Menzin was pointing up to the peak of the hill, which before had been obscured by dense trees. Now there was nothing but stumps of trees, broken in half by great force, and hurled to the ground.

All around, the grass was covered by thick brown mud which was marbled where it was beginning to dry out in some areas faster than others.

Stones and rocks had been tossed down the hill, and stood in newly formed piles at the bottom, and against the fallen trees. Sahlin couldn't speak but gazed open mouthed. However had any of them survived?

Menzin gently took her hand. "Come on," he said, easing her to where they had dug a grave for Rusnan.

The body was wrapped in the blankets they had found in the shack, and Sahlin recoiled as Menzin struggled to roll it over the edge into the hole, and it landed with a thud at the bottom.

Standing up again he prompted, "Do you want to say anything?"

She waited, then moving forward, she gazed pitifully down into the grave.

"I hope you find the peace that you never had in your lifetime here and on Spilon," she struggled to whisper, and then turned and fled.

Tamek and Menzin exchanged glances, and as he was about to follow, Tamek said gently, "No, leave her for a while. She is in shock, and needs some time alone."

Menzin nodded, and between them, they set out about covering the body with earth and filling in the grave. When they were finished Tamek said a small prayer asking that Rusnan be forgiven his sins and allowed to rest in peace.

Menzin laid down a little wooden plaque that he had fashioned with his knife while Sahlin slept, and stood for a few moments contemplating how they would all now resume their normal lives.

"I'll go and find Sahlin," he said, but Tamek pulled him back, asking if she could go. They looked at each other knowingly and Menzin nodded.

Sahlin was perched on a rock, head in hands, staring at her feet.

"How are you now, my child?"

"I'm fine."

"I see. Now tell me how you really are."

Sahlin looked up into her eyes, and smiled weakly.

"I don't know how I feel. Confused, I think. More than when my mother died."

"Is that surprising? Your mother dying was inevitable one day; you knew it had to happen. But with Rusnan it was different. He wanted to take Fulmin's life, and yours, for no reason and end them long before they were meant to. It wasn't a natural thing for you to have to hunt him down, and then to see Menzin have to kill him."

"I know, but I still feel we were wrong to kill him. Surely we could have helped him?"

"As I recall, you tried that several times, but he refused.

Nothing we could have done would ever have changed the way he felt towards us; the way he was."

"No, but I still feel sorry for him. At the end it was almost as though he wanted to believe me. I could almost see him fighting inside to believe what I said. But it was too late, he couldn't shake free."

She began to cry again, and Tamek placed her arms around her and hugged her tightly.

"Ssh now, child. It's all over. Ssh."

* * *

"What shall we do with it?" asked Tamek despondently.

"Do with what?"

"The shuttle."

"I don't think there's anything we can do. I think we will have to return home and send a party of men up here to destroy it."

"Destroy it? Couldn't we just leave it here?"

"No. I don't think so. In case they eventually trace where it is. Looking through the screen, we don't know what all the lights and switches on the control panel mean. They could be emitting some kind of signal that Spilon could lock onto. We can't take any chances. There could be another Rusnan, waiting to pounce."

The moment he said the words, Menzin felt the two women staring at him.

"Can you remember how to get there?" asked Tamek, trying to change the subject.

Woodenly Sahlin answered, "How could I ever forget?"

"Come on, let's go home."

"That sounds like a great idea to me."

The two held hands, and together with Tamek carrying Fulmin, began their descent, lighter in spirit than when they had set out, despite their ragged and bedraggled appearance. Menzin still limped heavily but seemed to find it less painful than before, and his face was cut and covered in bruises. One eye was so swollen it was almost closed. Sahlin knew that though her shoulder hurt, once it was cleaned and dressed properly, would heal. There would always be a scar she realised, but it would never be deeper than the emotional ones that would never go away.

"Oh, I understand that I should congratulate the future bride of Menzin," Tamek casually mentioned.

Sahlin cast a glance at Menzin, who looked sheepishly back at her. "Sorry, it slipped out."

She pretended to be cross with him, and let out a deep sigh.

"I'm sorry!" he repeated, not knowing what else to say.

"Stop apologising!" she laughed, unable to keep up her mock annoyance.

The clouds of worry lifted from his battered face, and he put his arms around her waist, trying to lift her up in the air.

Crying out in pain, he quickly thought better of the idea, and Sahlin gasped as the jolt sent her shoulder into spasms.

"You do still want to marry me?" he asked with a broad smile.

"I'll consider it," she teased back.

"Oh, I see, like before when you led me to believe that you were going to refuse me?"

"It seems to me, you need to make a commitment," Tamek interrupted.

"Yes, you're quite right." Menzin fished about inside his jacket and pulled out a small red stone on a chain.

"I want you to have this," he said, fastening it around her wrist. "I wasn't going to give it you until after I had asked

Latnor's permission. But after what's happened, I see that life can change so quickly, and I want to give it to you now. It was my mother's. She would have approved of you having it."

"Oh Menzin, it's beautiful. I don't know what to say."

"Just say that you are still going to marry me," he chuckled.

"Yes, of course I will. I have wanted nothing more since the day I met you."

"Promise me one thing?"

"Yes?"

Stepping back and looking her up and down, he grinned, "That you'll get a new dress for the wedding!"

"Oh! You!" She playfully slapped his arm and as they tenderly kissed, they heard a slight sound behind them. They parted to see Tamek crying.

"What is it?" Sahlin asked immediately concerned and hurrying to her side.

"Nothing. I'm just so happy!" she sobbed.

Sahlin laughed and placed her arm about Tamek's waist, gazing down at Fulmin who was peacefully asleep and blissfully unaware of anything that had taken place over the past few days. Indeed, unaware of the future that now lay securely in front of him once again.

"I thought we were going home."

"We are."

Thanks and Acknowledgements

Thank you to my family for being so patient while I tried to battle health problems, run a family and home, and try to achieve my goal of seeing my yellowing manuscript finally make it into a book after more than three decades sitting in a cupboard! To my husband Neil, thank you for being supportive and encouraging, and believing in me (because I didn't!) and to Hope and Jeremiah who live with a constantly worn out mother, but understood the need to do this and kept cheering me on.

To Lyndsey who gave me the extra shove, Alasdair who put up with constant questions, and Guy Bass who encouraged me it was worth a go, or it would still be sitting in the cupboard! And thanks mum for the lap top, which meant I could do it a lot quicker than waiting for times when the children didn't have ours to do their homework!

Finally, thank you to you the reader, who is holding my baby in your hands – please be gentle!

About the Author

Karen was born and raised in Brighton by the sea, and moved to Derbyshire six years ago with her husband and two children.

She has written much poetry and some short stories. "A Fight For Peace" is her first full length novel. It began its life over thirty years ago following the death of her father when she was sixteen. It has sat in a drawer all those years, until a conversation with children's author Guy Bass encouraged her to get it out again and consider publication.

She has taken the bare bones of the original story and changed and added to it, to make her debut novel of two parts.

Suffering from M.E. and fibromyalgia for many years, seeing "A Fight For Peace" finally published has meant a great deal to her, and stirred up her love of creative writing again.

The poems she has written mainly flow from her Christian faith, and she also hopes to see these published in the near future.

Printed in Great Britain
by Amazon

56830768R00224